"Cleverly merging two genres ... how have never met, *The Big B...* ... *... ....* is a hilarious cross-breeding of the lesbian pulp novel and the horse-girl fantasia. Authors Alisa Surkis and Monica Nolan clearly know their stuff, sending up a century of girl-loves-horse and girl-loves-girl stories with pitch-perfect language, pacing and plots."
—*Bitch Magazine*

"You know how the old adage goes: You can't judge a book by its cover. Well, *The Big Book of Lesbian Horse Stories* is an exception to the rule. The collection's tawdry tales of equine-loving lesbos are as vibrant, juicy, and pulpy as the sexy cover illustration. The stories are wildly entertaining . . . saddle up for this fun ride."
—*Out*

"The stories are perfectly written . . . if the title alone doesn't make you want to buy it, then you have a serious problem. If you aren't snorting with laughter by the time you get to the end of this book, then there is no saving you."
—*Gingerbeer.co.uk*

"The book can be loved for what it is—eight vintage stories of ladies, lust and the pretty ponies they love. It's kind of like *Black Beauty* for big girls."
—*Portland Mercury*

"If, like me, you have a section of a bookshelf devoted entirely to books you purchased solely for the sake of their glorious titles, you will undoubtedly be delighted to add to it the wonderfully named *The Big Book of Lesbian Horse Stories*. You might, too—as I did—actually enjoy the stories. Part of the fun of picking one's way through this book comes not just from anticipating which particular genre the authors will take on next, but also from discovering how they've worked an equine theme into possible unlikely settings."
—Sarah Waters, *The Erotic Review*

"Despite the wacky title and campy cover, *The Big Book of Lesbian Horse Stories* is no fluffy parody but the real McCoy: smart genre fiction with a horsey lesbian twist."
—*San Francisco Bay Guardian*

"Girls who love women who love horses—that's the gloriously tacky heart of this hilarious homage to the lesbian pulp fiction of yesteryear. In a seamless send-up of the genre made famous by Ann Bannon and Paula Christian, the authors have foaled an inspired cross-breeding of eager twilight lovers and equine-inspired orgasms. This spot-on parody is a galloping treat of a read."
—*Front Page*

Books by Monica Nolan

THE BIG BOOK OF LESBIAN HORSE STORIES
(with Alisa Surkis)

LOIS LENZ, LESBIAN SECRETARY

Published by Kensington Publishing

Lois Lenz, Lesbian Secretary

MONICA NOLAN

KENSINGTON BOOKS
http://www.kensingtonbooks.com

KENSINGTON BOOKS are published by

Kensington Publishing Corp.
850 Third Avenue
New York, NY 10022

All Kensington titles, imprints and distributed lines are available at special quantity discounts for bulk purchases for sales promotion, premiums, fund-raising, educational or institutional use.

Special book excerpts or customized printings can also be created to fit specific needs. For details, write or phone the office of the Kensington Special Sales Manager: Kensington Publishing Corp., 850 Third Avenue, New York, NY 10022. Attn. Special Sales Department. Phone: 1-800-221-2647.

Kensington and the K logo Reg. U.S. Pat. & TM Off.

ISBN-13: 978-0-7582-1422-5
ISBN-10: 0-7582-1422-7

First Kensington Trade Paperback Printing: August 2007
10   9   8   7   6   5   4   3   2   1

Printed in the United States of America

To the Group,
Kara, Corey, Meg, and sometimes Kristy;
and to Julie Ann.

Chapter One

A Date with the Career Counselor

Steam filled the empty locker room, drifting over the white sinks and rows of green lockers like mist rolling in from the ocean. Drops of water formed on the underside of the long benches, where the girls sat to change out of their gym uniforms, and dripped onto the gray and green tiled floor.

The steam wrapped around Lois Lenz like a damp towel as she stood just outside the shower stall. Her brassiere dangled forgotten from one hand as she gazed at her best friend, Faye. The steam blurred the outlines of Faye Collins's slender athletic body as she turned slowly this way and that under the spray, luxuriating in the hot water that pummeled her tender flesh. Lois's eyes devoured the white shoulders, the high breasts, the pouting mouth. That mouth, she thought. That pink, glistening mouth!

"Your lipstick—is it that new kissproof kind?" murmured Lois huskily.

"Yes," Faye replied, flashing a tantalizing smile at Lois, "it's called 'Strawberry Ice.'" Suddenly, she uncoiled one soapy arm and reached out to the other girl. "Come and try it," she whispered, pulling Lois under the spray.

"It's not—really—my color," Lois managed to gasp,

before she surrendered to Faye's embrace. The feel of her friend's satin skin against her own bare flesh, the touch of Faye's tongue on her own, set a fire burning inside Lois that no shower could put out. A moan escaped her when Faye's supple fingers trailed, light as mist, down the small of her back. The steady rush of water all but covered the faint sound; still, Faye stopped what she was doing to hiss, "Lois!"

"Sorry," muttered Lois, wrapping her arms around the other girl. She covered Faye's mouth with her own, silencing any further protest.

The two girls had been practice kissing for months now. It had been Faye's idea—one of her better ones, Lois had thought. They'd practiced every private moment they could find—after gym, before cheerleading practice, while the cupcakes for the Future Homemakers' bake sale were in the oven, in the janitor's broom closet before French . . .

The funny thing was, the more they practiced, the more practice Lois felt she needed. Even now, as she and Faye melted together, limbs entwined, Lois knew that if only they had more time, she'd be able to *really* get the hang of this kissing business, to get to the core—

Abruptly, Faye pulled away and turned off the shower. "We'd better get dressed," she said, "or we'll be late for Dom Sci again."

Lois stood for a second, breathing raggedly, as Faye stepped out of the shower and picked up the towel that lay on the bench. It was getting harder and harder to call a halt to practice—at least for Lois. Faye could start and stop as easily as she turned the shower knob, leaving Lois shaken, struggling to regain her usual poise.

Faye, having dried herself, pulled on a half-slip and reached around behind her back to fasten her brassiere. Lois watched, unable to tear her eyes away from the supple play of the muscles beneath Faye's skin.

"I got it the other day at Brendan's," Faye said. Lois realized with a start that her best friend was talking about her lipstick. "Go ahead, try it if you like."

Lois picked up a towel and began to dry herself off. "No thanks," she said, her practical self again. "It really *isn't* my color."

The two girls were a perfect study in contrasts. Faye was a honey blonde, with cornflower blue eyes and a peaches-and-cream complexion. Lois's brown hair was so dark it was almost black, and she had eyes to match. In the summer, Faye burned while Lois's warm, olive-toned complexion turned golden. Where Faye was tall and willowy, Lois was petite and curvacious.

"Zip me up?" said Faye. She slid her wristwatch on, murmuring, "Rod and Billy must be wondering what's taking us so long."

Lois zipped up the full-skirted, pink gingham shirt-waist dress Faye wore. "Well, *you're* the one who got me all wet again," she told Faye. "Just tell them that."

"Lois!" Faye took a deep breath. "Don't be silly. We won't tell them anything. It's good to be a little mysterious around boys."

"All right," Lois agreed as she fastened the cloth-covered belt that matched her periwinkle cotton. Faye always had the latest dating advice at her fingertips, and Lois was content to follow her lead.

Rod and Billy were loitering in the hallway outside the entrance to the girls' locker room, tossing a football back and forth. "Season's over, boys," chided Faye, ducking a pass.

"We have to do *something* while we wait for you two to finish primping," complained Rod.

"Rod, you know that as captain and co-captain of the pep squad, Faye and I have lots of work to do together," Lois defended earnestly.

Rod wasn't paying attention. He had taken Faye's hand and was giving her a kiss on the cheek. Lois flushed. She didn't approve of such public demonstrations of affection, even between steadies.

"Break it up, you two, hall monitor at six o'clock," quipped Billy Rivers as he took Lois's books from her and tucked them under his arm. A self-effacing lad with a wry sense of humor and a dirty blond cowlick, he'd been Lois's steady since sophomore year.

The four of them double-dated every weekend. Billy was as much a foil to the dark and brooding Rod as Lois was to Faye. Now they continued down the hall, four abreast, amid a flurry of greetings from their classmates: "Hi there, Lois!" "Great shot the other day, Rod!" "Hey Billy! Wasn't Art just awful today?" "Faye, that new sweater is the most!"

Usually Lois basked in the sensation of being a vital part of high school affairs, envied by the less popular students. She'd loved being an attendant when Faye was homecoming queen, and she knew Faye was right when her best friend told her dating athletic stars was good for their prestige.

But lately the things she'd once enjoyed had started to seem empty, purposeless. Sometimes she had the frightening feeling that all her activities—Class of 1959 Yearbook Advertising Secretary, Future Homemakers Secretary, Class Secretary—were just a frenzied effort to distract herself—but from what?

The only activity she still truly enjoyed was captaining the Nutshells, Walnut Grove High's pep squad. And next week that would be over, just like everything else.

With an effort, Lois pushed away the queer empty feeling. Faye was talking about the prom. Again.

"We'll have supper beforehand at the Club." Faye was reciting the plans she and Lois had put together last

LOIS LENZ, LESBIAN SECRETARY 5

month. "And then—Hi, Enid!" She interrupted herself to
greet the tall girl with dark, lank hair and thick glasses
who hurried along the hall hunched over a heavy pile of
books. Enid mumbled, "Hello," barely glancing up before rushing on.

"Is she on the guest list?" Rod asked with a laugh.

Faye shrugged. "Poor Enid! I feel sorry for her."

Enid lived next door to Faye, and their parents played
bridge together. Faye was always saying she wished she
could help the studious girl be more popular. "We used to
be good friends," she explained. "It's sad to see her so—
dateless."

Now Lois stood for a moment, looking after Enid's
hunched back in its mud brown blouse, as a new thought
occurred to her. "I don't think Enid wants Faye's help,"
she realized with a start.

"Lois! Lois!" Lois blinked and realized Faye was looking at her quizzically. "I said what do you think, should
we meet at the Country Club or at my house—maybe
have a Coke in the new fallout shelter Daddy just built?"

Lois sighed inwardly. Faye's parents were realtors who
were always making improvements to the modern ranch
house they'd built in the new Falling Leaves subdivision
just outside of town, and Faye loved to show off the latest additions to the picture perfect Collins home. Lois
thought she'd succeeded in convincing Faye that the submerged fallout shelter would *not* set the right tone for a
romantic prom evening, but Faye could be stubborn.

Lois took a notebook from the top of the pile Billy was
carrying and flipped it open, pretending to study the
"Prom To-Do" list inside. "I've already made the reservations at the Country Club and phoned the other girls and
their dates, Faye."

Faye pouted, and opened her mouth to argue, but Lois
forestalled her by adding hastily, "If we change the time,

the other girls will get all flurried and won't be able to appreciate the fallout shelter. Wait until summer vacation, we can have a fallout shelter pool party." She flipped to her calendar. "Maybe at the end of June. Or the Fourth of July."

Faye's home was the gathering place for their crowd. But while it was Faye's house, it was Lois who planned, organized, and executed each of Faye's social successes.

Faye brightened. "That's a good idea! When should we have it?" She turned to the boys, chattering excitedly, "Wait until you see it—it's dreamy! Daddy's already stocked it with canned goods and he says it will improve the resale value of the house by ten percent!"

But Lois had stopped listening. "Oh my gosh," she breathed, looking down at her calendar. "Oh my gosh and golly! My appointment with Miss Watkins is today!" Snatching her books from Billy, she sped away, calling over her shoulder to Faye, "Explain to Mrs. Bunn for me!"

Every senior at Walnut Grove High, from Rod on down to Enid Butler, was required to meet with Miss Watkins in the last two weeks of school. It was one of the many innovations the dynamic new career counselor had instituted when she came to Walnut Grove.

As Lois backtracked her way along the corridor and hurried up the stairs to Miss Watkins's office, she was appalled at how close she'd come to missing her appointment. She *never* forgot appointments. She couldn't let things like that shower with Faye and this strange empty feeling distract her from her responsibilities!

And it wasn't as if she was dreading her date with Miss Watkins. Lois admired the youthful guidance counselor, who was so stylish and seemed so sure of herself. It was quite the rage among the freshman girls to wear their hair like Miss Watkin's, and a scarf around their neck, in imitation of the silk neck scarf she always wore, jauntily knotted at one side. Of course, I've outgrown such crushes! Lois reminded herself.

Today Miss Watkin's scarf was a brilliant peacock blue, which echoed the blue piping on her tailored gabardine suit. "Sit down, Lois," she said, looking up from the file in front of her to smile at the flushed, panting girl.

Lois sat down and tried to slow her breathing, knowing that it was *her* file Miss Watkins was studying, the complete record of her years at Walnut Grove High.

"The Nutshells looked wonderful last weekend, by the way," Miss Watkins added. "You must be very proud of them."

"Why, I didn't know you went to the games!" blurted Lois, feeling unaccountably flattered and shy.

"I enjoy basketball, but it's really the cheerleading that thrills me," said Miss Watkins with a wink. She closed the file in front of her. "But let's get down to business. Why don't you tell me about your plans for after graduation. More school?"

"Well, sort of, I guess. I mean, in the fall Faye and I are going to Northridge Junior College for Girls, here in town," Lois explained. "I thought this summer I might get some sort of job, to help with the expense. Maybe clerking . . . or . . . I'm not really sure. I haven't any particular skills."

With Miss Watkins's keen gray eyes intently on her, Lois's plans suddenly sounded trivial to her own ears.

"I see." Miss Watkins stared thoughtfully at Lois for a long moment while the young cheerleader shifted uneasily in her chair. Then, as if making a decision, the guidance counselor leaned forward and clasped her hands together. "Lois, I can't say you seem terribly excited about the future you've sketched out for yourself so I'm going to jump right in and make a suggestion. Have you ever thought of a career as a secretary?"

"A secretary?" Lois's rosebud mouth was a round "O" of astonishment. "Me?"

Miss Watkins continued earnestly. "You've done superbly in typing and shorthand, and Mrs. Forester says you were her best student when your English class studied business writing. She said your memos were miracles of conciseness. You're overflowing with skills, Lois!"

"But—but aren't careers for girls who are greasy grinds—I mean smart girls," Lois corrected herself hastily. "Like Enid Butler?"

Girls who weren't likely to marry, was what she meant.

"Enid Butler will be majoring in mathematics at a very fine women's college," Miss Watkins told her. "Careers are for all sorts of girls these days. Look at me—I have a career." She smiled mischievously. "Would you call me a greasy grind?"

Without giving Lois time to answer, she asked the startled girl, "Why did you take the business vocational course all through high school?"

"My aunt Gertrude said it was good for a girl to have something to fall back on," Lois said slowly, "and once I started, I was enthralled!" She thought back nostalgically on the filing systems she'd learned, the labor-saving flow chart she'd invented for her mother that had earned her an A from Miss Grimes. She was sure she could have scored the highest in the typing time trials, if cheerleading practice hadn't taken up so much of her time.

"I wouldn't suggest such a step to just any girl," said Miss Watkins, "but there are also your scores on the Spindle-Janska Personality Penchant Assessment, and other aptitude tests to consider." She opened Lois's file. "Subject is highly organized," she read. She turned over a page.

"Highest score in managerial category." Another page. "Organization systems are this subject's strength. Subject should do well at the head of a large, multinational firm."

Lois's head was spinning. She'd completely forgotten the aptitude tests they'd taken last fall, another of Miss Watkins's innovations.

"You—you really think I could succeed in the business world?" Lois asked.

"Lois, I've never seen such an aptitude for the business environment in all my counseling experience." Miss Watkins closed the file again. "Which is why I'd like to recommend you for an opening in the Bay City office of Sather & Stirling. The office manager there, Ivy Gill, tells me she needs a girl for the secretarial pool. What do you think?"

Lois's cheeks had flushed a deep pink and her eyes were starry with excitement. A career! Bay City! All her inchoate dissatisfaction, all her nameless yearnings, bubbled up and pushed her toward this new world Miss Watkins was offering her. For a moment she couldn't identify the feeling that washed over her. Why, it was relief! Was it possible she'd been dreading another summer of fun in Walnut Grove, the familiar routine of double dates with Billy, Rod, and Faye, and the particular frustrations that went with them?

Faye. Lois's expressive young face grew serious. Faye was the one drawback. They'd been best friends since they both made the squad freshman year and they'd always done everything together. Briefly she wondered if they could *both* be secretaries. But she dismissed the thought instantly. Faye had never taken typing.

"I know the secretarial pool is starting at the bottom," Miss Watkins broke the silence, and Lois realized she'd been so absorbed in her thoughts she hadn't noticed the moments ticking by. "But it's really the fastest way to learn all aspects of a business—you know, the secretaries are the nerve center of any organization, privy to its innermost workings."

"Oh, I don't mind starting at the bottom," Lois felt she should explain. "To be honest, it sounds awfully exciting! But—you know, Faye and I have always done everything together—"

"Oh yes, of course," said Miss Watkins thoughtfully. She rubbed the bridge of her nose lightly. "Look, Lois, why don't you think of this summer as a kind of experiment? You said you were looking for a summer job anyway—why not take a job as a secretary?" She smiled. "It might not be a bad thing to stand alone for a summer. You may discover abilities you didn't know you had." She stood up, to indicate their talk was over, adding, "And if you decide you'd be better suited going to Junior College with Faye, why, back you come to Walnut Grove, no harm done." She opened the office door for the bemused young girl. "Why don't you think it over for a few days, Lois? I'm afraid I can't give you much more time—Miss Gill needs to fill the position soon."

The clamor of classes changing flooded into Miss Watkins's quiet office, bringing Lois back to the everyday world. "Yes—all right—I'll let you know as soon as I can," she babbled, and stumbled out of the office.

Chapter Two
At Cheer Practice

L ois walked through the rest of the afternoon in a daze. She attended classes, sat, stood, even answered questions, but her mind was in Bay City. It was as if she had walked into Miss Watkins's office a cheerleader, and come out a secretary. As Mr. Harrison droned on about the nineteenth amendment of the constitution in Civics, her last class of the day, she was picturing herself in the office of a skyscraper, studying papers through a pair of tortoiseshell glasses, her hair pulled back in a smooth chignon.

The picture in her head looked remarkably like that spread in the *Teenaged* magazine story about the girl who was a fashion designer in Bay City. Now she knew why she'd clipped that story and put it in her "fashion ideas" file. It wasn't the fashions, it was the big-city career that had attracted her!

Of course, I've always had twenty-twenty vision, Lois thought, mentally erasing the glasses.

And she had solved the problem of Faye. Faye could be a model, Lois had decided. Hadn't Miss Watkins said careers were for all kinds of girls? All the pep squad members agreed that Faye was the prettiest. Faye would go for that, Lois was sure. She was always poring over fashion magazines and adored clothes.

Lois drifted away into a new daydream. This time she was picturing the smart little apartment she and Faye would have. The slipcovers would be blue to complement Faye, and the drapes would be scarlet, to set off Lois's gypsy coloring. She could see the two of them, in satin lounging pajamas, maybe shaking up some cocktails, the way Mr. Collins did, when the Collinses had guests to dinner.

And best of all, there'd be no adults around to supervise them. Maybe in the privacy of their own apartment, she and Faye could get down to some serious kissing practice—or even go beyond . . .

So real had her daydream become, that it was almost a shock to see Faye already in her trim blue and white uniform, shutting her locker door and gathering up the practice pom-poms from the bin when Lois flew breathlessly into the locker room.

"Isn't Mr. Harrison the limit sometimes?" she greeted Lois. "I was so bored I almost fell asleep. I would have, too, if Rod hadn't kept pinching me awake. Why they make us take classes when there's only two weeks left is beyond me. Where've you been?"

"I stopped by Miss Kreplach's office," Lois explained, referring to the gym teacher who was also pep club moderator, although she was content to leave the pep squad in Lois's capable hands. Now Lois kicked off her ballet flats and opened her locker as she spoke. "I wanted to make sure she received my memo about reserving the gym for us on Friday." Then she hurried on, "Faye, you'll never guess what Miss Watkins said to me." Barely waiting for Faye's perfunctory "What?" Lois announced, "She's found me a job as a secretary in Bay City! She says I have 'managerial ability'!"

"You? A career girl in Bay City?" Faye hooted. "Of all

the nutty ideas!" She turned toward the door that led to the practice field, her arms full of blue and white pom-poms. "I'll get the squad warmed up. See you out there." And with a swirl of her short pleated skirt, she was gone.

Lois stood stock still for a moment, then swiftly stripped her clothes off and pulled on her uniform, trying to ignore a sudden sinking sensation in the pit of her stomach. "Faye will be as keen about being a career girl as I am, once I explain it carefully," she told herself. She shouldn't have blurted her news like that.

After practice, Lois decided. When they were sharing a Coke at the Korner Koffee Kuppe, Lois would tell her all the details, and make her understand what this meant for both of them.

The other members of the squad were doing stretches and jumps when Lois joined them on the field. "Chin up on your toe touches, Cathy," Lois called to the newest Nutshell. Cathy valiantly kicked both feet in the air simultaneously and touched her toes for a split second, a fixed smile on her red face. Looking at her effort, Lois remembered what it felt like, to care so deeply about making a perfect toe touch. Cathy would make a good cheerleader, Lois thought. She was glad she was leaving a well-trained squad behind her. "Leaving," she said softly, savoring the word. And her spirits lifted again.

"That's much better," she said to the flushed girl, who turned even redder with pleasure. Lois clapped her hands for attention. "Okay, girls, five more for stretches, and then we'll go over routine 3C02." At the blank looks of the squad she added, "The herkie-jerkie." Lois had made a chart of all the routines by number, but for some reason, the other girls could only remember them by nickname. "Dottie, you nearly collided with Marilyn on the cross last weekend, so we're going to work this until we get it right!"

The sky was as blue as their uniforms and the air had an intoxicating hint of summer warmth. The girls' spirited cries sounded small in the empty football field.

> *Oh, the nuts don't fall far from the tree* (clap
> clap)
> *Here in the land of the free* (clap clap)
> *Walnuts take us to vic-to-RY!* (clap clap clap)

It was the perfect day to be practicing cheers. Lois was everywhere at once, exhorting, correcting, encouraging.

"One, two, three, four," she chanted, beating the time with her foot while Marilyn and Dottie leapt one after the other, left to right and then right to left, front knee bent, back leg extended in a perfect herkie. Behind them Faye lifted her spectacular legs in an effortless toe touch while the rest of the squad did handsprings and cartwheels. "That's it," Lois applauded vigorously. "Just do that Saturday morning."

"Gosh, Lois, I don't know how we'll get along without you next year," Cathy burst out.

Lois put her arm around Cathy and gave her a quick squeeze. "You girls will do just fine. You have a great squad and Dottie's going to be a terrific captain." But Dottie was shaking her head. "Nowhere near as good as you," she said firmly. "They ought to hire you as part of the coaching staff!"

Lois laughed lightheartedly. "Maybe once that would have appealed to me," she admitted. "But I'm ready to move on, now that—" She stopped herself as Faye shot her a suspicious look. "Now that I've got plans," she amended hastily. Before anyone could ask what those plans were, she blew two sharp toots on her whistle. "Okay, let's run through the pyramid."

Obediently the girls assembled in formation, Faye in

the center with Dottie and Marilyn on either side. Cathy knelt in front of Faye, her hands cupped together. Lois bounced once on her toes, stepped into Cathy's hand, and was vaulted onto Faye's shoulders. Dottie and Marilyn spotted her on either side as she lifted her arms and began the chant:

Three two one, Oh!
One two three, Go!
Score! Score! Score!

They clapped three times in unison, and then Lois jumped down in front of Faye, who put her hands lightly around Lois's waist to spot her. Usually Lois went right into a somersault, but today Faye's hands stopped her, gripping her hips firmly.

"You're not thinking seriously about this secretary thing, are you?" Faye asked under her breath, her blue eyes boring into Lois like twin blue flames. "Let's talk about it later," Lois murmured, twisting out of Faye's grip. "Great job, girls!" she said hastily. "Let's do some tumbles and call it a day."

"I think we should practice the Up-and-Over," Faye spoke up suddenly. "What is it, routine 42B or something?" The other girls looked at her in surprise. Although Faye was nominally cocaptain, she was usually content to let Lois run the squad.

"It's 4A01," Lois corrected automatically. "I think we're a little tired . . ." Then seeing the dangerous glint in Faye's eye, she added hastily, "But maybe just once. Positions, girls!"

Routine number 4A01, or as the squad called it the "Up-and-Over," consisted of Lois and Faye doing double somersaults in front of the stands while the other girls did a combination of cartwheels and kicks. Lois flipped herself into position, standing on her hands with her face toward Faye's legs, as Faye grasped her ankles. As soon as she felt Faye's support, Lois shifted her hands to hold Faye's ankles, and in a carefully coordinated move, Faye sank backward, pulling Lois with her. Lois used the momentum of Faye's fall to pull herself upright, so that she was in Faye's starting position and Faye was in hers. Then they repeated the whole process again, in a series of slow rolls across the field.

"You *are* thinking of taking this secretary job, aren't you?" whispered Faye furiously as they completed the first roll.

"Faye, she said I have talent! That I could succeed in the business world!" Lois whispered back urgently, automatically bending her legs and sinking to the ground, her eyes fixed on Faye's dimpled knees.

"Lois, you never had the slightest inclination for the quote-unquote business world before Miss Watkins put the idea in your head," snapped Faye. "You just have a huge crush on her!" They were rolling more rapidly now, as Faye lunged up and down with energetic anger.

"I certainly respect her opinion," said Lois weakly, knowing that once again, Faye had seen through her.

"It's a crush," said Faye fiercely. "The way you had a crush on Pamela Prendergast when she was squad captain, the way Cathy has a crush on you! But when you're stuck in Bay City and Miss Watkins isn't around, then where'll you be?"

"Well, I'll be in Bay City," said Lois, trying to think logically, which was difficult when her head was spinning.

"You'll be alone," Faye sank down like a well-oiled piston, "friendless," Lois was upright now, "cooped up in some dull, stuffy office." Abruptly Faye pulled her ankles out of Lois's grasp and flipped herself upright. She was panting from the exertion, her half-opened lips full and pouting, her blue eyes sparking and snapping with emotion. "Don't you know I know you better than you know yourself?"

Lois's head was still spinning from the double somersaults. Was Faye right? Was she just under Miss Watkins's spell? She felt disoriented, and as she looked at Faye, her logic and the arguments she'd planned were swept away in one of those tidal waves of need that seemed to wash over her with increasing frequency. She wanted to pull Faye to her, put her hands under the tight blue sweater that was riding up around Faye's ribs right now, allowing Lois a tantalizing glimpse of her bare midriff. She wanted to nibble on the pink mouth that taunted her so. If only the rest of the squad would just vanish!

But where was the squad? Lois looked around, puzzled. Then she saw them, tiny dots at the other end of the field. While she and Faye had been talking, they'd rolled as far as the fifty yard line.

Faye's eyes were still on her, twin molten pools of blue. "I know what makes you tick," she said huskily. "And it isn't filing boring papers in some dusty office."

Lois's breath quickened. "I'd better tell the rest of the squad to hit the showers," she said, licking her suddenly dry lips. "Don't you think?"

"Oh yes." Faye nodded her head slowly. "They've practiced enough for today."

Chapter Three
A Talk with Mom

"Bye, Faye, see you tomorrow," Lois said as she got out of the blue convertible that had been Faye's sixteenth birthday present. "Thanks for the ride." Her brown eyes twinkled mischievously as she added, "And everything."

"It'll be just me picking you up tomorrow." Faye smiled. "The boys have early practice."

Lois watched the low-slung convertible back rakishly into the street, the expensive vehicle out of place on this block of modest homes. Then she turned up the concrete walk to her own house's side porch.

The Lenzes occupied half of a weathered frame house. It was a bit cramped at times, but comfortable. And there was more room now that Lois's older sister Marjorie had married and moved into a small apartment with her new husband.

" 'Lo, Mom, I'm home," Lois called in the direction of the kitchen before heading upstairs to the small room under the eaves she had shared with Marjorie. She set her books down on her tidy desk and then flung herself full-length on one of the twin beds (she still hadn't gotten around to rearranging the room), stretching and luxuriating in that sense of complete, physical well-being that came after a good workout.

How could she have considered, even for an instant, anything that would take her away from Faye? They'd been inseparable since freshman year. It wasn't just that they both liked cheering and throwing parties, or that they preferred Tab Hunter to Troy Donahue. Faye was the only one who could even partially quench those mysterious desires that swamped Lois without warning, like a flash flood in spring, submerging her sensible side so that she hardly knew herself.

She remembered the first time she'd felt that way. They'd been lying on Faye's ruffled canopied bed studying math together. Faye's bare leg had brushed hers and Lois had suddenly felt a zing of electricity that made her hands tremble and twisted her insides. She'd stopped in mid-calculation and looked at Faye, wide-eyed and open mouthed. And Faye had looked back at her as if she understood everything Lois was feeling.

That was when she'd suggested they practice kissing. So they'd be more confident on dates, she'd said.

But their practices were always too short, interrupted by their parents, or their schedules, or sometimes by Faye.

I'd like to practice going all the way, Lois thought wistfully.

She rolled over on her side and her eyes fell on her filing cabinet. She sighed a little. Billy had built her that filing cabinet in Shop, and given it to her for her sixteenth birthday. Lois sat up and pulled open the middle drawer. She felt a satisfaction spread through her at the array of neatly labeled, color-coded files. It was a different kind of satisfaction from what she felt with Faye, but important nonetheless.

A doubt nibbled at the edge of her mind. Did Faye really know her as well as she thought? So maybe she *did* have a crush on Miss Watkins, but the career counselor's suggestion also appealed to her at a deeper level. The problem was, Faye knew only part of what made her tick. She'd never understood Lois's fascination with filing.

But she does appreciate my organization, Lois argued with herself silently. She likes me to help her with her parties!

She brushed her fingers lightly over the files and then pulled out the blue one labeled SQUAD—FRESHMAN YEAR. She opened it to the squad roster: Pamela Prendergast, captain. Carol Claver, co-captain. At the bottom of the list were the two alternates: Lois Lenz and Faye Collins. She turned the sheet over. Underneath there was a photo, clipped from the school newspaper, of the whole squad. Lois was standing at the top of the pyramid, and Faye was kneeling at the side. In front of the pyramid was a stunning redhead doing the splits. Of course the photo was black and white, but Lois remembered Pamela's hair, the color of fine mahogany. Funny, Faye bringing her up after all this time. Lois had forgotten the desperate crush on Pamela she'd had most of freshman year, the lengths to which she'd go to win a smile from the squad captain.

Pamela had gone to work in Bay City after graduation, Lois recalled now. She had planned to attend State, but something had happened, Lois couldn't remember exactly what. Was it that the Prendergasts had lost their money? Or that Pamela's parents had caught her in a compromising position with her boyfriend? Either way, after the end of her freshman year, Lois had never seen Pamela again.

Suddenly the cloud of dissatisfaction was back, full force. The sense of physical well-being vanished like steam from the locker room. There was a whole world out there to be explored, and if she didn't get out of Walnut Grove, Lois felt she'd simply die of asphyxiation!

Abruptly she slapped the file shut and stuffed it hastily back into the drawer. Pushing the drawer closed, she bounced off the bed and went downstairs in search of her mother. She found her in the kitchen, folding up her sewing and putting the new portable sewing machine in its place under the pantry shelves.

She held up her handiwork for Lois to see, a panel of muslin printed with brightly colored vegetables. Mrs. Lenz had sewn a green ruffle to the bottom.

"Kitchen curtains?" Lois guessed.

Her mother nodded proudly. "Summery, hmmm? It's for your hope chest."

Ever since Lois could remember, her mother had been sewing curtains and bed shams, embroidering table runners, knitting afghans, and crocheting doilies. "It's my little hobby," she liked to tell visitors. Lois's hope chest was half full, without Lois having ever threaded a needle.

Now she glanced at the clock and told Lois, "Peel the potatoes, dear, your father will be home soon."

Lois fetched the vegetable peeler from the drawer and took four potatoes from the bin in the pantry, then put one back. It was hard to remember that Marjorie was gone. She knew that Marjorie hadn't been happy at cosmetology school, but she wasn't sure she'd be happy with Joe Jorgenson either. He'd been her reliable steady all through high school, but Lois had suspected that Marjorie would have dropped him like a flash if someone more interesting had come along or something.

Her mother was taking off the pink flowered smock she wore for sewing, and putting on a green and yellow plaid apron. She lifted the lid of a simmering pot on the stove and gave the contents a stir. The smell of pot roast filled the air.

"I had my meeting with Miss Watkins today," Lois told her mother as she began to peel the potatoes.

"A meeting with a teacher! Are you in trouble at school, Lois?"

"No, no," Lois corrected her, "Miss Watkins is the guidance counselor. All the seniors meet with her, so she can give them guidance in their careers."

"These modern methods," her mother murmured, getting down the china and going into the dining room. Her voice floated back to the kitchen: "I simply can't keep up!"

"She said I should be a secretary." Lois raised her voice so her mother would hear. "She said I have managerial capability!"

"What, dear?" Her mother called.

"Managerial capability!" Lois shouted.

Her mother bustled back into the kitchen. "Well, I should think so!" She glanced pridefully at the flow chart taped to the wall. "Who else could have designed such a wonderful work flow chart? Who else pointed out that I could get more sewing done if I moved the machine to the kitchen? Why, I'd never have gotten those curtains started today if I'd been running up and down to the spare room where it used to be!"

"Do you think I should take a secretarial job in Bay City?" Lois asked eagerly.

"Bay City!" Lois's mother turned pale, and put a hand over her heart. "Oh my, Lois, you know Bay City is no place for a young girl! Why, I clipped *Confidentially* just yesterday to show Mrs. Jorgenson . . . where is it?" Her mother rustled through a pile of clippings on the sideboard. "Here it is, 'White Slavers: City's New Menace. Men and Women Old in Evil, and the Unsuspecting Girls They Prey On.' It's all about naive young girls like you, who think they can make it in the big city and they end up drugged, and . . ." Mrs. Lenz's voice sank to a horrified whisper. "*Ruined.*"

Lois's heart fell. She'd forgotten how her mother relished Mamie McArdle's syndicated *Confidentially* column and the exposés the crusading journalist wrote about big-city problems. For weeks after Mamie McArdle's series on teenage delinquents, Lois's mother would barely let Lois out of the house.

"And you know, Lois"—her mother's voice sank even lower—"Mr. Bates at the processing plant said there are radicals in Bay City, even Communists! He said they were the ones behind the trouble they had with the shellers last year. No, dear," her mother continued, "this 'capability' of yours will make you a wonderful hobby after you're married, but it doesn't mean you should make a career out of it." She laughed a little. "Imagine if I'd made a career out of sewing!"

Lois, who'd often thought her mother could generate a nice little income making curtains and pillows for other homes besides the Lenzes', opened her mouth to reply, but her mother steamrolled on.

"Besides, you'd miss Billy and your other friends here in Walnut Grove," Mrs. Lenz concluded. "And I have a feeling that this summer Billy might be getting ready to ask a certain question!" She beamed at Lois coyly.

A cold chill went up Lois's spine. Could her mother be right? Would Billy propose to her this summer? The mere thought filled her with horror. But why was she surprised? Of course her parents expected her to follow Marjorie's path and marry in a few years. They looked forward to the day she and Billy would buy a small house in the new sub-division and come to dinner every Sunday. Lois felt panic rising in her at the thought. She liked Billy, but she'd rather be kidnapped by white slavers than marry him just yet!

"There's your father now." Lois's mother undid the plaid apron and tied on a ruffled one of crisp white dimity. "Put those potatoes in the oven and put Bay City out of your mind!"

Chapter Four
A Proposal for Faye

But Bay City was solidly lodged in Lois's brain now. She tossed and turned all night. She didn't want to leave Faye, and her parents certainly didn't want her to go to Bay City, and yet—

That picture of herself in an office—typing, filing, part of a bigger world—floated seductively in her mind's eye. She could see herself looking down from her office tower at the hustle and bustle of the city, where girls were drugged, and delinquents ran wild in the streets. The excitement was like a siren's call as she lay in her safe, sleepy little town.

Like Miss Watkins said, it's just for the summer, she argued silently with her phantom parents. It'll be an experiment.

If I can just persuade Faye, she thought. We've always done everything together. With her by my side, I know I can make a success as a career girl!

But without her? a small voice in her head whispered.

I'll persuade her, Lois told the voice. I didn't have a chance to really explain today.

Have you ever been able to persuade Faye? asked the voice. Or is it Faye who always persuades you?

Lois put a pillow over her head to squelch the little voice, and pictured again the apartment she and Faye would have, the gay parties they would throw, the admiration of their circle of sophisticated friends. She drifted to sleep, picturing herself and Faye demonstrating the latest dance step.

When Faye picked her up the next day, Lois plunged right in, before she could lose her courage. "You know Faye," she began, as Faye pulled away from the curb, "when I was thinking of going to Bay City, I was thinking we could both go."

"Bay City? Both go?" Faye repeated blankly. "What are you talking about?"

"I could take the secretarial job and you'd be a cinch for a model," said Lois eagerly. "We could get a cute little apartment, and decorate it all in—"

"You're forgetting one thing," said Faye. "I don't want to be a model."

"Well, what about working in an art gallery?" Lois persisted. "You've always done well in Art—"

Faye speeded up a little, taking a corner recklessly fast. "So I can be at the beck and call of a bunch of long-haired artists?"

"You could be a restaurant hostess—"

"Daddy would never permit it!"

"Or you could work at one of the big department stores—"

"Doing what?" demanded Faye.

"Demonstration cooking?" suggested Lois desperately.

"Look, Lois," Faye responded with controlled patience, "here in Walnut Grove we're tops, the two most popular girls in high school, and we'll be the most popular girls at Northridge Junior College. I know that Epsilon Epsilon Chi wants to pledge us. Why on earth," she continued more vehemently, "would I give that up to go to Bay City, which has a lot of queer types anyway, just to be ordered around by a bunch of greasy photographers or art dealers or businessmen? Why would you want to bury yourself in some boring office all day long?" She turned puzzled eyes to Lois. "I honestly don't get it."

"It's just . . ." Lois began helplessly. "It's just I feel like if I don't get out of Walnut Grove, I'll explode!" They'd reached school, and Faye had pulled into a parking space and turned off the ignition. Lois's last word echoed loudly in the sudden stillness.

"Well, of course we'll get out of Walnut Grove!" exclaimed Faye. "We'll go to Bay City later this summer for shopping, and we'll be going to State for weekend dances in the fall, and maybe to dances at other schools—"

"But—" Lois tried to interrupt.

Faye was just getting warmed up. "And after the boys get out of State and propose, we can have a double wedding, and buy houses right next door to each other in Falling Leaves."

Another proposal! Lois felt the familiar wave of sick dread.

"Billy's family is quite well-to-do, and Daddy will help me and Rod. We'll join the country club, and take over the bridge club and the garden club . . . why, we'll run this town!"

"But that's just more of the same old thing," Lois said helplessly. "I mean . . . listen, do you remember that trip our junior English class took to Bay City to see the exhibition on Elizabethan theater?"

"Yes," said Faye dubiously.

"Do you remember that girl who winked at us, the one with the short hair, who was unloading the delivery truck?"

"That was a boy," said Faye coldly.

"No, it was a girl," Lois insisted.

Faye's blue eyes were like twin beams of ice. "It was a boy," she repeated. "Just a dumb delivery boy, being fresh." She opened the car door with a jerk. "I don't know what point you're trying to make, but I'll tell you this much: The only time I'm going to Bay City is to buy my fall wardrobe!" With that, Faye slammed the door and stalked away.

Lois sat in the car lost in unhappy thought. The conversation hadn't gone anything like she'd planned! I didn't get to tell her about the apartment, Lois mourned. That's what would have convinced Faye. Instead she'd gone off on a tangent about the delivery girl. It had been a girl, Lois was sure of that. And she'd just wanted to point out to Faye that living in Bay City they'd meet all kinds of new and exciting people, people who didn't exist in Walnut Grove. She'd thought Faye had shared the funny little thrill it gave her, seeing a girl doing a boy's job. But now Faye was mad at Lois, as mad as she'd been that time after the Homecoming dance when Lois had spent the night and fallen asleep in Faye's bed. It was confusing, the things that ticked Faye off.

The distant ringing of the first period bell pulled Lois back to the present with a start. Classes had begun, and for the first time in her high school career, Lois was late!

Chapter Five

Detention for Lois

L ois sprang out of the car and sprinted for the high school entrance. Surely Miss Kreplach, who was on hall monitor duty first period, would understand and give her a pass! But Lois was out of luck that morning. Her entrance coincided with another group of stragglers, the kids her crowd mockingly called "the JDs." They were Walnut Grove's version of the teenaged hoodlums Mamie McArdle had described so chillingly. Except these boys and girls just spent the time before school sitting in their hot rods smoking cigarettes. They didn't belong to any of the school clubs, and the only school events they attended were the dances. Their biggest crime had been at the Winter Wonderland Ball last December, when Johnny Doone, the boy with the longest sideburns in Walnut Grove, had been suspended for spiking the punch.

Miss Kreplach's eyes widened with surprise as she saw Lois in the company of these disaffected youths, but she didn't hesitate. "You're late, all of you," she said curtly. "Report to Mr. Wolfe's office."

The group straggled down the hall toward the assistant principal's office. "Look," said one girl to another in an audible whisper, "it's the shadow! But she's got nothing to shadow!" The two girls giggled, casting sidelong glances in Lois's direction. After looking around curiously to see whom they were talking about, Lois realized, with a start, that they were referring to her! Never mind, she told herself. Faye always said girls like these were just jealous of her and Faye's popularity.

"How will she know what to do?" whispered the second girl to the first. "With nobody to copy?"

Lois couldn't help getting steamed. Just because she and Faye were good friends didn't mean she was a copycat! Just because this was the first morning in four years they hadn't walked into school together, after having coordinated their outfits the night before, didn't mean she wasn't her own person!

She eyed the two girls as they stood in line in Mr. Wolfe's office. They were the kind who wore their skirts tight, their lipstick red, and their hair teased. Suddenly the one with the blond bouffant demanded, "Whatcha staring at? Have I got a pimple or a hickey or something?"

"No, you look very nice," stammered Lois. "I was just admiring your lipstick."

The girl's aggressiveness changed to friendliness all at once.

"Try it," she suggested, taking a gold tube from her purse. "That shade you have on doesn't do a thing for you!"

"Why—all right." Lois applied the dark red lipstick carefully and examined the results in her compact. It made her look older, more daring. She took the late pass that would admit her to French and followed the two girls out into the hall. They studied her, lips pursed thoughtfully.

"Passion Fruit suits you. Listen, first period is for the birds. We're going to the bleachers for a smoke, wanna come?"

Lois was touched by the girl's friendly offer. Faye would

say no, of course; Faye was likely sitting in Madame Poiccard's class wondering where Lois was. Well—let her wonder a little longer! Lois felt a sort of carefree recklessness take hold of her. "Why—okay!" she said with a smile. "Only I've never smoked a cigarette before."

The girl and her friend laughed as if not surprised. "We'll show you how," the blond bouffant girl promised, introducing herself. "I'm Charmaine, and this is Wendy."

As they stole through the hallways quietly, on the lookout for Miss Kreplach, Charmaine and Wendy told Lois that they often cut first period.

"To tell you the truth, I'm usually so beat in the mornings, I just sleep through my alarm," confessed Charmaine as they pushed open the door to the athletic field. "What do I care about Dom Sci anyway?"

"Why are you so—so beat?" inquired Lois, imitating Charmaine's slang.

"She's a carhop at the new burger joint out on the highway," explained Wendy. Charmaine was busy cupping her hand around her match and cigarette to protect it from the spring breeze.

"And the tips are terrific!" Charmaine said when she'd gotten the cigarette lit. "Which is all gravy, because Momma needs some wheels. Her *own* wheels, dig? As soon as kindergarten's out, I'll be working 'round the clock, and then see my smoke!" She handed Lois the cigarette and exhaled through both nostrils, like a dragon. Lois wasn't sure if she meant smoke literally or figuratively.

"I'm thinking of getting a job after graduation, too," she confessed, coughing a little as she inhaled.

"Oh yeah? Doing what?" Charmaine asked.

"Miss Watkins has recommended me for a secretarial position—in Bay City," Lois told her shyly.

Neither girl evinced any surprise. "Well, that makes sense," said Charmaine, puffing away. "You're already secretary of everything around *here*!" She and Wendy laughed in a friendly way. "My cousin works as a secretary for Mr. Bates at the nut factory," Wendy volunteered as they climbed under the bleachers toward a group of other boys and girls at the far end. "She says the money's pretty good."

Her last remark barely penetrated Lois's consciousness. She'd been watching with curiosity a couple standing apart from the rest of the group, who seemed interested only in each other. The boy's back was to her, but she recognized the girl: She was Jane Phillips, the only Negro girl at Walnut Grove High. Lois didn't know her very well; the only class they shared was Dom Sci, and Jane hadn't joined any school clubs or taken part in any activities. Although, Lois remembered, she *had* briefly been a member of the Future Homemakers of America. But there'd been some sort of fuss, which Lois hadn't paid much attention to, and Jane had dropped out.

Now, as Lois watched, the boy lifted the girl's hand and pressed his lips to it, like the hero of a French movie. Good heavens! Was Walnut Grove home to an interracial romance, like the one in *Showboat*? As Lois watched, Jane pulled her hand out of the boy's grasp, and walked swiftly back toward the school building. She did a double take when she saw Lois, but hurried on without stopping.

"Jane, wait!" The boy hurried after her, but came to a dead stop at the sight of Lois. The boy was Billy.

Oh, thank goodness! thought Lois, feeling a wave of relief wash over her. Now not even Faye would try to pressure her into marrying her steady. Now Lois understood why Billy had argued so vehemently on the pro side when the debate club proposed the question, "Should You Marry Outside Your Faith?"

"Lois, what are you doing here? I mean—oh, Lois! This is a big mess!"

"Don't feel bad," she reassured him. "I think Jane is a swell kid." She took a drag from Charmaine's cigarette, feeling broadminded and sophisticated. It struck her suddenly that she and Billy had never necked, parked, or petted. It wasn't just that they'd never gotten to first base—Billy had never stepped up to bat.

And Faye and I spent so much time practicing! Lois thought bemusedly, as Billy launched into a long explanation of why he was courting Jane under the bleachers in the morning and taking Lois out on movie dates in the evening. He'd never meant to two-time Lois, he said. But Jane's father absolutely forbade Jane to date a white boy. "He's worried he'll get lynched or something." Billy dismissed Mr. Phillip's concerns. "So I thought, if I keep dating you, no one will suspect anything!" His shoulders slumped. "Except Jane says she's sick of being my secret romance. So you and I can't go steady anymore. Of course, I'll still take you to the prom if you want to go with me," he hastened to add.

"Well, of course I still want to go to prom with you!" Lois said, thinking it would be more fun than ever, now that she didn't have to worry Billy might propose. She searched for the words to wipe the guilty expression from her steady's face, and blurted out the first thing that came to her mind. "And don't worry about this summer—Miss Watkins found me a job as a secretary in Bay City."

"Oh?" Billy's eyebrows shot up to his dirty blond thatch of hair. "Gosh, I didn't realize! That's terrif!"

"Well, I'm not sure I'm going to take it," Lois added hastily. "You know Faye and I have already made plans to—"

"Not going to take it!" Billy exploded, "Why, Lois, you're nuts!" Several smokers shot quizzical glances at the pair and he lowered his voice.

"You have a chance to get out of this picayune town

and you're going to turn it down? For what, four more years of being Faye's stooge?"

Lois tried to protest, but Billy was going on, speaking more vehemently than she'd ever heard him speak. It was as if his easygoing facade had cracked open, to reveal a new, more passionate Billy underneath.

"What I wouldn't give to live in Bay City!" he continued. "Free lectures on social change! Integrated jazz clubs! Art galleries showing African art! To get away from the petty prejudices of people who think culture means a lecture at the garden club! To get out of Walnut Grove!"

"But—but you're getting out—you're going to State," Lois protested.

"Yeah, on a football scholarship! Do you have any idea how sick I am of playing football?"

Lois knew that Billy always weaseled out of practice whenever he could and had taken Art despite the teasing and heckling of his teammates, but she'd never thought about it much. Faye had explained it to everyone by saying Billy needed an easy A. Now, it seemed, there was another way of looking at it.

A low whistle came from Johnny Doone. "Second period in five minutes, for those who are going," he announced. There was a general scramble as the class-cutters snuck back to the school building by twos and threes. Lois fell in with Charmaine and Wendy, who ground out their cigarettes and sauntered back across the football field. The conversation with Billy was intriguing, but her next class was Business Methods, and she didn't want to miss it!

M iss Grimes was handing out statistical chart exercises when Lois slipped into her seat and took the cover off her typewriter. But Miss Grimes stopped her. "Not you, dear," said her favorite teacher with a twinkle in her eye. "Miss Watkins has told me about your exciting opportunity! Come with me, I have something special for you!"

It was turning into a most unusual day, Lois thought, as she put the cover back on the typewriter and left behind the clatter of her classmates pounding out numbers. She followed Miss Grimes to the teachers' lounge. Inside the restricted room, Lois looked around curiously. The off-duty teachers were all smoking, and Lois was struck by the uncanny resemblance to the scene under the bleachers, except that the teachers had comfortable chairs and mugs of coffee.

Miss Grimes was bubbling over with excitement as she took a parcel neatly wrapped in brown packing paper from a shelf and handed it to Lois.

"Oh, Miss Grimes!" breathed Lois. "You shouldn't have!"

"I'm sorry there's no ribbon," Miss Grimes apologized excitedly. "Go ahead, open it!"

"I like the brown paper," said Lois, taking the gift. "It's so businesslike." Her hands felt unusually clumsy as she tore the paper off, revealing a thick, heavy book bound in blue. Lois turned it over and gasped with pleasure at the title: *Standard Secretary's Desk Reference, Fourth Edition.*

"Oh, Miss Grimes," was all she could say. She opened the book at random as Miss Grimes burbled, "It's a few years old, but still quite up-to-date! All the postage rates are still accurate, and so many things never change!"

Lois's eyes had fallen upon a section titled, "Efficient Methods of Preparing Letters and Handing Them In." Suddenly the page blurred as her eyes filled with tears. One of them fell on the open book, making an ugly wet splotch on the words "proofread slowly."

"Why, Lois, what in the world?" exclaimed Miss Grimes. Lois sank down on one of the lounge's comfortable chairs. "It's just, it's just, this is so nice, and I'm not sure what to do!" she half sobbed, half laughed. "I'm not sure I can be a secretary, even though I really want to!"

"Really want to *be one*," corrected Miss Grimes automatically, sitting down next to her. "What seems to be the problem, Lois?"

"Faye wants me to go to Northridge Junior College with her," Lois explained, taking the neatly folded white handkerchief that Miss Grimes handed her. "She'll be furious with me if I don't, and meanwhile my mother thinks Bay City's too dangerous and I'll be kidnapped into a white slave ring . . ." The tears flowed again. Could I be having hysterics? Lois asked herself in astonishment.

"Your friends and family mean well, I'm sure, but Lois, you have to think of what *you* want," said Miss Grimes firmly. "After all, it's your life!" Lois blinked back her tears. This was a new thought. "I'm sure Faye will recover if you don't accompany her to Northridge, and you'll continue to be great friends!"

Lois wondered if she could explain to Miss Grimes the exact nature of her special friendship with Faye.

"As for your mother, I have a solution that might reassure her! That's the other reason I wanted to see you." She handed Lois a card, saying, "I didn't know if you'd thought yet about your living arrangements."

Lois wiped her eyes and looked at the card with interest.

THE MAGDALENA ARMS
A Residence for Women
220 W. 47th Steet
Bay City
"Let he who is without sin
cast the first stone"

"That should satisfy your mother," Miss Grimes continued gaily. "It's a supervised boardinghouse, with a curfew and a sort of housemother who acts as a chaperone for the girls who live there." She stood up. "Of course, there's often a waiting list, but I have a little influence with Mrs. DeWitt, so you needn't worry about *that*."

Lois stood up as well. "Thank you for the recommendation, and the book. I'll certainly think about what you said."

Miss Grimes patted her arm. "No need for thanks, Lois dear," she said. "I know senior year is an emotional time. But when you're settled in Bay City, you'll look back on this and realize it was all a tempest in a teapot!"

Lois still wasn't certain, but she hadn't the heart to burden Miss Grimes with more of her doubts. This was the woman who had taught her that Mc comes before Ma, after all.

The day continued to be out of the ordinary. The oddest thing, Lois realized at the end of it, was that she'd barely glimpsed Faye. After Business Methods her third period was Business Math, while Faye had third-period Art. Usually they met for fourth-period lunch, but today Miss Watkins intercepted her in the hall and whisked her downtown to apply for a social security card, which she would need, Miss Watkins told her, for her job. When Lois confessed that she was still uncertain about whether or not she would take the job, Miss Watkins merely smiled, and said, "It's good to be prepared either way, don't you think?"

With everything that happened, Lois didn't see Faye until sixth-period Civics. "Where in the world have you been today?" the beautiful blond girl demanded as they slid into their seats. Lois shrugged helplessly. Mr. Harrison was announcing a pop quiz and the events of the day were too involved to get into. "Well, never mind," murmured Faye. "Meet me at my locker and we'll go to the Korner Koffee Kuppe for a malted."

"I can't!" remembered Lois. "I have detention seventh period."

"*Detention!*" Faye twisted around, her eyes wide with shock. Mr. Harrison, passing out test papers, hushed her sternly.

When Lois entered the library for detention after Civics, Charmaine and Wendy waved to her from the back table as if they were old friends. To Lois's astonishment, Enid Butler was sitting with them. Enid seemed equally startled to see Lois. "What are you in for?" she asked as Lois hesitantly pulled out an empty chair next to the brainy girl.

"I was late this morning," Lois explained. "How about you?"

"I cut Dom Sci to work on a proof for trigonometry,"

said Enid. She ground her teeth. "Dom Sci is the dumbest waste of time ever!"

"Here's my math homework," Charmaine interrupted, handing Enid a piece of paper. Lois was startled when Charmaine gave her a dollar bill as well. "And here's the payola for last time. Remember, jazz it up with a few mistakes, or even a square like Mr. Schultie will catch on."

"Charmaine pays you to do her homework?" Lois asked, torn between horror and fascination.

"Sure," said Enid. "She doesn't have the time and I need the money. College isn't cheap, you know. Unless, of course, you're Faye Collins! What a waste of time, going to Northridge Junior."

It was funny to hear Enid, who ducked her head and hurried on whenever Faye said hello, calmly criticizing the most popular girl in school. "Well, Faye's not a brain like you," Lois defended her friend.

Enid snorted, and the librarian glared at her. Lowering her voice, Enid said, "Faye was better at math than I was in eighth grade when we used to study together. Then she got that popularity bug in her head."

"Really?" stammered Lois.

"Oh yes, back in eighth grade, when I'd sleep over at her house, we'd argue over where we should go to college, Radcliffe or Smith." Enid took off her thick glasses and rubbed the bridge of her nose. With her dark brows and square jaw, she bore a startling resemblance to Rod. Then she put her glasses back on and the resemblance vanished.

The librarian was frowning at them, so Lois opened her *Secretary's Desk Reference* and bent her head over it. But the words whirled before her eyes as she tried to make sense out of her unusual day.

For the first time in four years, Lois wondered about Faye's belief that popularity was the be-all and end-all of

existence. "Poor" Enid was thinking about college tu-
ition, not dates, while Charmaine, far from envying Lois
and Faye, was wrapped up in her carhop job and the
"wheels" she wanted. Then there was Billy. Faye had always said he and Lois were a perfect couple. But how
was it Lois had dated him for three years without ever
suspecting that he was carrying on a secret romance? Or
that he hated football?

Faye was waiting for Lois after detention, leaning
against Lois's locker, a faint pout on her lips. "For
heaven's sakes, tell me what on earth happened to you
today," she demanded as Lois dialed the combination to
her locker. "Did you really have detention? Was it for
cutting French?"

"No, it was because I was late this morning, and then I
cut French to smoke under the bleachers with Charmaine
and Wendy," Lois explained.

"Smoke under the—Lois, are you crazy? You don't
want to get the kind of reputation those girls have!"

"They were awfully nice!" Lois protested. "Charmaine
loaned me her lipstick. Then I found out that Billy and
Jane—"

"Oh, you poor thing." Faye put her arm around Lois
comfortingly. "No wonder you're upset."

"You mean you knew?" Lois asked in surprise.

"Well—I'd heard the rumors." Faye stepped back and
fiddled with the clasp on her gold wristwatch. "I hoped
Billy would come to his senses before you found out."
She sighed. "I guess we'll have to ask Rod to fix you up
with someone else on the team for prom."

"Oh no, I'm still going with Billy to prom," Lois said,
shutting her locker.

"Lois, you can't! Not with a fellow who's been two-
timing you with a Negro girl! You'd be the laughing stock
of the school!"

"But I like Billy," Lois argued. "We're old friends. I don't want to date someone else."

Now Faye was distracted by the heavy *Secretary's Desk Reference* that Lois had under her arm. "Where did you get *that*?"

"Miss Grimes gave it to me. And guess what else I got— Miss Watkins took me downtown during fourth period to get a social security number!" Lois wanted to tell Faye how Miss Watkins had taken her out to lunch afterward, and the thrill she felt when their hands touched as Miss Watkins passed her the cream for her coffee, but Faye was rolling her eyes.

"I thought you'd given up that crazy idea of being a secretary."

"Well, no," said Lois hesitantly. "I've been thinking maybe it's not so crazy. Everyone I've talked to, except for Mom, seems to think it's a grand idea."

Faye changed her tactics. "Come with me to the girls' washroom. I need to refresh my lipstick—and so do you," she said enticingly.

Lois felt a flicker of warmth start inside her, as if a Girl Scout had put a match to a pile of kindling in her stomach. "Well, okay," she agreed, even though she realized what Faye was doing. She was counting on her ability to turn Lois topsy-turvy as the best way of persuading Lois to stay in town. Yes, Lois knew exactly what Faye had in mind, but she was helpless in the grip of those strange urges that Faye inspired in her. As she followed Faye to the bathroom, her whole body felt alive and her knees began to quiver in anticipation.

Faye stood in front of the mirror and slowly outlined her full lips with Strawberry Ice. Lois watched her, her stomach doing the queer little flip it always did when she gazed at Faye's profile. She felt her resolve weakening. Would there be anyone in Bay City like Faye? Could there be, anywhere?

Stop it! she told herself firmly. I'm not going to let Faye get me all hot and bothered. She bent down to splash cool water on her face. But while she blotted her flushed cheeks with a paper towel, Faye's arms encircled her from behind. They snaked under Lois's arms, and Faye's hands began to undo the buttons of Lois's crisp plaid blouse. Lois tried to be stoic, watching their reflection for a moment in the mirror, Faye's blond loveliness next to Lois's dark beauty, as if they were two other girls who had no connection to her.

Then Faye turned and with a lick of her pointed pink tongue lapped up the drop of water that was trickling down Lois's flushed cheek. All at once desire reared up in Lois, tearing away the last shreds of her resistance, drying up her uncertainties in its white-hot blast. She gripped the edge of the sink so hard her knuckles turned as white as the porcelain.

She didn't want to feel this—she didn't want to let her rational mind dissolve in this whirlwind of sensation—but every nerve of her was conscious of Faye's body pressing against her, of the heated trail left by Faye's kisses, of the uncanny expertise with which Faye teased and tortured Lois's suddenly aching breasts.

She twisted in Faye's grasp, so that she was facing the blond girl, and pulling Faye's head down, she kissed her ravenously. Faye responded with equal appetite.

Abruptly Lois pulled away. She yanked up Faye's soft cashmere slipover and savagely pulled at Faye's pink brassiere until the ripe young breast was free. Then she attacked it with her mouth, like a vampire pursuing the scent of blood.

"Oh—Lois—no," gasped Faye, "we never—not third base!" Her hands, poised on Lois's shoulder, ready to push her away, remained still. Lois's tongue teased the quivering girl's erect nipple, and Faye's protests died away in a low moan.

Lois reveled in Faye's weakness. There was something to be said for ignoring Faye's advice! Why hadn't she ever taken the lead in their practices before?

But now what? A phrase from a novel she'd once read at the drugstore flitted through Lois's head: "And she fell into a whirlpool that spun around until she floated away on a sea of rapturous release." But what did that mean exactly? She tried to think back to last year's hygiene class, and the *Guide to Marital Happiness* book, which Miss Gillhooly had kept on the restricted shelf.

I'll research this in Bay City, where they don't have any restricted shelves! she told herself.

While she'd been thinking, Faye's moment of weakness had passed. With a long quivering sigh, she pulled herself away from Lois, and straightened her disarranged clothing. "Goodness, Lois," she scolded lightly. "What were you thinking?"

Lois leaned back against the sink and panted, "I've been thinking I *will* take that secretarial job!"

Chapter Seven
Bay City

"Taxi!" called Lois breathlessly, and to her relief the yellow cab stopped at the curb with a jerk. The former Walnut Grove cheerleader-soon-to-be-secretary was happy to slide into the backseat and lean against the worn leather while the driver stowed her six-piece set of "French Tan" luggage in the trunk. It had been a long, hot train ride, and she was perspiring in the gray poplin suit that her mother thought correct for a visit to the city.

Through the cab window, Lois watched the constant stream of people going in and out of the train station. She couldn't get over the number of people the city held. Only three people had boarded the train in Walnut Grove, but here there were hundreds! And to Lois they all seemed to know exactly where they were going.

So do I! she reminded herself. But when the cab driver got in and grunted "Where to?" Lois had to hunt through her purse, pulling out her lipstick, her compact, her comb, a handkerchief, the envelope of "emergency money" her father had given her, and her change purse before she found the card with the address of the Magdalena Arms.

"Take me to 220 West Forty-Seventh Street," she told

the driver, and they were off with a jerk that threw Lois back against the brown leather seat.

It was only two weeks since Lois had stunned Faye with her decision. Yet so much had happened in those two weeks that Lois felt she'd been living in the path of a hurricane.

She'd raced from the restroom, not even bothering to refresh her lipstick, to tell Miss Watkins she'd take the job, before she could lose her nerve. Miss Watkins had immediately put in a long-distance call to Miss Gill in Bay City, and with her pulse still pounding and her nipples still tingling, Lois had secured a place in the typing pool of Sather & Stirling. In the excitement of the moment, fresh from the stimulating encounter with Faye, Lois almost embraced Miss Watkins, whose snug-fitting navy suit showed off her trim figure to perfection.

The letter to the Magdalena Arms had been less successful. How Lois's heart had plummeted like a penny tossed in a wishing well when Mrs. DeWitt had written her that there were no rooms available. The best Mrs. DeWitt could promise her was the first vacancy that came along.

Lois had felt even more hopeless as the days passed and nothing turned up. The prices apartment agencies quoted astounded her, and she knew of no other girl who could share living expenses with her. "What with the white slavery kidnappings and murderous teens, I'm surprised there aren't more vacancies," she'd fumed to Miss Grimes.

Then the miracle happened. The day before graduation Mrs. DeWitt had called. "You're a very lucky young lady," her voice crackled over the wire. "One of our girls had to leave very suddenly—sickness in the family."

With a place to stay assured, Lois broke the news to her parents. She'd enlisted the help of Miss Grimes and

Miss Watkins in reassuring her mother, and among the three of them, they'd managed to gain her parents' reluctant blessing. Lois touched the little silver whistle she wore around her neck. Her mother had given it to her so that if she found herself in danger, she could signal for help. "Promise me you'll never take it off!" Mrs. Lenz had begged her tearfully at the train station.

Lois knew her mother hoped her youngest daughter would be back by the end of the summer, ready to attend Northridge with Faye.

Faye. That had been the hardest part of the last two weeks. From the moment Lois had made her decision, Faye had tried a thousand different ways to change Lois's mind. And Faye could be very good at coaxing. She'd painted their life in Walnut Grove in enticing hues: Lois married ("If not Billy, someone even better!") and well off, fulfilling her ambitions by becoming secretary of the garden club, the pinnacle for every Walnut Grove social climber. She pictured their homes, right next door to each other ("Who will help me decorate? No one has your taste!"), the long afternoons when their husbands would be away at work, and they would have leisure to—Faye left the promise unspoken but it was in her eyes.

She was even more persuasive when she wasn't talking. And she'd been almost reckless in her attempts to show Lois what she'd be leaving behind. There'd been the time at prom, when Faye had pulled Lois outside the crowded gym "for some fresh air." Even the lace-ruffled, whalebone reinforced strapless basque of Lois's yellow formal was no barrier for the heat between them. Then there was the fallout shelter barbecue, when Faye's father demonstrated for the giggling crowd what it would be like when the bombs fell. As soon as he'd herded them inside and shut them in darkness, Faye had crushed Lois against the stacks of canned pork and beans, and her mouth had found Lois's for a long hungry kiss before the emergency lights came on.

There was one moment when Lois had weakened, when she'd come close to calling the whole trip off. Faye had stopped by the Lenz house the night before Lois was to leave. Lois had been double-checking her packing lists, wearing a faded pink sleeveless blouse from last summer and some old pedal pushers she'd inherited from Marjorie. Faye had been perfection, of course, in the latest fashion trend, a solid colored accordion pleated skirt and a matching striped sailor shirt. She'd carried a small, gift-wrapped box.

"It's not really a farewell present," she'd explained as she looked around Lois's bare room, not bothering to disguise her distaste for the partially filled bags that represented Lois's upcoming departure. "It's a 'come back soon' present." Lois had carefully undone the wrapping paper. Inside was a velvet box from Walnut Grove's finest jeweler. When she'd opened it up, there were two little charms for her charm bracelet, two tiny houses of delicate gold filagree.

"Oh, Faye," she'd said, and then the two girls were in each other's arms, and in the time it took for Faye's arms to tighten around Lois, the embrace went from mournful affection to white-hot desire. Lois's senses had reeled under Faye's passionate onslaught. She'd clung to the other girl and kissed her with a thirst that grew rather than lessened with each moment. Suddenly Faye had pushed Lois onto the bed and straddled the supine girl. "If this is what it takes to make you stay," she'd panted, her eyes glittering with desire, "then—"

If only Mom hadn't come in at that moment, with a pile of clean linens! Yet, perhaps it was for the best that she had interrupted them, gently scolding the pair for "roughhousing like children." Lois knew that if she and Faye had been left alone for even another minute, she would have been promising Faye to spend the rest of her life in Walnut Grove!

Peering from the window of the speeding taxi, Lois wondered, for the hundredth time, if she'd made the right decision. They'd reached the business district and were moving slowly through the traffic-clogged streets. Sunlight slanted down in the narrow slits between the tall gray skyscrapers of glass and steel, and the sidewalks overflowed with people. Lois pressed her face against the cab window, eyes wide as she watched the endless stream of humanity. Harried businessmen glanced at their watches and raised imperative hands for cabs, while beautifully dressed women sauntered more slowly, their arms heavy with shopping bags that bore the names of famous stores. A trim girl in brown linen darted across the street right in front of Lois's cab, and the girl from Walnut Grove blushed red to the roots of her dark brown bob as the driver leaned out the window and bellowed a curse. But the city girl hurried along without even glancing back.

There was an invigorating energy about the scene that lifted Lois's spirits and made her forget how hot and tired she was from the long train ride and the emotional whirlwind of the past weeks. Which one of these gleaming office towers housed Sather & Stirling? Would she, too, learn to skip blasély through traffic, like that other girl?

North of downtown, the cab turned off Broadway, Bay City's main thoroughfare, and headed west toward the waterfront. Now the streets were narrower and packed with four- and five-story brick buildings, all lined up right against each other without even a breathing space between. Lois wondered if these were the slums she'd read about in the newspaper. She wrinkled her nose. The neighborhood was certainly dirty enough.

The cabdriver stopped abruptly, and again Lois almost slid off the worn seat. Why are we stopping here? she wondered. It wasn't until the cabdriver had gotten out and begun tossing her new luggage on the sidewalk that Lois spotted the granite lintel over the doorway of a building that was both more imposing and more dilapidated than its neighbors. On the lintel were engraved the words MAGDALENA ARMS.

Lois's heart sank. I guess I should be glad Mom can't see it, she told herself as she slid out of the cab. Unlike its neighbors, the Magdalena Arms was set back from the sidewalk, and a narrow strip of dusty grass and shrubbery bordered it in front. Lois noticed with dismay a beer bottle tangled in the branches of one of the bushes. There were three chipped marble steps up to an imposing double door of glass with an intricately worked, if tarnished, brass grille.

The driver had piled Lois's luggage on the bottom step, and after she paid him—I guess I won't be taking any more cabs! Lois thought wryly—she picked up her overnight bag and pushed open the heavy door to her new home. Maybe it's nicer inside, she told herself hopefully.

Chapter Eight
The Magdalena Arms

"Hello?" Lois called into the dusty emptiness of the cavernous reception hall. The room echoed the faded grandeur of the exterior. It was wood paneled, and there was a mosaic M in the center of the marble floor. To her right and left were paneled double doors with flaking gilt trim. An elaborate chandelier hung from the ceiling, but the only light came from a modern fixture over a sort of reception counter, which was tucked into the curve of a grand staircase. Behind the desk was a wall of pigeonholes, holding the tenants' mail.

"Hello?" she called more loudly.

"Coming!" replied a muffled voice. The next moment a section of the pigeonholes swung outward and a girl emerged from what seemed to be a little closet under the stairs.

"May I help you?" the girl asked.

"I'm Lois Lenz," Lois explained. "I've come to live here." She looked around dubiously at her surroundings as she spoke.

"Lenz, Lenz . . ." The girl flipped open a ledger and ran a finger down a column of names. "Oh! You're the girl taking over 504!" She cast a searching glance at Lois.

"I'm in 506 so we'll be neighbors. My name's Netta Bean."

The two girls studied each other. Netta was a plain girl, wearing glasses as thick as Enid's. Her hair—that no-color between blond and brown, was strained back into a tight bun. There was a sprinkling of freckles across her nose, which she'd made no attempt to conceal.

Lois's heart sank even further. This girl was a far cry from the glamorous career girl in the *Teenaged* magazine!

Abruptly Netta said, "I'll get Mrs. DeWitt."

Lois watched her hurry from behind the desk to knock on the left-hand set of doors. She had the strangest impression that the desk girl had sized her up and found her lacking. But why?

The door opened a crack and Netta whispered something, of which Lois only caught the words "Miss Lenz." The door opened wider, and a tall woman with an old-fashioned pompadour emerged. Her lined face was made up with bright spots of rouge and lipstick, which had been applied with a shaky hand. She held a highball glass in one hand and gave the other, heavy with rings, to Lois.

"Miss Lenz," she intoned in a deep, carrying voice. "Welcome. You arrive at twilight time, *l'heure de l'apéritif,* or as the poet said:

> *"Between the dark and daylight,*
> *When the night is beginning to lower*
> *Comes a pause in the day's occupations*
> *That is known as the Children's Hour."*

Lois was engulfed in a powerful odor of gin, which Mrs. DeWitt exhaled with her verse.

"Let me show you around, my dear," said Mrs. DeWitt,

keeping hold of Lois's hand. "I know you're going to love being part of the Magdalena family. We have quite a special atmosphere—so gay, so liberal, yet closely supervised and cared for all the same." She looked around vaguely for a place to put down her highball glass, and Netta took it from her. "Now, if you'll follow me, I'll familiarize you with our facilities."

"My luggage—" Lois began.

"I'll bring it in, while Mrs. DeWitt shows you around," Netta volunteered.

Lois thanked Netta and followed Mrs. DeWitt. I must have imagined her dislike, she thought.

Mrs. DeWitt was opening the right-hand set of double doors. "This is our visitors' parlor," she announced, ushering Lois into a narrow, dusty room with a horsehair sofa and a white marble fireplace. Over the mantelpiece was a large oil painting in garish colors. It depicted a woman in Victorian dress leaping up from a piano, while a laughing man grasped her around the waist. The woman's eyes had a wild look, and the brass tag on the frame read *The Awakening Conscience*.

Mrs. DeWitt noticed Lois studying the painting. "That's an original copy of an original," she told Lois proudly. "One of our girls painted it during her European tour many years ago."

Lois followed her back into the entrance hall, where Netta was dragging Lois's Pullman suitcase through the door. Mrs. DeWitt led Lois past the grand staircase and pointed to a narrow flight of stairs leading to the basement. "Breakfast is served from seven to eight. As I explained on the phone, you are responsible for your own lunches and dinners." She paused and deepened her voice. "Absolutely no food is allowed in the rooms! It attracts vermin." She opened a door at the back of the hall. "This is the lounge, what I like to call our rest and recreation room." She laughed lightly, ushering Lois in. "For when the girls are home from the wars, you know."

The big room ran the width of the building and was furnished in a homey hodge podge of divans, sofas, overstuffed armchairs, and daybeds. End tables and kidney-shaped coffee tables held piles of magazines, and there was even a Ping-Pong table. At the far end was a bookcase and a quite modern hi-fi. As Lois entered, a girl in plaid Bermudas was cha-cha-ing to "Everybody Likes to Cha Cha" as her friends laughed and egged her on. In another corner, four girls were smoking and playing bridge, while others sat reading, or chatting in low-toned pairs.

"Girls, this is Lois Lenz, the newest member of our little family," Mrs. DeWitt's carrying voice cut through the buzz of conversation. There was a chorus of hellos and welcomes, and Lois smiled and nodded, feeling both self-conscious under the gaze of so many frankly curious eyes, and conspicuous in her gray "city suit." She couldn't keep track of the string of names Mrs. DeWitt rattled off, as she noted that most of the girls were casually attired in capri pants and blouses, their feet thrust into ballet flats or slippers. I guess you don't dress up for the city when you live there! she realized.

She followed Mrs. DeWitt back to the reception desk, and was alarmed when the older woman suddenly swayed, pressing her blue-veined hands to her temples. "I'm afraid I must leave you now, Lois," she murmured, closing her eyes. "I am a sufferer of la migraine, unfortunately, and I find it's best to retire before the onslaught. My rooms are here." She opened the left-hand double doors and drifted inside. Lois glimpsed a dim, crowded room, and sniffed the mingled scents of lavender and gin. "If you ever need me, my door is always open," Mrs. DeWitt added, as she closed the door behind her. Lois heard the sound of a bolt sliding into place.

"I'll help you take your bags up," said Netta behind her. "I put them by the elevator. Your trunk came yesterday—it's already in your room."

Lois turned with relief. "But what about the reception desk?"

"My shift is over, and Kay's on duty," Netta replied. Lois noticed that a redheaded girl was behind the desk now, reading a paperback novel. She gave Lois a friendly smile and nod. Netta was already heading back behind the stairs. When Lois caught up with her, she was pushing Lois's luggage through the door of a tiny old-fashioned elevator. Lois, who hadn't noticed the elevator, was relieved she wouldn't have to carry her luggage up all those stairs. She joined her efforts to Netta's, and when the luggage was all inside, the two girls managed to squeeze in as well.

"Oh, here's your key, Miss Lenz," said Netta, digging a silver key out of her skirt pocket and handing it to Lois. Despite the shabby surroundings, Lois felt a little thrill as she took it. It represented her new home in Bay City!

"Please call me Lois," she told Netta. Back in Walnut Grove, Lois would have automatically classed the other girl as "not my type." But here in Bay City, Lois had a dim suspicion that those high school hierarchies no longer held. And despite her librarian looks, Netta had a dependable quality that made Lois feel instinctively that she was more to be relied on than—well, Mrs. DeWitt, for example.

"Are you Mrs. DeWitt's assistant?" she asked curiously.

Netta shook her head. "I just mind the desk, three afternoons a week. I'm a teacher in training." As the elevator stopped with a jerk, she added, "Several of the girls here take shifts at the front desk to help pay their board. If you're interested . . ." She pulled the mesh gate aside and pushed open the door to the fifth floor.

Lois shook her head. "I'm starting a full-time job as a typist tomorrow," she announced proudly. "I think that will keep me busy enough." She started to say she wanted to keep her evenings free for dates and fun, but then realized that Billy and Faye and the rest of the gang were far away, and she knew no one. For the first time in four years, her evenings were hers to do with exactly as she liked. No one expected her to go to a double feature or out for a soda every night to prove she was popular. Why, if I wanted to stay home and practice my number technique, no one would even notice! she thought. The idea was both exhilarating and frightening.

"Good for you," said Netta, unaware of the thoughts racing through Lois's mind. "So many girls come here looking for a job and run through their savings before they find one." She dragged a suitcase into the corridor. "I hope it pays well."

Her salary—$175 a month—had seemed like a fortune to Lois, but already she was realizing the big city was expensive. Her father had given her two crisp twenties at the train station this morning, and in less than a day she'd spent over three dollars. Almost ten percent of my nest egg, she calculated, as they got the luggage out of the elevator.

Netta was leading the way down the shabby hallway, lugging the heaviest bag. Lois picked up her overnight bag and followed her. There were three doors on each side of the hall. Netta stopped at the middle one on the right-hand side. "Here's 504," Netta announced. "Welcome to the fifth floor."

Lois unlocked the door and opened it. The room was

medium-sized and furnished with only a bed, a bureau, and a desk. Lois's trunk stood in the middle of the room, its newness striking a discordant note. The walls were painted buff, pockmarked with nail holes, and there was a discolored spot on the ceiling. The bare floorboards were painted dark brown. A single narrow window looked out on the dreary brick apartment buildings across the street.

Lois's eyes welled up with sudden tears. There were no two ways about it. This place was awful! And such a far cry from the apartment she'd dreamed of for herself and Faye.

"We're both lucky we face the street," said Netta behind her. "It's cooler in the summer." She went over to the window and opened it, letting in a gust of hot, sooty air. The faded beige curtains flapped listlessly.

Lois stared at Netta. She seemed sincere. Could she really find something to like about this dingy room? She tried to say something polite, but her throat closed up and she could think of nothing.

"Ramona—the girl who used to live here—put up some old paisley shawls on the wall," said Netta, looking around reminiscently. "And she had a pink lampshade, and an old red rug . . . I hardly recognize the room now." She shot Lois a piercing glance, and shrugged. "It's not everybody's cup of tea. Let's get the rest of your things."

"I'm sure it has possibilities," said Lois, feeling again she'd been found wanting. "I guess I'm just feeling a little—overwhelmed. The Magdalena Arms isn't quite what I expected—my business typing teacher spoke of it so highly." She trailed Netta back to the pile of luggage by the elevator.

"She probably remembers it from its heyday, when Mrs. Payne-Putney was still alive," said Netta, picking up another bag. "Have you heard its history?" Lois shook her head as she tucked her train case under one arm. "It was founded by Mrs. Payne-Putney of the timber Putneys. She had a friend from boarding school who went to Bay City to become an actress—this was before World War I. Anyway, the friend didn't make it as an actress and went "astray," as they used to say. Mrs. Payne-Putney blamed it on the lack of decent, affordable housing for young working women, and so when her husband died and she came into her fortune, she started the Magdalena Arms. It used to be quite elegant, and I've heard they served tea and sherry every evening, even through the Depression, but it hasn't been properly kept up—something about the trust losing value. *We* still like it," she added defensively. "And it's one of the cheapest places to live in the city."

As Netta talked, the girls made another trip and now Netta added a hatbox to the growing pile of luggage in room 504. "There used to be mostly just aspiring actresses living here," she concluded as they sank down on the bed. "But now it's all sorts of people—secretaries, teachers, bookkeepers, publicity girls."

"That's quite a romantic story!" said Lois, intrigued. "Does anyone know what happened to the friend, the girl who went astray?"

"She's here—Mrs. DeWitt is the friend," replied Netta with a sudden grin. She flexed her hands. "I think there's one more bag—"

"I'll get it." Lois sprang to her feet. "You've done enough!"

She was wondering what she could do to thank Netta for her help—perhaps invite her to have dinner with her? Lois was a little nervous at the idea of dining alone, and she thought Netta would probably know some inexpensive place, like the Korner Koffee Kuppe at home. But when she lugged the last suitcase into her new room, Netta had left.

Well! Girls in Bay City evidently didn't stand on ceremony. Lois shrugged. She would knock on the door of 506 in a little while. Meanwhile . . .

She surveyed her new domain. At least it's all mine, she thought. And no parents down the hall to scold me if I stay up late rearranging my files. With the setting sun gilding the old woodwork and the gathering shadows camouflaging the water stain, Lois could see that the high-ceilinged room had a certain charm. She crossed to the window and leaned on the sill. A very faint breath of cool air lifted the hair from her damp temples.

I'll write Mom the window measurements tomorrow, she decided. Some new curtains will make a world of difference. And I'll dig that rag rug out of my trunk and . . . I should hang up my navy suit for tomorrow.

Humming a little tune, Lois unlatched her wardrobe case and opened the closet door. But the tune died on her lips and she stopped in her tracks. Netta Bean was on her hands and knees, feeling delicately over the bare closet floor!

"Netta!" cried Lois.

Netta scrambled to her feet. "I lost a hairpin," she explained, one hand on her bun. "I was looking for my hairpin."

"You startled me so," said Lois. "I thought you'd gone back to your room."

"I'm sorry," Netta apologized. "Here, let me hang that up for you."

But as Netta took the blue suit from Lois and hung it up, Lois couldn't help wondering what Netta had been doing in the closet in the first place.

"But what . . ." she began. "But why . . ."

Before she could formulate the awkward question, there was a stir in the corridor. Footsteps were heard, then a lilting voice called, "Hellooo! Anybody home?" Doors opened and closed and there was a buzz of conversation and laughter.

"Maxie's back!" said Netta quickly. "Come on, Lois, you can unpack later—come meet the gang!"

Lois followed Netta into the hall. Doors were open on both sides of the corridor, and there was a cluster of girls in the middle of the hallway.

At the center of the group was a petite girl with a heart-shaped face framed by jet-black locks cut pixie fashion. She wore a boxy pink suit of nubby linen, which even Lois's inexperienced eyes could tell was the height of fashion. In one hand she carried an overnight case, and in the other a large pasteboard box.

"Maxie, m'love, what'd you bring us?" demanded a tall girl with tortoiseshell glasses, hands on her hips.

The girl in pink set down her suitcase and lifted the lid of her box to reveal a jumble of pastries and tiny frosted cakes. "Spoils from 'the wedding of the season': Goose liver mousse turnovers and petit fours. In other words, dinner."

"Yum!" said a third girl, bending to peer nearsightedly into the box so that her frizzy, blond hair almost touched the rim. "And I thought it was going to be another soup and a roll night!"

Maxie caught sight of Lois looking at the scene over Netta's shoulder. "Oh, hello!" she smiled widely. "You're welcome to join us—unless, of course, you two have other plans." She winked at Netta.

For some reason Netta turned a dull red. "This is Lois Lenz. She's just moved into 504."

There was a sudden stillness, as Lois's new neighbors exchanged covert glances. They all seemed taken aback by this news. Didn't they know the room had been rented? Lois wondered. But that's silly—with a waiting list, they must have known it wouldn't be vacant long.

Maxie was the first to recover. "In that case, you must join us," she told Lois. She rapped imperatively on the door across from Lois. "Wake up, Dolly! Dinner in my room!" Without waiting for a reply, she led the gaggle of girls to room 505.

Maxie's room was in the back corner of the building,

and it was as different from 504 as day from night. The walls had been painted pink, and the furniture white. There were white dimity curtains at the two windows, and the bed was covered with a quilted pink silk comforter. Instead of a desk, there was a dainty dressing table. It was hard to believe this luxurious boudoir, fit for the pampered daughter of a millionaire, was concealed behind the worn brown door. Two slipper chairs were upholstered in pink velvet, and Maxie insisted Lois take one. She pulled out the dressing table stool for the blond girl, and Netta disappeared then reappeared carrying a straight chair from her room, while Maxie busied herself setting out the food on dainty china plates.

While Lois was wondering at finding a girl with such obviously expensive tastes living in a place as down-at-heel as the Magdalena Arms, the girl with the tortoiseshell glasses, seated now on the other slipper chair, was making introductions.

"Welcome to the Arms Lois, I'm Janet Kahn," she said. She was several years older than Lois, and looked the very picture of a career girl with her smooth chestnut pageboy, and her tailored clothes. Lois felt drawn to her at once. "This is Phyllis Densher." The frizzy-haired girl gave a little wave and a shy smile. "And our benefactress for the evening, Maxie Mainwaring. We put up with Maxie even though she's a rich dilettante and we're all working girls, because she bribes us with goodies like these." She ducked Maxie's pretended swat. "How *was* the honorable Muffy Mainwaring's wedding?"

"Ducky!" replied Maxie, handing Lois a plate. "Five assorted aunts, uncles, and cousins told me my turn was coming next."

"Are you engaged?" asked Lois.

The girls all looked at Maxie, as if curious to see how

she'd answer. "Not at the moment," said Maxie airily. "But enough about weddings. Where's Dolly?" She reached over to pound on the wall. "Dolly, hurry up!"

"Who's Dolly?" Lois asked Netta, as she bit into the rich pastry.

"Dolly is Dorian Dingle, in 503," Netta explained. "She's an actress although she hasn't worked much lately. Did you ever watch *At Home with the Jarvises* when you were a kid? She was the teenaged daughter, who was always getting into trouble."

"Yes, I remember her! Judy Jarvis, and she had a steady, Fred! Goodness," exclaimed Lois. "I never dreamed I'd be living with an actress! Are the rest of you as glamorous?"

The girls shouted with laughter. Janet, it developed, worked in a law office and went to night school. "I'm studying for a law degree, part time," she explained. Lois, who had never met a lady lawyer, was more impressed than ever. Phyllis worked for the Harbor Commission, investigating living conditions in Bay City's notorious slum district. "Aren't you frightened?" wondered Lois. But Phyllis said she mostly sat at a desk all day typing up statistics. "My supervisor, Miss Ware, is the brave one," she said, her eyes lighting up.

"What about you, Maxie?" Lois asked her hostess curiously.

"Me? I haven't any particular talent or training, like the rest of you." Maxie, stretched out on her bed with a plate of food, gave a shrug. "I do a little of this, a little of that."

"She was an artists' model for a while," said Phyllis.

"Then she went to secretarial school," put in Netta.

"And now I'm taking art classes at the Art Alliance," finished Maxie.

"A dilettante," summed up Janet. "Wasting her talents."

"My family expects me to marry, and it would be one

solution—if I found the right man." Maxie stretched her arms languorously and leaned back on the bed.

"You mean a man who wouldn't interfere with your goings-on," said Netta acidly. "I say, better no marriage than a farce!"

Maxie shrugged. "What can I do? I'm not cut out for a career, like the rest of you."

"Don't say that, Maxie," said Janet earnestly. "You know you don't mean it."

"Not cut out for a career!" a new voice boomed. "Why, you're more of a career girl than the rest of us put together!"

Dolly—for Lois recognized the girl who had once played Judy Jarvis on television—entered carrying a cocktail shaker and several glasses. She was considerably older than the teenaged girl from the show, and she'd filled out some. It was as if the fresh-faced girl Lois remembered had blurred around the edges. She wore a worn satin dressing gown and a chin guard was strapped around her head. Imagine, Judy Jarvis worrying about a double chin!

"Dolly, finally!" Maxie's eyes lit up. "And you brought martinis! How did you know?"

"What did you think I was doing? Twiddling my thumbs?" demanded Dolly, pretending indignation. Then her eyes fell on Lois. "Hello-oo! Something new has been added! Who's this luscious little morsel?"

"Lois is the new girl on the floor," said Janet hastily. "She'll be in 504. She just arrived today—from a small town, I believe." Was Lois imagining it, or was there a warning note in Janet's voice?

"Welcome, Lois!" said Dolly jovially. "Maybe you can drive the ghosts from 504, hmmm, Netta? Gosh, I wish I had another glass for you." She began filling glasses from her cocktail shaker.

Netta jumped to her feet. "I can drink out of my toothbrush glass," she said in a strained voice, and left the room.

"Isn't that nice?" beamed Dolly, as she handed Lois a brimming glass. "She's got a soft spot for you already."

Lois wanted to ask Dolly what she meant by ghosts in 504, but Janet asked swiftly, "What's your line of work, Lois?"

"I'm starting in the secretarial pool at Sather & Stirling, the advertising agency," replied Lois.

"That sounds fascinating," said Maxie enthusiastically. "I've always thought advertising would be fun to try." Janet nodded her head in agreement. "They're a solid firm, with an excellent reputation."

Lois expanded under the interest she saw in the faces around her. How different this was from the blank, uncomprehending faces of the girls on the Pep Squad and her other friends in Walnut Grove, when she'd told them. "I never really thought of myself as a career girl," she confessed as Netta slipped back in, carrying a glass. "But my guidance counselor thought I had managerial ability, so I'm giving it a try!"

"Once you get used to having a career, you'll never want to give it up," Dolly assured her. "Speaking of which," she turned to Maxie, "where's your girlfriend, the career girl to end all career girls?"

Suddenly all the girls were busy sipping their martinis. "Dolly!" said Maxie with an attempt at a laugh. "You're determined to be an *enfant terrible* tonight, aren't you?"

"What?" asked Dolly, looking around. "You're worried about Luscious here?" She leaned forward and put a hand on Lois's knee. "You like girls, don't you?" she queried.

The sudden silence in the room was thick with a tension Lois didn't understand. "Well, of course," she said curiously. She thought of Faye for the first time in several hours, her sparkling blue eyes, her red full lips. "My very best friend is a girl!"

"See?" said Dolly triumphantly.

Lois wanted to ask Dolly what she meant by her odd question, but Netta had jumped in with an inquiry about an audition Dolly'd gone on, and Dolly turned gloomy and began discussing the vagaries of casting directors. Janet asked Lois where she'd gotten her suit—she just *loved* the scalloped pockets. Soon Lois, Janet, and Phyllis were deep in a discussion of clothes. Lois was glad of the opportunity to ask Janet's advice on the all-important subject of office attire. Then Dolly joined the discussion, telling Lois that in advertising, image was everything.

"I was going to wear a navy suit my mother made last fall," Lois worried aloud. "She's an excellent seamstress, but . . . I don't know. Do you think it will be all right?"

"I'm sure it will be fine," Phyllis said encouragingly. "You can't go wrong with navy!"

Lois was not reassured by fashion advice from a social worker who wore a shapeless chemise dress in a peasant print with sandals and no stockings. She was relieved when Janet interposed, "Why don't you show us the suit? We can tell you if it looks homemade or not."

"Or too small-town," said Dolly. "That would be the kiss of death."

"You're exaggerating, Dolly," said Netta impatiently. "What matters most is that she's a competent typist." She turned to Lois, who was finishing her second martini. "You might want to take it easy on those."

"You know, I bet we're just the same size," interrupted Maxie, jumping up from her seat on the bed. "Why don't you try on my mauve Claire McCardell. It would be stunning with your coloring." She opened her closet door and pulled an attractive ensemble from the rack of gay attire.

"Oooooh." Lois was breathless with admiration. This was more stylish and sophisticated than anything she'd owned—in it she'd outdo even Faye! While in her heart she knew Netta was right about the typing, she couldn't help thinking that an outfit like Maxie's would give her confidence a big boost. "But I couldn't, Maxie—why, you barely know me!"

"It's all for one and one for all on the fifth floor, right, girls?" Maxie insisted, thrusting the dress into Lois's hand. Lois found it impossible to resist the impulsive generosity, and the rest of the girls encouraged her to accept Maxie's offer. Even Netta said bluntly, "You might as well—sooner or later Maxie will collect a favor from you. That's the way it works around here."

"Well," said Lois, taking the outfit. "I'll try it on, anyway." She opened the door to the hallway but then stopped in amazement. There was a boyish redhead standing in the threshold to Maxie's room, one hand raised to knock.

"Why, Pamela!" Lois exclaimed after a stunned moment. "What are you doing here?"

Chapter Ten

An Old Acquaintance

Pamela Prendergast seemed even more startled than Lois. "Lois? Little Lois Lenz?" Her low contralto was as thrilling as Lois remembered, but after the first moment of recognition, she couldn't believe how the older girl had changed.

The mahogany hair was cropped short, and Pamela's athletic figure was encased in a pair of tailored linen pants and a crisp white blouse, the sleeves rolled halfway up. She wore sporty saddle shoes, and carried a dress box in one hand. It was strange to remember this same girl in a cheerleading uniform.

"You're so—so different!" exclaimed Lois.

"So are you!" said Pamela, who'd been surveying Lois with equal attention. "You used to be such a skinny kid—you've filled out nicely!" Her dark blue eyes were frankly appreciative.

A voice behind Lois reminded her that she and Pamela had an audience. "I hate to interrupt this interesting moment," said Dolly dryly. "But catch the rest of us up. How do you two know each other?"

"Why, we were cheerleaders together, in Walnut Grove," Lois explained.

"Cheerleaders!" the other girls chorused. They seemed as startled as if Lois had said she and Pamela were in a girl gang together. "Pam, you were a cheerleader?" asked Phyllis in disbelief. She twisted around. "Maxie, did you know?"

Maxie evidently had not known. She sat up on the bed, as open-mouthed as the rest.

"Oh, you naughty girl, keeping that a secret!" said Dolly, wagging a finger playfully at the redheaded girl.

"It wasn't a secret," said Pam. "Nobody ever asked me." She walked into the room with the familiar athletic stride that bordered on a swagger, unable to take her eyes off Lois. "I just can't believe Lois Lenz, junior cheerleader from Walnut Grove, has shown up at the Magdalena Arms!"

Lois blushed happily. "I'm squad captain now—I mean, I was my senior year. It's good to see you, too, Pamela!"

The fashion show was forgotten. The girls chattered excitedly about the unexpected meeting, as Dolly mixed up another batch of martinis, in honor, she said, of the Walnut Grove High School Pep Squad. Only Maxie seemed strangely subdued as she hung the purple suit back in her closet. Lois was eagerly telling Pamela about Miss Watkins's advice, her decision to come to Bay City, and the job she was starting the next day at Sather & Stirling.

"That's quite a coup, Lois," said Pamela, in frank admiration. "They're a top-drawer firm." Basking in Pamela's praise, Lois felt the stirrings of her old crush. Only now Pamela was treating her as if—well, as if they were equals!

"S&S do most of Gruneman's advertising, so I know a few people in their organization," Pamela added.

"Gruneman's? Is that where you work?" asked Lois, impressed at the casual way Pamela named the famous department store.

"Yes, I'm an assistant buyer, in sportswear," Pamela replied.

"She started at the hosiery counter, but got promoted right away because of her keen business sense," Netta explained.

"And her uncanny nose for fashion," put in Janet.

"And her charm," murmured Maxie.

"I guess I still don't understand how you girls know Pamela," said Lois curiously.

"Why, Pam used to live here!" they chorused. "In 504—your room!"

"We still think of Pam as an honorary member of the fifth-floor gang," Dolly explained.

"In my room?" The thought pleased Lois. "Where do you live now?" she asked.

Pamela explained that with a raise in salary she'd moved to a little apartment in Lincoln Heights. She lived by herself, she said. She'd tried to persuade another girl to join her and share expenses, but it hadn't worked out. "And actually, I'm not as lonely as I thought I'd be," she told Lois.

For some reason, Dolly, Janet, and Phyllis all turned their heads like marionettes toward Maxie, who was lounging back against the pink silk pillows. "I always told you you'd be better off having a place to yourself," Maxie remarked. "So, Lois, you must know Carol Claver—weren't you good friends with Carol Claver once, Pammie? Didn't you once think of—sharing an apartment with her?"

"I knew Carol, she was co-captain of the Nutshells," Lois told Maxie. She turned to Pamela. "I didn't know you and Carol—"

Pamela interrupted her hastily, "Oh, Carol joined the WACs a few years ago and left town. But tell me, is Miss

Kreplach still coaching the squad? Are you still friendly with Faye what's-her-name?"

"Yes, and yes," laughed Lois. She was getting used to this new Pamela. The lack of makeup which had seemed so strange at first now seemed appropriate for Pamela's strong features. "Faye thinks I was crazy to come to Bay City."

"Why?" asked Phyllis earnestly.

"She—well, she doesn't believe in careers for women, I guess." Lois admitted.

"What does she think you should do?" Janet interposed indignantly.

Lois tried to think back on Faye's more compelling arguments. "Take over the garden club?" she offered.

"Women don't have to limit themselves to garden clubs—why, they can go straight to the top these days," Pamela declaimed. "One of the most highly placed executives at Sather & Stirling is a woman—Mrs. Martha Pierson."

"A woman executive!" said Lois. She'd never before imagined a woman rising that high.

"She's as tough as any man," Pamela boasted. "The copywriters call her 'the hyena,' because of the way she laughs whenever she bests someone in a deal."

A woman whose staff called her the hyena! The thought scared Lois a little.

"Anyway, I'll just be in the typing pool," Lois said, to reassure herself.

"Not for long, I'll bet," Pamela predicted. "I remember how organized and dedicated you were on the squad." She contemplated Lois. "We're a lot alike, I think."

"Really?" To her embarrassment, Lois found she was blushing.

"You know what would be awfully fun," Maxie suggested. "We should take Lois to Francine's—to celebrate her first night in the big city."

"No!" The other girls were unanimous. "It's nicer here," said Janet firmly.

"What's Francine's?" asked Lois. Maxie opened her mouth, but Pamela beat her to it.

"It's just a bar in the neighborhood, where we have a beer every once in a while. It's amusing, in an—an off-beat way, but it can get a little rough late at night."

Lois was intrigued at the idea of having a beer in an off-beat bar. But wouldn't they need escorts?

Come to think of it, no one had mentioned a boyfriend or a date all evening! Yet they were almost all attractive girls. Even Phyllis was cute, in a studious sort of way, Lois mused, looking around the circle. Were they just too dedicated to their careers to have time for boys?

Netta, of course, was already a classic old maid. She was one of those prickly girls who simply couldn't be bothered. You could tell by looking at her she'd given up even trying to make the best of her appearance. Her skirt was a sensible beige drip dry, her white blouse was plain, and her black ballet flats were scuffed. No longer listening, or participating in the conversation around her, she looked melancholy as she nibbled at the olive Dolly had put in her drink.

She's probably always been a wallflower, Lois thought, pitying the blunt-tongued girl. And as she watched Netta's lip curl in a disdainful sneer, she thought: And she's beginning to turn bitter.

"Don't worry, Netta, I wasn't suggesting it for you," Pamela was laughing. She'd opened the dress box she'd brought and was holding up a simple rose-colored frock of sheer wool. "It's for our fall collection."

"Dreamy!" Janet put it succinctly. She explained to

Lois, "Pam always brings the samples here for Maxie, since she's a perfect six."

But Maxie said airily, "I don't need another red dress. Why don't you give it to Lois, Pam? We were just discussing her wardrobe when you got here." Turning to Lois, "You're a size six, too, aren't you?"

"Well, yes, but no, I mean, I don't really need new clothes," protested Lois, embarrassed. But Pamela was beaming. "That's a wonderful idea." She pulled Lois to her feet, and held the dress up to her. "You're a bit bigger in the bust than Maxie, but this sheer wool has some give."

"No, but if Maxie always gets the samples . . . I wouldn't want to cut in on her territory," Lois continued to protest weakly.

"Don't worry, no one cuts in on me unless I let them," Maxie laughed, as Pamela said simultaneously, "Maxie likes to be independent—except of Daddy and his allowance."

Lois felt a little unsteady on her feet, and the feel of Pamela's firm hands on her waist as the older girl measured the dress against Lois's figure only increased her dizziness. What's the matter with me? she scolded herself. I'm much too old for crushes! And why were Maxie and Pamela staring at each other defiantly, as if each was daring the other to blink first?

"Well, if neither of you minds . . ." Lois said doubtfully.

"We don't," they chorused, still looking at each other.

"I'm going to put some music on." Janet got up and went to the portable phonograph in the corner. Dolly peered into her shaker, saying, "Let's finish this batch off. I propose a toast." She splashed some into Maxie's glass. "To new dresses." Then she poured a little in Pamela's.

"Old friends." And finally she emptied the rest in Lois's.
"And a successful career for Lois!"

Music began to pour from the phonograph, and Maxie
finally looked away from Pamela, clinking her glass
against Dolly's shaker. "And to the Nutshells!" she pro-
claimed.

"To the Nutshells," everyone echoed, and drank.

"Pamela had the highest kick in the state!" Lois told
them proudly.

"I'm not surprised," drawled Maxie. "Pamela's always
been very limber."

"Do you remember the time at the State Champi-
onship when I taught everyone on the squad to jitter-
bug?" said Pamela to Lois. "Do you still remember how?"
Taking Lois's hand and snapping her fingers, Pamela twirled
the petite brunette around the tiny space.

Soon chairs were pushed aside, and the rest of the girls
were dancing, too, laughing immoderately as they bumped
into each other in the small room. Lois hadn't had so
much fun in years. The other girls were a blur as she spun,
passed from one girl to the next. She danced with Maxie
(We are the same size, she thought) and then Dolly (I'm
dancing with an actress! she told herself, awed), Janet,
Phyllis, even Netta. "You girls are the nize—nicest girls
I've ever met," she told Netta earnestly as they swayed
together to a crooner's ballad. Netta peered at her. "Are
you feeling all right?" "Grand!" said Lois. If only the spinning hadn't made her so dizzy. She stumbled and fell heavily against Janet, who was dancing with Phyllis, knocking
the law student's glasses to the floor. "I'm sorry," she said,
bending down confusedly to pick them up. But bending
down didn't work and she found herself on all fours. She
picked up the glasses and peered through them. To her
surprise, they were made of clear glass. "Here you are,"

she said, attempting to hand them to Janet from her position on the floor.

Pamela helped her to her feet. "Lois, how many martinis have you had?" she asked.

Lois thought a moment. "Maybe three? And a half?"

"We're on our third shaker," said Dolly apologetically. "I'm afraid I kept refilling her glass. She just looked so cute."

Pamela clicked her tongue impatiently. "Walnut Grove High School girls don't have cocktail hour every night like you do, Dolly," she scolded. Lois sank down on the bed, her head spinning. Lying down seemed like a good idea, so she did that. She closed her eyes.

"Is she going to pass out on my bed?" she heard Maxie's dismayed voice.

It's a good thing these girls aren't white slavers, Lois decided, because she'd be absolutely powerless in their clutches. Her muscles no longer obeyed her mind's commands. Yet, although they weren't white slavers, Lois realized in a moment of drunken clarity that there was definitely something a little strange about the girls on the fifth floor. Why was Janet pretending she needed glasses when she didn't? Why had Pamela and Maxie made such a fuss about giving her a dress she couldn't even wear until fall? What had Dolly meant when she asked if Lois liked girls? Were there girls in the big city who didn't like other girls? And what had Netta been doing in her closet?

In the midst of these reflections, Lois felt a firm hand on her arm, hoisting her to her feet. "I'll take this side," she heard Netta say, as if from far away. With Netta on one side and Pamela on the other, she lurched across the hall. She suddenly wanted to tell Pamela what Faye had said about Lois having a crush on her; in fact, she wanted to tell her all about Faye and their practice kissing, and how worried she was she'd get out of practice in Bay City, but unfortunately her tongue was too heavy in her mouth to form the words. "Mmmwhaaazzz," she said. Then she was sitting in a chair in her barren new room. "I'll make up the bed," she heard Janet's voice. She heard the sound of her trunk opening, and Dolly's voice saying, "Here's sheets and—oh, lookee here!" Lois remembered, through the haze, that she'd wrapped a picture of herself and Faye, flanked by Billy and Rod, in one of her pillowcases. "Putitonsideable," she said, opening her eyes, "a'right?"

"Your intuition's on the fritz, I'd say," Janet said low as she tucked in the sheets. Dolly put the picture on the nightstand. "This doesn't mean anything," she told Janet firmly. Lois closed her eyes again. More mysteries, and she wasn't up to puzzling them out.

"I don't feel very good," Lois told Pamela, leaning her head against the other girl's shirt front. But it wasn't Pamela, it was Netta, who said, "Drink this, and take these." Lois obediently washed down the pills with a glass of water. "You're not a white slaver, are you?" she asked. "No, I'm a school teacher," Netta reassured her.

Hands undressed her and put her between cool sheets. "Wherezz Pamela?" asked Lois. "Gone to get what she came for, before you distracted her," said Dolly enigmatically, and two other voices said, "Shush!" There were more whispers, and the click of the door closing. A siren wailed in the distance, but Lois didn't hear it.

Chapter Eleven
The Typing Test

Lois's head pounded as she blearily looked through her purse for the address she'd already memorized. Sather & Stirling, 333 Lake. Get off at Lake and Broadway, Netta had instructed her.

Lois peered out the bus window at the dizzying panorama of buildings passing by and wished she'd had something more substantial than a cup of coffee and a sweet roll this morning. She thought of the breakfasts Mom would make at home, oatmeal and toast, sizzling sausage patties, a soft-boiled egg and a fruit cup. Then her stomach lurched as the bus turned a corner and she decided it was just as well she'd eaten lightly.

Thank heavens Netta had woken her up this morning, knocking repeatedly on the door until Lois had staggered out of bed. Imagine if she'd slept through her interview with Miss Gill! She smoothed the collar of her white blouse. It had been awfully sweet of Janet to iron it. She was very lucky to have fallen in with such nice girls. In the glare of the hot summer sun, it seemed as if last night she'd created mysteries and undercurrents out of nothing more than her own overactive imagination. Why, take Janet's glasses, for instance. When she'd asked Janet this morning, rather hesitantly, why she wore glasses with clear lenses, Janet had laughed.

"They make me look older," she'd explained. "And my coworkers and teachers at night school take me more seriously."

I have to remember things are different in the big city, Lois reminded herself. That's why I came here, after all.

And the best thing was that she'd found Pamela again! Even though she'd changed so much, Lois sensed the same wonderful squad captain underneath the rising young merchandiser. She'd left a note under Lois's door, wishing her good luck and inviting her to lunch later that week.

Of course, that was another odd thing. Lois frowned a little, remembering. She'd woken up briefly, just as the early dawn light was filtering into her dingy room. As she came back from the washroom (she'd felt a little sick to her stomach), she'd glimpsed a figure going down the stairs. Even in her half-asleep state she'd thought it was Pamela. But why would Pamela have spent the night when she had her own apartment? I must have been mistaken, Lois told herself. It was probably one of the other girls.

"Lake Street!" called the driver, interrupting Lois's thoughts. Lois jumped up and joined the crush of people pushing their way out the bus door. "Excuse me," Lois murmured, but she was jostled, shouldered aside, and finally carried along in the crowd, clamped between two businessmen, until she popped out the door.

Goodness! Lois twisted her skirt back into place and looked around bewildered. She had to jump back to avoid being bowled over by a gaggle of chattering office workers, and stumbled into a delivery boy.

"Excuse me, which way is 333 Lake?" she asked, pulling herself upright.

"You're standing right in front of it, sister," he said with a jerk of his chin toward the glittering glass-and-steel building in the center of the block.

Lois's nervousness increased as her shoes clack-clacked across the marble-lined lobby. How stylish everyone looked—even the men! She was more self-conscious than ever about the navy suit Mom had made last year for the father-daughter luncheon. How at ease the others were as they squeezed onto elevators, chatting casually, yawning, or skimming their newspapers.

One girl in particular caught Lois's attention. She wore a summer dress in a striking print of chartreuse, black, and pink, with shoes and purse to match, and a chartreuse sweater slung casually over her shoulders. Her hair was a close-fitting cap of pale gold. She'd pushed her gold-framed sunglasses back on her head as she entered the elevator, and as they ascended with a whoosh, she studied the advertising spread of a magazine intently. Lois felt an unreasonable delight when the girl got off with her on the twenty-seventh floor. Maybe she'd see the girl again!

For now, the blond girl disappeared through a door-way behind the reception desk, while Lois approached the busy receptionist. "I'm Lois Lenz, Miss Gill is expecting me," she told her.

"Take a seat, please. I'll let her know you're here," said the receptionist, not even listening to Lois's thank-you as she plugged in a phone line and said, "Sather & Stirling, how may I direct your call?"

Lois had only time to rub her temples in a vain effort to lessen her headache before an older woman entered the room briskly, hand extended.

"You must be Lois Lenz, good morning. I'm Ivy Gill and we're delighted to have you here. Doris Watkins spoke very highly of your abilities."

Miss Gill was thin and wiry. Her dark hair was streaked with gray and pulled back into a neat chignon. She scarcely paused for Lois's murmured greeting before continuing, "Follow me and I'll give you the two-minute tour." As she led Lois through the doorway behind the receptionist into what seemed to be a warren of corridors and small offices, she added, "I hope you're ready to dive right in, because we're going to put you through your paces this morning. Oh, just a formality! Miss Watkins's recommendation is good enough for me. But Mrs. Pierson insists on you taking a typing and dictation test. This is the Art Department."

Lois peered into the large, sun-lit room with row upon row of heads bent over drafting tables, while she tried to pay attention to what Miss Gill was telling her. Mrs. Pierson—that was the executive Pamela had mentioned last night, the woman they called "the hyena." Was she in charge of the secretaries? Miss Gill was moving on and Lois hurried to keep up with her rapid stride. She seemed to have the energy of a much younger woman.

"This is the secretarial pool." Miss Gill opened another door, and the clatter and bang of a dozen typewriters enveloped them at once. Lois scarcely had a chance to look for the empty desk that would be hers before Miss Gill had closed the door and was moving on. The younger girl made a mental note to get some earplugs.

"Copywriting." Miss Gill gestured to the left. In one of the cramped little offices Lois glimpsed the blond girl from the elevator. She was leaning back in her chair and idly tapping a pencil against her chin, while a man was hunched over the desk in the opposite corner, writing furiously. But Miss Gill turned right, down a carpeted hallway lined with framed advertisements for beer, brassieres, cigarettes, soap, and perfume. "Our account executives are along here," she said. "And here's Mrs. Pierson's office." She opened a heavy wooden door.

Lois gasped. She couldn't help it. The corner office had floor-to-ceiling windows that gave her the sensation of floating in the sky. Lois's feet in their navy pumps sank into peacock blue carpeting that matched the walls. I clash! she thought, looking down in dismay. The furniture was all made of blond wood, and a large desk sat in the center of the room, beneath a modern clock of metal rods and brass balls with no numbers. Behind the desk a woman sat, riffling impatiently through piles of paper.

"Mrs. Pierson, this is Miss Lenz," said Miss Gill.

The woman behind the desk lifted her head and looked at Miss Gill impatiently. "Miss Lenz?" she said coldly. "Who is Miss Lenz?"

She was a striking woman, with a hawk-nosed profile and icy gray eyes. She wore a simply tailored suit of gunmetal gray, and her short hair was the silver of an ice-skating rink on a winter evening. Yet despite the white hair and black-framed glasses that hung on a chain around her neck, Lois guessed she was not much more than forty.

She's old enough to be my mother, Lois thought. But how different she is!

"Lois Lenz," repeated Miss Gill patiently. "You remember, we thought she might do as your secretary, at least temporarily."

Lois was rooted to the floor in astonishment. Her heart quaked at the idea of working for this forbidding woman whose underlings referred to her as "the hyena."

"I—I thought—Miss Watkins said the position was in the typing pool," she said faintly.

Mrs. Pierson turned freezing eyes on Lois. "Would you

prefer the typing pool, Miss Lenz? Have you no ambition? No drive? Pah! Girls today!" She took a cigarette from the box on her desk and waited with barely contained impatience as Miss Gill leapt forward to light it.

Lois flinched at Mrs. Pierson's scorn. "No," she said. "I mean, yes, I am ambitious. That is—"

"The clock is ticking," Mrs. Pierson interrupted her. "Do you want this position or not?"

"Yes," said Lois weakly. Such was the force of Mrs. Pierson's personality that she felt she had no choice. And somehow she wanted to prove to this hyena woman that she, Lois, was different from those girls of today whom Mrs. Pierson held in such low esteem.

Mrs. Pierson pulled a sheet of paper from a drawer. "Very well," she said with a sudden indifference Lois found more galling than her scorn. "Have a seat and type this up. Miss Gill will time you." As soon as Lois had taken the paper, Mrs. Pierson picked up the phone on her desk. "Miss Wallis, give me Herb Hathaway."

Miss Gill directed Lois to a small blond wood desk, with a peacock blue typing table and typewriter, in a corner of the office. Shakily Lois deposited her purse, sat down, removed her gloves, flexed her fingers, and placed the paper on the typing stand. She found typing paper neatly stacked in one drawer, carbons in another. She glanced up at Miss Gill, who was peering at her wrist watch. Miss Gill gave a nod and Lois began.

The spidery handwriting was almost impossible to read, and several words were misspelled. Lois typed as fast as she could, making corrections as she went along. She tried not to be distracted by Mrs. Pierson's phone conversation, but it was difficult not to listen to that whiplash voice: "I needed that copy last week, Mr. Hathaway. Maybe they believe in pampering their copywriters at J. C. Birch, but here at Sather & Stirling we do things a little differently!"

"Time," called Miss Gill, just as Lois reached the last sentence of the business letter she was typing. Lois pulled the sheet from the typewriter and handed it to Miss Gill. "Very good, Lois. That's seventy words a minute."

Mrs. Pierson slammed down the phone. "Let's check her accuracy," she said, holding out her hand. Rapidly she scanned down the handwritten and typewritten pages. Then she turned to Lois and said, "You corrected the spelling errors, I see."

"Yes," said Lois modestly. "I'm an excellent speller."

"No!" cried Mrs. Pierson, slamming the papers down on her desk with a bang that made Lois jump. "We're not looking for improvements, Miss Lenz, we're looking for accuracy! Do you know that when I started out in the business, secretaries were still referred to as 'typewriters'? Because they were nothing more than machines! And that's as it should be. Nowadays all you girls want to add your 'creative' touches!"

Lois felt the criticism was unfair. There was nothing creative about accurate spelling! But remembering one of Miss Grimes' favorite dictums, "The secretary who always disagrees makes herself disagreeable," she kept her mouth shut.

Mrs. Pierson sighed and let the papers fall to her desk. "Well, let's try your dictation skills, and see how you do there," she said wearily. Picking up the phone, she said, "Miss Wallis, tell Miss Winstead and Mr. Hathaway I'd like to see them."

A moment later a man and a woman filed into the office. Lois's heart leapt when she recognized the golden-haired girl from the elevator. The man was short, and rumpled, wearing a bow tie and glasses. He looked nervous and jittery, but the girl—Miss Winstead—seated herself indifferently, as if she was called into her boss's office every day. Mrs. Pierson ignored them both. "Hold up those comps, Ivy," she said. Miss Gill obligingly picked up a heavy rectangle of cardboard that was leaning against the peacock blue wall behind Mrs. Pierson's desk. As she turned to face them, her face and torso were concealed by a large photo of a red lipstick and the silhouette of a woman's profile. Miss Gill had nice legs for a woman her age, Lois noted irrelevantly.

"Paula Winstead, Herb Hathaway, this is Lois Lenz, who wishes to join the Sather & Stirling family." Mrs. Pierson made the introductions rapidly. Paula Winstead shot Lois a pitying look while Herb Hathaway gulped nervously. "This is the new Norvell lipstick. It hasn't got a name. I want you two to brainstorm. Miss Lenz will take down everything you say."

Cold sweat ran down Lois's back. This was quite different from dictation in Miss Grimes's Business Methods class!

"You—you want us to name the lipstick?" asked Herb uncertainly.

Mrs. Pierson pounced. "Naming a new product is not something I generally entrust to my junior copywriters," she said triumphantly. "Particularly those who can't get me some simple girdle copy when I need it." Herb winced. "I just thought it would be an opportunity for you to test your creative juices. I know Miss Winstead has complained of feeling frustrated in that department." Paula Winstead arched an eyebrow. "And sometimes the most unlikely people come up with half-decent ideas."

Lois flipped open the steno pad and gripped her pencil with a sweaty hand.

"Crimson?" Herb said uncertainly. "Cherry. Red Delicious."

"Old hat, Herb!" barked Mrs. Pierson. "We did the fruit theme last year."

Lois scribbled Mrs. Pierson's comment as well as Herb's. She hoped Miss Gill would stay quiet. Three was bad enough!

"Luscious Red, Delirious Red, Fever Red, Jungle Red." Paula fired off each suggestion with the rapidity of a machine gun.

"None of your usual lazy recycling, Paula." Mrs. Pierson's scorn was palpable. "Think new, different, better!"

"Luscious Ruby," muttered Herb. "Ruby Slipper."

"*Cerises d'Amour,*" said Paula thoughtfully. "Maybe something more abstract? *Echt* Red. Philospher's Red. Philosopher's Blood. *Sang d'Amour?*"

Lois's head was awhirl as she tried not to let the avalanche of foreign words throw her. Ekt—what language was that? How did you spell that gargling sound?

"Okay Paula, we all know you were finished in some French boarding school in the Alps," broke in Herb desperately. "But Mrs. Housewife doesn't care for foreign phrases."

"My school was Swiss," retorted Paula. "You may be selling 'Jungle Red' to Mrs. Housewife, but I'm selling '*Rêve d'Amour*' to Miss Sorority Girl, and her older sister, Miss Career Girl, who have more money to spend on lipsticks!"

"*Rêve d'Amour* is too pink," interjected Mrs. Pierson. Even in the midst of dictation, Lois couldn't help thinking that Miss Gill's arms must be getting tired of holding the heavy poster board. Is this what it's like working for Mrs. Pierson? she asked herself, a little frightened. Being treated like a piece of furniture? But Herb was trying again.

"True Red," he said with fresh determination. Paula snorted. "That's what *I* said, I just said it in German."

"True West, Western Red, Western Sunset," continued

Herb, so fast now that Lois's pencil raced across the page. "Western Sunset, Flaming Red, Flame Red! Set your lips afire with the reddest red that won the West . . ."

"Ouch," commented Mrs. Pierson caustically.

"Café Red," countered Paula. "Espresso Red . . . yes, yes!" She held up her hand for attention, the fire of inspiration in her eye: "Listen to the insistent thrum of the throbbing bass as the beat poet recites and you slide across the dance floor, a strange languor stealing over you as you give in to some primal instinct and press your lithe body against the cool cat who will take you places you've never been, places you've never dared to go until now—now when you know you've got the reddest lips in the room, the sinful, kissable, unmistakable—Bongo Red!"

Paula sagged with exhaustion when she'd finished, and Miss Gill put down the comp to applaud while Herb spread his hands helplessly. "It's the woman angle," he said, attempting a smile. "It's got me all beat to heck."

Miss Gill consoled him. "It was your 'fits you, supports you, loves you' campaign that sold a million Helga brassieres."

Lois didn't write down either remark. She'd felt for a moment that she *was* that girl, slinking across the dance floor. Except the mysterious stranger's face kept changing—first it was Faye's, then Pamela's, and even Paula's.

Mrs. Pierson, who'd been slumped back in her chair, listening, now roused herself. "The beat angle is rather last year," she said dismissively.

Paula leaned forward, her aristocratic chin jutting out. "I've been looking at our research department reports and I know the Norvell people are eager to expand into the youth market. The beat angle may be last year to you, but it's still news to most people."

Herb cleared his throat. "I guess I better get back to work on that girdle copy." He hesitated, then sidled out when Mrs. Pierson took no notice. She nodded at Paula, a reluctant smile creeping onto her face almost in spite of itself.

"So you've done your homework. We'll see about 'Bongo Red.'" Paula, dismissed but satisfied, exited with a triumphant look. Mrs. Pierson turned to Lois and asked acidly, "Are you planning on transcribing your notes today, Miss Lenz?"

Lois hastily fed paper and carbon into the typewriter. Miss Gill carefully set the comp back down, but Mrs. Pierson exclaimed, "Oh, take it back to the art department, Ivy, I don't want it cluttering up my office anymore."

As Lois set about untangling her steno notes, her thoughts whirled around in her head. Was Mrs. Pierson always so rude to her staff? How did Paula have the nerve to contradict the fearsome woman? Lois felt like Little Red Riding Hood, left alone with the wolf.

"Here you are," she said, pulling the neatly typed sheets from her typewriter and laying them on Mrs. Pierson's desk.

Mrs. Pierson glanced over them. "You misspelled *echt*, Lois. I thought you were the champion speller? I guess not in German."

"I took French," said Lois, keeping her temper in check.

Mrs. Pierson shuffled through the sheets. "In the future, remember to make *two* carbons of everything, not one."

In the future? "Then I have the job?" Suddenly the woods weren't so dark and the wolf had a benevolent look.

"Heavens, yes, I have to hire someone since my last secretary took it into her head to elope without giving notice. You can start by getting me coffee."

Lois refused to be deflated. She had a job! And strangely enough, she wouldn't have taken the typing pool now if Miss Gill had begged her. Working for Mrs. Pierson would be irritating, frustrating, and make her furious, but it was also sure to be stimulating!

"How do you take your coffee?" she asked.

"Well, I suppose that's all I can expect from you today, Miss Lenz." Mrs. Pierson leaned back in her chair and looked at Lois, disappointment and resignation simply oozing from every pore. "You may go."

With trembling hands, Lois carefully placed the typewriter cover over the peacock blue typewriter, then bent her aching back to pick up her purse.

"Miss Lenz!" Lois flinched for the hundredth time that day at Mrs. Pierson's whiplash voice. "I hope you're not a clockwatcher."

"No, Mrs. Pierson," Lois replied faintly. "Do you— shall I stay a little longer?"

For a moment Mrs. Pierson toyed with the idea as a cat might toy with a mouse. But just then the door opened and a stunningly beautiful redhead in a snug-fitting knit suit walked in. "Shall we—that is, did you still want to take me to the art show?" She looked adoringly at Mrs. Pierson. "I've been waiting in the lobby. I can wait longer if you're not ready."

"Ah! Gloria, my pet. No, I was just leaving." Mrs. Pierson got to her feet, picked up her purse, and set a modish hat carefully on her head. Lois covertly studied the redhead. There was something familiar about her. Then it came to her—she was the girl in the Helga brassiere ad. She was even prettier in color than she had been in black and white.

"I've been looking forward to seeing the Monette paintings," Gloria said, like a pupil trying to please her teacher.

"*Mo-nay*, the artist's name is pronounced *Mo-nay*, first name Claude." Mrs. Pierson's voice was one of strained patience and Gloria wilted visibly. "And call it an exhibition, not an art show." Mrs. Pierson took Gloria's drooping chin in her hand and waggled the model's face back and forth. "Oh, that there was a little more of a brain beneath all that beautiful hair," she said caressingly. As they departed, she called over her shoulder to Lois, "See Miss Gill before you go. I believe she has some paperwork for you to fill out."

Lois sank back in her chair as soon as Mrs. Pierson was out the door. It had been a grueling day. Mrs. Pierson had been unrelenting in her criticism from the first cup of coffee Lois brought her. "Two sugars," she snapped after the first sip. "That's what I put in," protested Lois. "Well then, you should have made it three," Mrs. Pierson replied.

Later it was, "You need to ask for Louis when you make reservations at Le Cheval Blanc, you silly fool! Who told you they were all booked up, the hatcheck girl?" And when Lois asked what brand of cigarettes she should buy to refill the box on Mrs. Pierson's desk, the executive had sighed in exasperation before answering, "Dunhill's, of course."

In between she'd taken dictation and typed steadily, producing a mound of letters and memos which Mrs.

Pierson had demolished with her rapid signature. She'd gone to Miss Gill to learn how to make an entry in the petty cash book. The petty cash had been for lunch— sandwiches and cartons of iced coffee which Mrs. Pierson and two junior account executives ate while they discussed the financial details of a bid and Lois took notes. She'd managed to cram down half a chicken salad sandwich while Mrs. Pierson had a brief conference with Mr. Sather. She'd typed up a contract in triplicate, and then retyped it after Mrs. Pierson corrected the spelling of a name that appeared on almost every page.

I wonder why on earth they chose me for this position? Lois asked herself as she made her way down the corridor to Miss Gill's office. Mr. Stirling's secretary, Miss Emery, and Mr. Sather's secretary, Miss Weber, were both women in their thirties. It must just be luck, Lois decided. Or maybe they couldn't find anyone else who would take the job!

Miss Gill wasn't in her office. Lois poked her head into the typing pool, which was empty except for one forlorn typist, who said Miss Gill might be in the file room. After going down the wrong corridor, and opening a door that proved to be a broom closet, Lois spotted a door labeled FILE ROOM. Peering inside, she saw row upon row of gleaming metal file cabinets. "Oh!" she breathed in delight. She pushed open the door and trailed her fingers lovingly along a row of cabinets. Going down one aisle and up the other, she found Miss Gill bent over an open drawer, rapidly thumbing through its contents.

"Excuse me, Miss Gill," Lois said to the engrossed office manager. Miss Gill jumped and slammed the drawer shut. "Lois! What are you doing here?"

"Mrs. Pierson said you had some forms to fill out," Lois said.

"Oh yes! This way." Miss Gill ushered her out of the file room and to her own office. "I've been spending my evenings straightening the files," she explained. "I'm afraid your predecessor, Miss Ravenal, left things in rather a disarray." She sighed wearily.

"Would you like me to help you?" Lois asked eagerly. "Back in Business Methods, filing was sort of . . ." She was going to finish with ". . . my forte," but Miss Gill was smilingly shaking her head. "I approve of your attitude, Lois, but I think you should concentrate on your immediate task, which is assisting Mrs. Pierson. Remember the secretary's creed: Learn your basic duties thoroughly before adding new ones. How was your first day?" As she spoke, she was busy pulling a form out of a drawer.

"I felt I was in a little over my head," admitted Lois. "Maybe this isn't something most new employees say, but I couldn't help wondering why you hadn't hired someone more experienced!"

"Mrs. Pierson requested someone with no previous secretarial habits, someone she could mold to all her special quirks and tastes," Miss Gill explained, handing Lois an employee information form. "And do keep in mind, Lois, that the position is yours on a trial basis, until Mrs. Pierson decides whether or not you'll suit in the long term."

Lois nodded. "I understand." She picked up a pen and began to fill out the form.

A kettle on a hotplate in the corner began to whistle. Miss Gill made tea while Lois wrote, and set a cup of tea at Lois's elbow as Lois pushed the finished form across the desk. While Miss Gill reviewed the form, Lois sipped her tea and looked around the office manager's office. It was spartan in its simplicity. There were no windows, and a large bulletin board behind the desk held a series of clipboards, neatly labeled PERSONNEL, INVENTORY, CONTRACTS, and so on. On the wall over the hotplate was a framed piece of needlepoint embroidery, red on a white background. After a moment's puzzlement, Lois realized it was a motto, embroidered in the hooks and dashes of shorthand.

"Now, I just need your social security—Oh!" Miss Gill looked up at Lois with an expression of confusion. "You're living at the Magdalena Arms?"

"Why yes," said Lois. "Is there anything the matter?"

"Most girls prefer to share an apartment these days." Miss Gill's brows were drawn together.

"My mother would only let me take this job in Bay City on the condition that I lived in a supervised residence," Lois explained, wondering a little at Miss Gill's evident concern.

"Yes, of course. Perfectly normal. Well, thank you, Lois, I'll see you tomorrow."

Although she had only half drunk her tea, Lois could see that Miss Gill was anxious to get back to work. It was only when she reached the lobby that she realized she'd never given Miss Gill her new social security number. Should she go back upstairs? Miss Gill had been so preoccupied with Lois's address that she'd forgotten all about it.

Well, tomorrow will be time enough, Lois decided. Miss Gill was probably back in the file room by now.

The file room—that was another odd thing. How could a secretary who had left Lois's desk in such perfect order have disarranged the files so badly that Miss Gill had to work late reorganizing them?

Her reflections on these puzzles were dried up by the blast of heat that engulfed her as soon as she pushed her way through the revolving door to the street. The heat seemed somehow more intense in the city, hotter than the hottest summer day in Walnut Grove. The automobiles in the street, the steel and glass office towers, the mass of people pushing their way along the sidewalk, all seemed to reflect the heat and magnify it.

Goodness, how do people stand it? Lois asked herself as she stood at the bus stop. But when the bus came, it was full, and she couldn't bring herself to join the crowd of people trying to cram themselves on. I'll walk a bit, she decided. The bus pulled away, and she choked on the gust of hot exhaust. She pulled a handkerchief from her purse as she walked down the street, and wiped her forehead. The handkerchief came away gray and she looked at it in distaste.

"Lois! Lois!" The sound of her name, dimly heard above the traffic and bustle, drew her attention away from hygienic concerns, and she looked around in every direction.

"Over here!" called the voice, and finally Lois spotted Dolly Dingle, wearing a floppy black straw hat and waving to her frantically from the window of a cab stuck in traffic.

"Hop in! Quick!" she called. Lois squeezed through the automobiles and jumped into the cab just as it began to move.

"What luck!" she gasped. "Of course I really shouldn't—but I couldn't stand the idea of the bus."

"It's on me, kid," Dolly assured her. "I just got paid." She flashed two crisp twenty-dollar bills, before tucking them into her purse.

"Paid? An acting job?" Lois asked with interest.

"No, I get by between acting jobs by doing photowork," Dolly explained. "You know, modeling for calendars, and magazines. Between you and me, you get paid more for less work, but it's all short-term stuff."

"I see," said Lois. She looked at Dolly, who had encased her voluptuous frame in a brown and black flowered summer silk, and put her hair up. Despite the dress and tidied hair, Dolly still didn't look the modeling type.

Dolly folded away the newspaper she'd been reading. Lois caught a glimpse of the *Confidentially* headline: EVEN AT THE COUNTRY CLUB: COMMIES INFILTRATE HIGH SOCIETY, and in smaller letters: RED DEB TELLS ALL. For a brief moment, Lois felt a pang of homesickness for her mother.

"So how was the first day? Did the suit pass inspection?"

Lois told Dolly about the unexpected job with Mrs. Pierson, and Dolly was impressed. "A promotion practically before you started," she marveled. "You're going straight to the top, kid, straight to the top—even if you have to ride a hyena to get there!"

Lois's spirits lifted, and she giggled a little at the idea of riding Mrs. Pierson around the office. Her first day in the world of business hadn't been at all like she'd imagined it, looking at the career girl spread in *Teenaged*. But it hadn't been dusty and boring, as Faye had predicted, either!

The cab stopped with the jolt all the cabs in Bay City seemed to feel was necessary. Lois tried to give Dolly some money for the fare, but Dolly categorically refused, and Lois contented herself with repacking the contents of Dolly's bag, which had spilled on the cab floor: a riding crop, a feather boa, and a black silk mask. "Props for the photo shoot," Dolly explained. The actress headed toward the lounge "to scare up a bridge game" while Lois stopped by the front desk to see if she had any mail.

A gay postcard was poking out of pigeonhole 504 and

Lois snatched it eagerly. A postcard from Faye! She slowly boarded the elevator drinking in the familiar picture of Buffalo Bluff, the scene of so much vacation fun. Then she flipped it over and read Faye's hastily scrawled message: "Cookout at the bluff this weekend—won't be the same without you. I told Billy he'd bring Jane Phillips over my dead body! Some people don't know their proper place. When are you coming back to Walnut Grove? Missing you a lot. Love, Faye."

Lois leaned against the elevator wall as it creaked upward, staring blindly in front of her, seeing not the peeling brown paint of the elevator wall, but the cool blue waters of Lake Tonga, and the boys and girls she'd gone to high school with splashing and playing. She saw Faye coming up from a dive, her wet blond hair clinging to her cheeks, her red lips, pearled with droplets of water and parted in a tantalizing smile, her eyes the same color as the lake.

Sure, Faye was still kidding herself that Lois and Billy would get back together and they'd be a happy foursome again, but even though Lois recognized Faye's foolishness, she couldn't help missing her best friend—missing her so badly it hurt.

The elevator came to a halt, bringing Lois back to the reality of Bay City. The hot, humid reality, she thought glumly. Feeling her fatigue anew, she pulled open the elevator's mesh gate, and then pushed open the heavy outer door.

Netta was standing in the corridor, just outside Lois's room. She stepped back and turned toward Lois, but not before Lois had seen Netta's hand on the doorknob to room 504!

"Lois," said Netta. "You got home so quickly."

Lois explained about Dolly and the unexpected cab

ride, all the while wondering what Netta had been doing at her door. But Netta was scolding her testily. "You forgot to lock your door this morning, and the wind must have blown it open. I was just going to lock it for you with the pass key from downstairs." She held up the key reproachfully.

"Why—why, I was sure I locked it this morning," said Lois uneasily. Of course she'd had such a bad headache—could she have forgotten? "But it's all right, isn't it? No one can get in downstairs—there's someone at the desk."

"In the big city, you can't be too careful," lectured Netta before retreating into her own room.

Lois closed the door behind her, locked it, and looked carefully around her room. As far as she could tell, everything was just as she'd left it. She peered in the closet. Why, there was a bobby pin on the floor! Hadn't Netta found it yesterday? No more martinis, she admonished herself sternly. Too much about the previous evening was a blur.

She stripped off her hot navy suit, and wearing only a slip and brassiere, busied herself for the next half hour in unpacking and putting her room to rights. Her clothes were quickly hung in the closet, or stacked on the bed. Lois found a collection of nightclub matchbooks the previous tenant had left behind in the desk drawer, and threw them away. The bureau drawers were grimy, and Lois decided to strip the soiled paper liners and put in fresh ones before she put away her undergarments, scarves, and gloves.

She pulled the old paper out and crumpled it into the wastebasket when something caught her eye. A piece of carbon paper clung to the liner. Lois detached it and smoothed it out. It was a fragment of what seemed to be a letter.

an acquaintance in common, someone
a publicity girl, when your politics
ker than the current color scheme permits.
e so many mementos from that period;
hip cards that others would be sure to

might find a place in your organization
ho has such a knack for finding out
hers.

that I am a competent typist and filer,
ht course in stenography, in which
dly.

ition to get ahead, something you
for. I feel sure you and I can
ill be beneficial to both of us.

he phone numbers to the Federal
at hand.

How funny, Lois thought, rereading the fragment. It seemed to be a job application. But what kind of job combined politics and color schemes?

A light tap sounded at the door. "Just a minute," called Lois, carefully folding the cryptic note and putting it in her purse to examine later. Hastily slipping on a flowered cotton frock, she opened the door.

Chapter Thirteen

A Night Out with Maxie

Maxie stood in the hallway, a wide smile on her vivid face. Today she was dressed in scarlet toreador pants and a cream-colored peasant blouse, which clung to her smooth shoulders and dipped daringly low in front. A wide black belt emphasized her slender waist.

"Hi, Lois!" she greeted her neighbor gaily. "I thought we'd celebrate your first day as a working girl with a beer at Francine's."

"Thanks, Maxie, I'd love to!" exclaimed Lois with real pleasure. "Who are we going with?"

"Why, I thought it would be just the two of us," said Maxie with a little pout. "I'd like us to get better acquainted."

"But won't we need escorts?" asked Lois, puzzled.

Maxie's brow cleared. "Escorts? Oh no! Not at Francine's. In fact, it's more fun to go *without* male company, if you know what I mean."

Lois didn't but she was prepared to follow the sophisticated girl's lead. She picked up her hat and gloves, but Maxie laughed and took them from her. "Francine's isn't formal," she said, tossing them onto Lois's bureau.

Francine's proved to be a medium-sized establishment

only two blocks and a short flight of steps away. The dim cellar room was basic, with a long bar stretched along the left-hand wall and a profusion of small tables and chairs scattered around the rest of the room. A jukebox took center stage on the right. Lois wondered, as she entered, what made this bar a favorite with the gang on the fifth floor. The place was deserted, save for a matronly woman feeding the chrome and glass jukebox, and two nurses talking quietly at a table.

Maxie seemed disappointed at the bar's emptiness. "Usually there's more of a crowd," she murmured as they settled themselves at the bar. Doris Day began singing about her sentimental journey, and the older woman leaned on the jukebox, a rapt expression in her eyes. "Two beers, Jo," said Maxie to the bartender.

It took a second glance for Lois to realize the bartender was a woman. With her short hair and crisp white shirt, her lined face unsullied by makeup, Lois had at first mistaken her for a man. The door opened and a gaggle of girls came down the stairs, college girls from the sound of it, as they giggled about something their "psych" professor had said.

Now Lois realized what was special about Francine's—it was a women-only bar. They must be a feature of big-city life, like women-only boardinghouses. She relaxed a little and looked around with a smile. Of course she and Maxie didn't need escorts!

"Here's to big-city life." Maxie clinked her glass against Lois's, echoing the young girl's thoughts. "Here's hoping it agrees with you."

"Oh, it already has." Lois sipped her beer daintily. "There's certainly lots that's different, but I'm getting used to it all. And it doesn't seem half as dangerous as Mamie McArdle's *Confidentially* column makes it out to be!"

Maxie leaned forward eagerly. "Oh! Are you a *Confidentially* fan?"

"My mother is," Lois admitted. "And that column got her so worked up she almost didn't let me take this job!" She ticked off the items on her fingers: "She worried I'd be kidnapped by white slavers; or that I'd witness a gangland shooting and have a contract taken out on me; or that a drug peddler would turn me into an addict; and I won't even go into her worries about juvenile delinquents, Communists, and deviants!"

Maxie laughed sympathetically. "It's a good thing Mamie never ran that column on women-only residences. Your mother would have flipped! She was going to call it 'Secret Dens of Sin.'"

Lois shuddered at the thought. "A darn good thing," she declared, pouring the rest of her beer into her glass. "But if she never ran it, how do you know about it?"

"Because she wanted to use the Magdalena Arms for some pictures, but we wouldn't cooperate," said Maxie mischievously. "She wanted to send a photographer and have us pose in the lounge, smoking, and playing cards, and reading books and magazines with lurid covers."

"That doesn't sound very honest," said Lois doubtfully.

"Well, she tried to sweeten the deal by offering us cash," Maxie defended the popular columnist. "Dolly and a few of the other girls who always find themselves short at the end of the month were all for it, but most of the girls were like Netta—they have to keep their reps clean. They put the kibosh on the whole scheme. Even Pam got sticky about it, and she'd already moved out!"

Lois wished she had her steno pad so she could record Maxie's vivid slang for future reference. Maxie was exactly the kind of person she'd hoped to meet in the big city, someone with a different angle on life. However, Lois couldn't help being disturbed by the casual way Maxie talked about Mamie McArdle's lack of journalistic integrity. "I don't think Miss McArdle should use such deceptive methods," she told the other girl.

"You don't know the pressure she's under," Maxie argued back. "She's got an editor to answer to who expects her columns to sell papers—lots of papers. I got to know her a little bit when she was working on the story, and she's okay."

Lois thought Maxie's attitude toward Mamie's ethics would have made a good foundation for a column on the poor values of today's youth, but Maxie was continuing:

"I did think she went too far with the break-in."

"Break-in!" Lois's eyes widened.

"Are you sure you want to hear about it?" Maxie looked at Lois coyly. "I don't want to frighten you."

"You won't frighten me, honestly," Lois promised. And with no further coaxing, Maxie leaned forward and, lowering her voice, told her story.

"It was just a few weeks ago. The whole gang was here, at Francine's. Ramona, the girl who used to be in your room, had just gotten a raise and was treating us all to a night out.

"It was rather late by the time we headed back home to the Magdalena Arms. Luckily, Netta has a duplicate key to the front door, so she can let us in when we stay out past curfew. There sure are advantages to working every job you can find, the way she does! It was dark inside and we all tiptoed up the stairs, bumping into each other and shushing ourselves, and then just giggling even more. You know we're not supposed to use the elevator after ten o'clock, and we didn't want to risk any noise for fear we would wake up Mrs. DeWitt, who might have one of her attacks of conscientiousness and go all housemothery on us.

"When we got to the last flight of stairs, Ramona suddenly grabbed my arm and whispered to everybody to be absolutely still. We could hear there was someone on the fifth floor—there was a kind of rustling and bumping noise. And we knew nobody *should* be up there, because everyone who roomed there was standing on the stairs, petrified!

"It couldn't have been more than a split second we stood there, and then Ramona shot up the stairs. We all followed, of course, and just as we got to the top of the flight, someone came running out of Ramona's room—your room—and just crashed right through us!"

"Did you catch the intruder? Who was it?" breathed Lois, who'd been listening with shining eyes, lips parted in fascination. "Was it Mamie McArdle?"

"Oh no." Maxie waved a hand dismissively. "She has assistants to do her dirty wor—research. And anyway, Mamie's kind of short and plump; this person was taller, although I can't say more than that. Why, it could have been a man, even! It was too dark on the stairs to see much, and it all happened so fast. He or she was wearing a trenchcoat with the collar turned up and a hat pulled low over the face."

"Well, then how do you know it was someone working for *Confidentially*?" demanded Lois logically.

Maxie pulled thoughtfully at her lower lip. "Why, I suppose because Ramona said that's who it was. She said Mamie knew she had some pictures of the gang having a party. And her room had been ransacked! I mean, torn to pieces! So someone was looking for something. It's funny, I never thought before . . ."

"Never thought what?" prodded Lois, when Maxie trailed off into a thoughtful silence.

"I was just thinking it was odd, the way Ramona left so suddenly, the very next day," replied Maxie.

"But Mrs. DeWitt told me she was called away . . ." Lois was going to finish her sentence with, ". . . by a sudden family illness," but there was a gentle tap on her shoulder and she swiveled around on her bar stool. It was the woman who'd been playing the jukebox.

"Do you have a light?" she asked. She was an older, good-looking blonde, quietly yet expensively dressed in gray sharkskin. She held an unlit cigarette in one hand.

"I'm sorry, I don't smoke," said Lois politely. But Maxie picked up a box of matches from the bar and struck a light. "Hello, Sylvia," she said as the woman leaned toward the flame. "Has it been so long you've forgotten me?"

"Maxie!" Sylvia inhaled the smoke deeply into her lungs and exhaled a blue cloud that settled gently over the three of them. "I didn't recognize you in the bullfighter getup." Her eyes slid from Maxie to Lois and back. "I hope I'm not interrupting anything."

"Not at all," Maxie assured her. "In fact, I was just about to go powder my nose." She slid off the bar stool. "This is Lois Lenz, Sylvia. Lois, this is an old friend, Sylvia Loring." She spun gracefully on her heel. "I'll leave you two to get acquainted."

Sylvia promptly sat down on the stool Maxie had vacated. "Maxie's a sweet girl, isn't she?" she said, leaning forward confidentially. She signaled the bartender. "The ususal, Jo." Then, turning back to Lois, "Jo always remembers my drink, no matter how long it's been. Isn't that wonderful? It's simply heavenly to be here—to be free to be oneself. I only wish I could come more often." Her eyes traveled slowly over Lois. "I always find a new friend who makes it worth the trip."

Lois straightened instinctively as Sylvia examined her admiringly. Sylvia was sitting so that their knees touched, and Lois could smell Sylvia's perfume. Lois felt a tension between them that was oddly familiar.

"Why don't you come more often?" Lois asked the older woman.

Sylvia sighed. "I'm married," she said, as if admitting a horrible defect. "We live in Poinsettia Estates, outside the city. I'm here tonight only because my husband is away on a business trip and I found a babysitter for my daughter. She's six." She leaned forward and lowered her voice. "My need had been building for the past three months— and tonight I just couldn't be alone anymore! I was drowning in it! Can you understand that?"

"Of course I can," Lois assured her, thinking of some of the desperate young mothers she'd babysat for back in Walnut Grove.

The bar grew more crowded as they talked, and once a girl in a delivery uniform interrupted to ask Lois to dance. Thinking of the delivery girl who'd winked at her during junior year, Lois was about to say yes, when Sylvia said sharply, "Hands off, Terry!"

Just as Lois was telling Sylvia how much she missed Faye—Sylvia had a friend who'd moved away and sympathized—Maxie reappeared. And now Netta and Phyllis were with her! The two girls looked hot and breathless, as if they'd been running. Netta had fixed her gaze accusingly on Maxie, whose usual carefree look had changed to one of cowed resignation.

"We're going to dinner," she said, like a little girl prompted by her mother. "Netta thought you should— you'd like to join us."

"There's an inexpensive little Italian restaurant not far from here, where we often go," Phyllis added in her gentle voice.

Lois looked at her watch. Why, it was half past seven! Time had certainly flown by as she sat talking to Sylvia. She had resolved this morning to get to bed in a more timely fashion, so she excused herself to the older woman, who looked terribly disappointed. "Wouldn't you like to come back after you've eaten? Or come up to my room later—I'm at the Leighton Hotel." She insisted on writing the address and room number down, although Netta was frothing with impatience. "Your friend is awfully nice," Lois told Maxie as they emerged from Francine's, blinking their eyes in the sunlight. "Although she doesn't seem very happily married."

The restaurant nearby was unassuming but clean, and the prices quite reasonable. Maxie ordered the veal plate, which came with soup and salad, while Phyllis, who said she was dieting, ordered a bowl of minestrone. Lois followed Netta's lead and ordered the cheapest and most filling dish, spaghetti with meatballs. In high spirits again, Maxie entertained the girls with droll imitations of Mrs. Lenz's fearfulness for Lois. She had all of them laughing uproariously at her outrageous picture of Lois trapped in a den of Communist spies.

"But honestly, that attitude has ruined thousands of innocent lives," said Phyllis earnestly, pushing her glasses back up her nose.

"Yes, it is sad," agreed Netta, twirling her spaghetti expertly around her fork. "One of my professors at Teacher's College in Minnesota was forced to resign, just because he'd signed some petition about the Scottsboro Boys!"

Lois spoke up. "But Netta, if they asked your professor to leave his position, he was probably much more deeply involved than just signing a petition. Why, he might have been a sleeper agent, teaching you Communist doctrine without you even realizing it!" Lois had read selected chapters from J. Edgar Hoover's masterly *Masters of Deceit* her sophomore year and had been vigilant about the Communist conspiracy ever since.

"It was a class called 'Math Methods for Junior Learners,'" said Netta drily. "If he could squeeze any Communist doctrine into that, he deserved a prize." She pointed a fork at Lois. "You could write some of Mamie McArdle's columns without half trying."

"Just because a Communist fights for a cause doesn't make it bad," Phyllis said. But Lois ignored this radical idea. Netta's remark had opened a new train of thought.

"Maxie was telling me about Mamie McArdle and the break-in at Magdalena Arms," she began. "Doesn't it seem like an awfully strange coincidence, Ramona leaving right afterwards? How can you be sure it was someone from *Confidentially*? Is it possible that Ramona left for some other reason than illness in her family?"

The other three girls exchanged looks—worried, guilty, and accusing. "I'm sorry Maxie told you about the break-in," said Netta, looking murderously at Maxie. "We all agreed—that is, we thought it would worry you needlessly if you heard about it."

"There's never, ever been a break-in before or since," Phyllis assured Lois.

"Maxie forgot to tell you we found a *Confidentially* card on the stairway, which clinches Mamie's guilt in my view. And Ramona *was* called away by a family illness," said Netta firmly. "Right, Maxie?"

"I believe she wrote Mrs. DeWitt a note saying just that," murmured Maxie, her eyes on her plate.

"The only reason this has even come up is that Ramona forgot to leave a forwarding address," Netta continued. "I've been trying to find one so I can return a—a book I borrowed."

"Have you checked with her employer?" asked Lois as she buttered another slice of the crusty Italian bread. "Surely she left word with them, saying where to send her final paycheck."

"Why, I never thought of that," said Netta. She looked at Lois with surprised respect.

Phyllis, Lois noticed, was eating the rest of Maxie's veal chop. At some point in the meal, Maxie had quietly switched plates with her. Whatever Maxie's flaws, Lois decided, she was generous to a fault.

And Netta was certainly conscientious, Lois decided as she continued analyzing her new friends. Taking so much trouble over a borrowed book! Netta had stopped eating, and was gazing at the tablecloth, a frown line creasing her forehead.

Phyllis was sweet, too, although Lois was concerned about her weakness for Communist ideology. They argued earnestly all the way back to the Magdalena Arms, walking through the soft summer dusk that gilded even the dingy tenements.

"I'm as patriotic as any American," Phyllis defended herself. "But isn't independent thinking a basic American value? Wasn't America, like the Soviet Union, founded as a result of a revolution?"

"But Phyllis, independent thinking is just what the Communist Party is against!" argued Lois. "They excel at using thought control to exert blind obedience to all party doctrine!"

"What about the loyalty oath program our own government instituted?" shot back Phyllis. "Isn't that, in a way, a form of thought control?"

Lois was speechless. Phyllis had shocked her into silence with her twisted logic.

"I wish you could talk to Miss Ware, my supervisor," Phyllis continued. "She's much more persuasive than I am."

They'd reached the front steps of the Magdalena Arms and Lois bade the other three girls goodnight as they headed for the elevator. She wanted to look in the lounge for a foreign phrasebook Netta had told her she might find there. And she was concerned about Phyllis. The young girl seemed naive enough to be duped into joining a Communist cell! I should do something, thought Lois.

Reluctantly, she decided that it was her duty to speak to Mrs. DeWitt about her worries. After all, wasn't Mrs. DeWitt responsible for her charges' morals? It said something like that in the "Magdalena Arms Rules and Regulations" pamphlet.

Still, she hesitated outside Mrs. DeWitt's door and perhaps would have gone upstairs to bed, if the door hadn't suddenly swung open and Mrs. DeWitt appeared on the threshold, an empty gin bottle in one hand.

"Why Miss—Miss Linzer, isn't it?" She peered at Lois nearsightedly.

"Miss Lenz," corrected Lois. "Lois Lenz. I wonder if I—"

"Isn't it past curfew?" Mrs. DeWitt fumbled with an enameled watch-brooch, attached by a long gold chain to the lapel of the quilted dressing gown she wore. She peered at it, shook it, and peered at it again. "Dear me, it's stopped." Dropping the brooch, she swept across the hall into the visitors parlor, murmuring to herself:

> *"I hear in the chamber above me*
> *The patter of little feet,*
> *The sound of a door that is opened,*
> *And voices soft and sweet."*

Lois followed her, determined to do her duty no matter how distasteful.

"Mrs. DeWitt, I wonder if I might speak to you a moment?"

Mrs. DeWitt was rummaging under the faded cushions of the horsehair sofa. "Aha!" she said triumphantly. She pulled another gin bottle, this one half full, out from under the cushion. "Of course, dear girl, whatever you like," she replied when she realized Lois was waiting for a response. Absently, she tucked the empty back under the cushion, and led the way to her room.

Mrs. DeWitt's room was dim and crowded with heavy Victorian furniture. The walls were thick with pictures—some hunting prints, but mostly photographs, caricatures, and sketches of actors and actresses from days gone by. Mrs. DeWitt poured a generous amount of gin into a lipstick-stained tumbler. "Purely medicinal," she explained to Lois before taking a gulp. "Prevents *la migraine*."

"I'm concerned about one of my neighbors on the fifth floor," began Lois, seating herself on a red brocade hassock. She was feeling more dubious than ever about her patriotic mission, but determined to go through with it. "I'm worried she might have fallen under the influence of a nest of Communists!"

"And what of it, my dear?" Mrs. DeWitt took another long draught from her glass. "Youth is the time for grand passions, is it not?" She sighed reminiscently. "I knew a most dashing anarchist in ought-nine."

"But Mrs. DeWitt . . ." Lois groped for words. "Today's Communist conspiracy is much more serious than early twentieth-century anarchists! They're organized and deadly, determined to extend their influence into every sphere of American life!"

"Oh my dear!" Mrs. DeWitt trilled a little laugh. "The Communists, organized! Some of my best friends were rather red, and the time it took them to put together a simple benefit performance for the Spanish refugees! Yet it was awfully fun in the end. I have a picture some-where—Edgar Villiers, the famous Iago was there . . ." She pulled a leather-bound album off a stack by the love seat, and began flipping through pages of yellowed clippings. "Now, where is it? I was just showing it to one of my other girls a few weeks ago."

Lois had resigned herself to the failure of her mission long before she could get away. She had to look through an album of clippings from Mrs. DeWitt's career, and another of famous former residents of the Magdalena Arms before Mrs. DeWitt would let her leave. "I do enjoy these little chats with my girls," she said in parting. "We'll find that picture another time." Communists no longer seemed important as Lois wondered whether she'd have time to wash her gloves, as she'd planned, and whether they'd be dry by tomorrow morning.

With my first paycheck, I'll buy another pair, she promised herself. I wonder if I could afford a small fan for my room?

Her room was hot and airless when she collected her toiletries and the soiled gloves, and stepped down the hall to the communal bathroom. But before she could push the door open, the sound of her own name made her stop.

". . . and Lois will probably write a letter reporting you to J. Edgar Hoover," giggled someone. "Honestly, Phyllis, why don't you lay off politics once in a while? You're worse than Senator McCarthy ever was!"

Lois recognized Maxie's voice.

"Oh hush up," said Phyllis grumpily. "Are you done with your pin curls yet? I'd like to brush my teeth."

"You're one to talk." That was Netta's matter-of-fact voice. "What was the idea of taking her to Francine's? You might have exposed us all, and I don't think Pamela would have thanked you!"

"I just wanted to see her face," Maxie sounded more subdued. "Besides, Dolly said—"

"Dolly's an incurable optimist," put in Phyllis.

"Well, anyway, she didn't pick up a single trick—that girl is thicker than the Bible!" The laughter was back in Maxie's voice.

"Don't underestimate her," Netta replied. "She's made the first practical suggestion for finding Ramona yet."

Lois backed silently away from the door without waiting to hear anymore. One thing was clear: The girls on the fifth floor were hiding something!

Chapter Fourteen
Bay City Life

B ut even when you lived with five girls who were up to something, life followed a regular routine. Whether her floor-mates were Communist conspirators or pushing dope on small schoolchildren, they all still ate breakfast in the morning and hurried off to catch the bus, except for Phyllis, who walked to save carfare. They all still had stockings to mend, or nails to file; in the evenings Janet studied her law books, Dolly memorized lines, Netta graded papers.

As she, too, fell into a routine, Lois almost forgot what she'd overheard that second night. When Maxie urged the loan of her tangerine silk scarf—"It will give your gray suit some dash"—or Phyllis saved her the cherry Danish at breakfast; when Dolly asked her to "run lines while I touch up my hair" or Janet said she was going to the drugstore did Lois need anything; then, oh then, it was impossible to think that the girls on the fifth floor were anything but hardworking young women trying to forge a life for themselves.

Yet Lois's suspicions never quite died away. There was the way a conversation would sometimes stop when she entered the room; or the way Netta had quickly stuffed a book under her pillow, that evening Lois had returned her hairpin; and although the girls often invited her along on their excursions, they'd never gone to Francine's again. She tried to explain her feeling to Pamela one day, when they'd met for lunch downtown. But Pamela laughed it off.

"Secrets? What secrets? Nobody has any secrets. City girls are just naturally more private than the girls at Walnut Grove High. Anyway, the fifth-floor gang likes you—Maxie's told me so."

"And I like them. It's just—"

"Do you?" Pamela leaned forward eagerly, pushing aside her egg salad sandwich. "What do you think of Maxie? She's pretty swell, isn't she?"

"Maxie is swell," Lois admitted. You couldn't help but like the high-spirited society girl, even though her habits were quite irregular. She always skipped breakfast, and ever since she'd made a duplicate of Netta's duplicate front door key, she'd completely ignored the Magdalena Arms curfew, staying out as late as two or even three in the morning. Lois wondered if Pamela knew how much the fifth-floor gang had begun to worry about their black sheep. Only yesterday, in the lounge, Janet had said to Dolly, "The arty phase was bad enough, but this new beat kick Maxie's on—she may get into real trouble!"

"It's just a kick," Dolly had replied, with a confidence that rang hollow. "You know Maxie. Next month it will be something else."

Now Pamela sighed. "Maxie's one in a million." She stirred the melting ice in her glass as she added, "Although there are times when I wish she was a little less carefree, a little more industrious—more organized, more . . ." Her eyes rested on Lois thoughtfully. "More like you, I guess."

Hurrying back to the office afterward, dress box in hand (the third sample Pamela had given her), Lois thought of another odd thing: None of the girls on the fifth floor ever talked about their beaus or crushes. They never discussed the kind of man they hoped to marry, or how many children they wanted to have, the way the girls back home did. Most of the time Lois didn't even notice it; it seemed, well, *normal*, not to have that eternal buzz about men and marriage.

Still, Janet *did* introduce me to her date last week, Lois reminded herself. That young man, George or maybe Harold, who had escorted the young legal secretary to her law firm's Fourth of July dinner-dance. The one Dolly referred to as "Janet's beard," which made no sense to Lois—he'd been clean-shaven, not a beatnik at all!

As she sat down at her desk in Mrs. Pierson's office and called the receptionist for Mrs. Pierson's messages, Lois thought about her plans for the evening ahead. She was going to wash her hair, play Ping-Pong with Dolly, and read a chapter of the book Miss Gill had loaned her, *Mind Over Matter: On the Efficient Management of Materials*. Lois knew it would sound dull to Faye and the other girls back home, but she secretly reveled in her date-free nights. Herb Hathaway, the young copywriter she'd met her first day, had asked her out twice, but both times she had turned him down. His desk is so untidy, she reasoned, even though she could hear Faye's voice, whispering in her ear that she was acting crazy. What could we possibly have in common?

"Do you think I'm foolish, preferring an evening like this to a date with a perfectly harmless man?" Lois had asked Dolly the second time she'd told Herb no. They were in the lounge, playing Ping-Pong. "Lord, no!" said Dolly heartily as she returned Lois's serve with a forceful *whap!* "It makes perfect sense to me."

And Lois certainly wasn't staying in every night. There was always something new and exciting to do in Bay

City. Maxie had taken her to hear a jazz singer last week—how novel it felt, being the only white girls in the whole place! Another night she'd gone with Phyllis and Dolly to a strange French movie about a pickpocket. And Lois loved to accompany Janet on walks around the city, exploring different neighborhoods, and visiting odd little shops, where Janet bought foreign delicacies, like lox and bagels.

But she liked best the nights with the girls at the Arms, when they would hold informal "bull sessions" about office politics and career management. Janet and Netta both advised Lois to take some college courses at night, while Phyllis and Dolly argued she would benefit most right now by trying to learn as much as she could on the job.

Almost as rewarding was the time she spent alone in her room, much improved with curtains Mom had made, a rug on the floor, and pictures and her Nutshells pennant strategically hung to cover stains and cracks. There she worked late into the night, practicing her typing (she was still weak on charts and numbers), or pondering which was more efficient, putting the most recent item at the front or at the back of a file folder. She'd even begun to devise a filing system that would combine the chronological with the alphabetical in a revolutionary new way.

Lois knew she needed to work hard—every day she realized how much she had to learn about the complex job of being a secretary. Her biggest fear was that Mrs. Pierson would grow tired of putting up with Lois's lack of experience and hire someone else. Something she'd overheard, quite by accident, fed this fear.

It was the day Lois had borrowed a dress from Maxie, a slim raw silk number with a matching jacket, the exact same peacock blue as Mrs. Pierson's office. Lois had been fretting to Maxie about Mrs. Pierson's acid "country clod" comments, and the way she'd started calling Lois "Miss Frumpsville," as if it were her given name. "This should shut her up for a while," Maxie had said, taking the fashionable ensemble from her closet. "And there are shoes to match."

So there was Lois, not only at her desk before even Miss Gill, but looking as chic as any model. She stood up expectantly when she heard the door open, Mrs. Pierson's appointment list ready in her hand. Mrs. Pierson entered, in mid-sentence. ". . . certainly *seems* like an idiot, but maybe she's not as stupid as she seems, which means the risk is all the . . ." She was halfway to her desk before she noticed Lois. She started violently, dropping her leather satchel and newspaper. "Good lord, Miss Lenz, what's the idea of sneaking up on me like that?" she exploded irately. "You practically blend with the walls in that dress!"

"I'm sorry, Mrs. Pierson, I merely wanted to get a head start on work today," Lois said, hurrying to pick up Mrs. Pierson's satchel and newspaper. The *Confidentially* headline jumped out at her: COMMUNISTS, JAZZ MUSICIANS FUEL CITYWIDE REEFER PLAGUE!

"Very commendable, I'm sure," commented Miss Gill, who had followed Mrs. Pierson in.

"Yes, yes, commendable," said Mrs. Pierson icily. "But a better head start would have been to have a cup of coffee on my desk, rather than ambushing me by camouflaging yourself!"

"If I'd put a cup of coffee on your desk, it wouldn't be hot anymore," Lois couldn't help pointing out. "But I'll get you one now."

"Do that, Lois," said Mrs. Pierson, sitting down at her desk and rubbing her temples. "Do that and we'll call it square."

So the dress hadn't been a success, and Lois was left

with the disagreeable impression that *she* had been the "idiot" Mrs. Pierson was referring to! Of course, Mrs. Pierson called her an idiot to her face all the time, as well as a number of other insulting epithets. But this overheard remark was different, and Lois was worried.

She was tempted to ask Miss Gill about it. She'd developed the habit of visiting Miss Gill at the end of the day, and asking her advice about the difficulties she ran into, the ones even her *Secretary's Desk Reference* couldn't help her solve. Usually it was some off-the-wall request from Mrs. Pierson: "She told me to buy some expensive lingerie for Gloria Drake, but when I asked her Miss Drake's size, she just snapped at me not to be an idiot," Lois had worried one day. Miss Gill had the solution: The art director for the Helga campaign would know Miss Drake's size.

There was a comfort to sitting in Miss Gill's spartan, windowless office, with the kettle bubbling on the hotplate, and the Helga ad production schedule tacked up below the clipboards on the bulletin board. Lois liked to look at the framed motto Miss Gill had embroidered in shorthand: "Only through struggle will concrete results be achieved." The young girl would often ponder the motto's meaning, its applicability to almost every situation.

When Lois had asked about it, Miss Gill had replied: "I made it in a period of despair. It reminds me that the small, immediate tasks that face me every day are part of a greater good—a smoothly running office and the happiness of all who work at Sather & Stirling."

It was difficult to imagine Miss Gill in despair. Each morning found the office manager in the office before anyone else, cheerful and even-tempered. When Lois left at the end of the day, Miss Gill was still hard at work in the file room, reorganizing the files. Lois didn't know where she got the energy, unless it was the diet pills she swallowed with her cups of tea.

And no detail of office life was too small to interest Miss Gill. Just now she was helping to train a new paste-up artist, reorganizing the files, and smoothing out a quarrel between the marketing and research departments. Yet she still found time to ask Lois about the progress Mrs. Pierson was making in the education of the Helga model, Gloria Drake.

"Does Mrs. Pierson seem extra edgy after her dates, er, lessons with Miss Drake?" Miss Gill probed one evening. Lois admitted that her boss *had* been awfully insulting the past few days. "I wouldn't worry about keeping Miss Drake's size and other personal information in your BUSINESS ASSOCIATES file," advised Miss Gill. "I think by next week or the week after, we'll be seeing much less of Miss Drake."

After Miss Gill had shown Lois another "apartment to share" advertisement—the office manager still insisted Lois would be happier in a share—the young secretary went to Gretchen Wallis for information. Sather & Stirling's receptionist knew all the office gossip and was always happy to share it.

"Gretchen, tell me honestly, am I dumber than Mrs. Pierson's previous secretary?"

Gretchen looked up from her movie magazine and thought for a moment. "You're younger. You're different. But no, you're not dumber."

"Different how?" Lois pressed.

"Well, Miss R. was more forceful, somehow. She didn't knuckle under to Mrs. P. the way you do."

"Shouldn't a secretary knuckle under?" wondered Lois aloud. Gretchen ignored the interruption.

"She dressed swell, and she'd go to lunch with Mrs. Pierson at the Cheval Blanc, or leave early on Friday for a theater date. I figured she was one of those girls that went to a swank secretarial school and thought it would be fun to work in an office in between social engagements. You know the type." Gretchen looked at Lois kindly. "She didn't have more brains than you, honey, just more *chutzpah*."

Another sophisticated girl, thought Lois, feeling more inadequate than ever. Miss Ravenal had left behind a little box of exotic-looking cigarettes, buried in the back corner of the bottom drawer of the desk, with a matchbook from an exclusive nightclub.

"Mrs. Pierson never takes me to Le Cheval Blanc," said Lois a little sadly.

"Who wants to go? Give me a pastrami on rye at Lou's deli any day. Anyway, my personal belief, if you want to know, is that Miss R. was related to some big client, and that's how she got the job with Mrs. P. The old hyena seemed kind of relieved when Miss R. eloped."

Lois had made another friend at the office. She'd developed the habit of bringing Paula a cup of coffee in the morning, when she went down to the drugstore to get Mrs. Pierson's. Paula always rewarded her with a ravishing smile, and sometimes a "*merci mille fois*," when she was abstracted and lapsed into her finishing school French. Lois had stayed late one evening to help Paula organize her copy into a sample book, and Paula had entertained her with stories of the exclusive Haute École pour les Jeunes Filles, perched high in the Swiss Alps. Gretchen said Paula's background made her the go-to girl for any account that required a cosmopolitan touch.

However, Gretchen had only shrugged when Lois asked who was responsible for the diamond Paula wore on her left hand. "Some guy, who's always abroad somewhere," was all she knew, and she opined further, "Paula doesn't miss him much. All she thinks about is her career."

It was true, Paula was as dedicated as Miss Gill and

more ambitious. For where Miss Gill existed to serve, Paula wanted to lead. She'd come by Miss Gill's office at the end of the day, as Miss Gill was telling Lois, "Be tractable with your superiors, even when they lose their temper," one of her favorite maxims.

"I intend to stay late and review the Helga campaigns from 1952 on," Paula had announced. "The file room seems to be locked, may I have the key?"

When Miss Gill explained about the disorganized files and told Paula she'd pull the campaign material herself, Paula had bitten her lip in frustration and left without another word.

"Miss Winstead will go far," the office manager had commented. "She's got the executive spirit."

"Yes, she certainly does," sighed Lois, who'd been admiring the snug fit of Paula's white sweater. Was it because both girls were blondes that Paula always made Lois think of Faye, and feel that sharp ache of missing her?

She had a whole stack of postcards from Faye by now. Yet, she had to admit she enjoyed the letters Billy sent her more. Was it Faye's wooden style? She never wrote more than a few sentences, and one of them was usually about something she needed. "I'm having a cookout next week—who did we invite last year?" or "What was that marshmallow jello dish everyone liked so much? Send me the recipe." or "Write down some good records for me to play, will you?" They were an uncanny echo of the demands Lois faced every day at work and sometimes she was tempted to throw Faye's postcard across the room. Didn't Faye miss any of the other things they'd shared?

"Gosh, I've been having such a whirl I still haven't looked for that drugstore book or the marriage manuals," Lois realized with a start. "And it's almost August!"

Lois resolved that Tuesday, without fail, she'd visit the

library after work. However, she was thwarted again. Late on Tuesday afternoon, as Mrs. Pierson handed her a stack of employee evaluations with a brusque "I need these tomorrow morning," the phone buzzed and it was Gretchen. "You have a visitor in reception," she said. "A Netta Bean."

Chapter Fifteen
Netta's News

Netta Bean stood in the reception room, looking out the window at the city below. She was wearing her usual much-washed skirt and blouse, and with her hair pulled back in her usual tight bun, she looked as out of place in Sather & Stirling's sleek offices as a weed in a florist's bouquet. "Hello, Netta," Lois said curiously. Of all the girls at the Arms, she felt she knew Netta the least well.

Netta turned around and Lois saw at once that her eyes were red-rimmed. "I want to see that piece of paper you found in Ramona's room," she said fiercely.

Lois looked at her blankly. "What piece of paper?"

"Dolly said you told her you'd found a scrap of some letter when you were cleaning out the bureau drawers—and I want to see it!"

Lois remembered now—the scrap of carbon she'd found the night she and Maxie went to Francine's. She must have mentioned it to Dolly the other night, to illustrate the secretarial habit of saving every piece of paper, even those that seemed without value.

"Of course you can see it," she told Netta, wondering at the other girl's manner. "You came all the way down here for that? What's so important about this scrap of paper?"

Netta hesitated and then plunged in. "I followed your suggestion and went to Ramona's employer to find her forwarding address. But they don't have it. Her superior at the West Side Branch Library told me she gave notice five months ago!"

"Five months ago!" Lois's jaw dropped. "Did she get a new job?"

"No one knows!" Netta's voice wobbled. She paused a moment, fighting for control. "She didn't say a thing about it to any of us! In fact, she followed the same routine as ever, getting up and getting dressed as if she were going to work, and coming home in the evening tired, as if she'd had a hard day." A tear squeezed out, and rolled down Netta's cheek. "Oh Lois, What does this mean? Why didn't she tell me? Where has she been going every morning at eight A.M.? What's she been living on all these weeks? I'm at my wit's end, and that's why you've got to show me what you found!"

Lois patted Netta's shoulder helplessly, feeling a little frightened. "I'll help you any way I can," she assured her neighbor. Some of her mother's darker predictions flashed through her mind, and she fingered the silver whistle around her neck, asking Netta, "You don't think she fell into the clutches of a white slave ring, do you?"

"You have white slavers on the brain," Netta replied impatiently. "Believe me, they're less of a problem in Bay City than you think. Honestly!" She blew her nose with a snort.

The staff of Sather & Stirling were beginning to depart, and a few of the employees waiting for the elevator glanced curiously at the two girls.

"Look," said Lois, feeling snubbed but still sympathetic, "let me get my things and we'll get a bite in the neighborhood, and hash this over. Sometimes it helps just to have a fresh perspective on the problem. It sounds like you've been stewing over this by yourself for too long."

"Maybe you're right." Netta managed a watery smile. "I certainly appreciate your helpful attitude."

"I'll just be a minute," promised Lois. Netta was such an odd mixture—first prickly and condescending, then vulnerable and grateful.

Fortunately, Lois was able to make a quick exit without Mrs. Pierson's usual comment about clock-watchers. The executive was huddled in conference with Gloria Drake in the far corner of the office. When Lois walked in, she immediately snapped, "You're through for the day, Lois." Lois was able to simply snatch up her purse and hat and exit, closing the door carefully behind her as Mrs. Pierson continued berating the beleaguered young model: "I simply won't allow it! I've put too much time and effort into you to let some cheap stylist spoil everything!"

Poor Gloria! thought Lois sympathetically. It must be hard to be a model and face the competing demands of so many different people. Gloria had looked quite distraught.

Out in the reception room, Netta had taken off her glasses and was polishing them carefully with her handkerchief. Lois noticed for the first time how unusual Netta's eyes were, a changeable mixture of brown and green and gold. A gold tweed suit and some fashionable tortoiseshell frames would do wonders for Netta, Lois thought. Paula had worn such a suit the other day.

As if her thoughts had produced the ambitious copywriter, Paula Winstead walked into the reception room and picked up a package from Gretchen's desk. Lois clutched Netta's arm. "Look! There's Paula Winstead!" she whispered. Netta peered nearsightedly at the blond girl. "Who's that?" she asked, putting on her glasses as Paula disappeared through the door that led to the offices. "Someone famous?"

"No, just a copywriter here." Lois released Netta's arm, feeling a little ashamed of her excitement. The special feeling Paula inspired in her was not an emotion the staid school teacher would understand.

"She looked familiar," Netta remarked. "I wonder if I've seen her before. Maybe at the Magdalena Arms?"

"Oh, I doubt it," said Lois with certainty. "Paula moves in very different circles. She's quite the up-and-coming writer here at the agency, and she has a very cosmopolitan background. Why, she was finished in Switzerland!"

"She might have been started anywhere," Netta pointed out as they got on the elevator.

The two girls went to an inexpensive café Lois had heard Gretchen mention. The young secretary splurged on the blue plate special, while Netta settled for a tuna salad sandwich. As they ate, Netta studied the carbon fragment Lois had pulled from her purse.

"I thought it was probably a job application," Lois said, "from that phrase, 'find a place in your organization,' and then she talks about her skills. That would certainly make sense, wouldn't it, that Ramona had found another job? She had to be getting money somewhere, unless she had a family allowance like Maxie."

"No," said Netta, still absorbed in the carbon. "Ramona had no family. She was an orphan."

"Then that note she wrote Mrs. DeWitt was a lie! Why, you and the rest of the gang have known about this all the time, haven't you?" Lois accused.

Netta colored. "We didn't think it was your concern."

There it was again. The way the rest of the fifth-floor girls didn't trust her. And she had an inkling that Netta was the ringleader in some way! Lois couldn't help feeling confused and hurt. What had she ever done to earn Netta's dislike? She sawed viciously on her tough swiss steak.

As if she sensed Lois's hurt feelings, Netta said swiftly, "It wasn't really a secret; we think Ramona probably just wrote that to save time and explanations. None of the other girls are worried about it. But Ramona wrote me a note saying she'd left me a key and I can't find it. That's why I need to find her."

"A key to what?"

"I don't know. Perhaps her trunk? It's still in the store-room."

"Well . . ." Lois was willing to help again. "Perhaps Ramona got a position in another library. It shouldn't be too time-consuming to check—"

"Ramona was never happy at the library," Netta said immediately. "She wanted a more glamorous job from the first day we arrived from Minnesota. But she'd quali-fied as a library assistant at Teacher's College, and that was the only job she could get, besides teaching, which she hated. She only ended up at Teacher's College with me because some orphanage benefactress had endowed a scholarship there." Netta fell silent and Lois remembered something she'd learned from Phyllis.

It was the evening she and Phyllis had gone to an ex-hibit of Mexican paintings at one of the galleries in the riverside neighborhood nicknamed "Little Bohemia." The gallery was crowded with the mix of races and col-ors Lois had become accustomed to in the big city and she drank in the atmosphere, enjoying it as much as the artwork. Snippets of conversation drifted through the air, about the folk revival, what was happening down south, and how to go about "organizing." Lois's ears had pricked up at that last—it sounded like her kind of topic!

"It's too bad Ramona's not here," Phyllis had said as

they looked respectfully at a painting of a laborer with a machete. "She was so interested in Mexican culture."

"Really?"

"Oh yes. She was studying Spanish on her own, and I used to see her around the harbor sometimes, practicing her conversational skills on some of the Mexican dock workers."

This had revealed a new side of Ramona to Lois, who had heard plenty of stories about Ramona's high-spirited pranks and quick wit.

"What did Ramona look like?" Lois had asked curiously.

"Oh, she was pretty, I guess. Brown hair, brown eyes. She was always so—so animated, you didn't think about how she looked. She loved clothes. Netta used to scold her for spending her salary on new outfits."

"It seems funny, she and Netta were so close," Lois had mused. "They sound so different."

"Oh well, you know what they say about opposites attracting!" Phyllis had replied, then added hastily, "What I mean is, they were old friends, from attending teacher's college together."

Now Lois wondered if Ramona had been planning to use her language skills in some new career, perhaps as a translator or in the diplomatic service. She asked Netta, "Didn't Ramona talk to you about her ambitions?"

Netta stirred uneasily, as if at unpleasant recollections. "When we first came to the city, we did everything together. But lately, I guess we'd started to drift apart. I was spending more time on my teaching, while Ramona fell in with Maxie and . . ."

Netta fell silent, and Lois prompted, "What happened with her and Maxie?"

"Oh, it was all innocent, I'm sure," Netta said with an impatient shrug. "But they both have a yen for thrills, and they used to urge each other on. One time they went to an after-hours jazz party and came home smelling of reefer. Ramona and I had a huge quarrel—"

"Reefer? Do you mean loco-weed? Deadly marijuana?" asked Lois, shocked to the very core of her being. "Why, Netta, this explains everything! You shouldn't be phoning libraries, you should be combing the city's opium dens and hospitals if you want to find her!"

Not that it would do any good if they did, Lois thought despairingly. Ramona was almost certainly addicted to heroin by now. And once that poison was in your system, you were never free again. They'd watched a movie on the topic in health class last semester.

To her amazement, Netta burst out laughing. "Lois, for someone so smart, you can be awfully dumb!" she giggled. "Or naive is a better description. You're even worse than me, and Ramona used to call me an old-maid school teacher."

"Maybe she said it because of your hairstyle, not your opinions," retorted Lois, smarting at Netta's insults.

"My hairstyle?" Netta put her hand self-consciously to her bun. "What's the matter with my hairstyle? I've always worn my hair like this."

"It's just not very stylish," said Lois, regretting her hasty remark.

"It's comfortable and practical, and I save money other girls spend at beauty parlors," retorted Netta defensively.

"Well, so long as you're happy," murmured Lois, wishing she'd never said anything.

"Ramona liked my long hair. She said it was pretty when it was down."

"But you wear it in that bun all the time," objected Lois. Then as Netta opened her mouth, she added hastily, "Anyway, about Ramona, I guess you should probably see if she said anything to any of her reefer-mad acquaintances. That is, if they haven't already lost all sense of moral responsibility."

"I already questioned Maxie. She swears it was just that one party."

"As far as she knows," countered Lois. "And I wouldn't be surprised if Maxie knew more than she was telling you."

This time Netta didn't laugh. "I wouldn't either," she said thoughtfully. "Is that all you can suggest?"

"I'm afraid so," said Lois, irritated at Netta's evident disappointment. After all, she was a secretary, not a private detective! "It's going to be pretty difficult to track down Ramona's new occupation in a big city like this." She stood up. "I ought to be going. I left some unfinished typing that needs to be completed by tomorrow." Lois had decided it would be easier to do the work tonight, rather than get up early the next day.

"Oh! I'm very sorry to have imposed on you," said Netta a little stiffly. "I'd be happy to help you with your typing."

Lois shook her head. "That's not necessary."

"Dolly said you were supposed to have a job in the typing pool, and then they made you this Mrs. Pierson's secretary," Netta said as they left the restaurant and walked along the block. "Isn't that a little odd? I mean, that they would make a girl like you, fresh out of high school, personal secretary to one of the most important executives in the company?"

"I was first in my business classes all through high school," Lois defended herself. "And I was highly recommended by my career counselor, who knows the office manager."

"Yes, but still . . ." Netta broke off. "Never mind."

The two girls walked along in silence, each preoccupied with her own thoughts, each feeling a little dissatisfied with her companion.

The nerve, fumed Lois inwardly, suggesting that I'm incompetent. I got an A+ in stenography! I would have been first in the typing time trials! My business memos were miracles of conciseness!

But it was no use. Netta's words had tapped into an unease that had been growing inside her, a sense that there *was* something odd about being catapulted so quickly to such a responsible position. Deep down she knew there were loads of girls more qualified than she, and still moldable. So why *had* Miss Gill and Mrs. Pierson decided to give the job to her?

She remembered the remark she'd overheard. "Not stupid enough," Mrs. Pierson had said. But why would anyone want a stupid secretary?

Netta broke Lois's train of thought. "Here's my bus. I'd better run, or I'll be late for my class."

Netta was taking jujitsu at the Central Y, so she could defend herself against the troubled youths at the city high school where she taught.

"I do appreciate your help," the school teacher added formally.

Lois was equally polite. "I'm sorry I couldn't be of more assistance." There was something thorny and private about Netta that made the easy banter that Lois enjoyed with the other girls impossible. She only confided in me tonight because she was driven to it, Lois thought. And I'm sure she didn't tell me everything.

Lois had to sign in with the night guard at 333 Lake. "After seven," he said phlegmatically. A cleaning woman was vacuuming the reception area and Lois wondered if she had the office to herself. But no, there was a light on in the file room.

"Hi, Miss Gill," she said. Miss Gill whirled around from an open file drawer.

"Lois, you startled me," she said with a laugh, her hand to her heart. "Working late?"

Lois nodded. "Some typing to finish before tomorrow's deluge." She pointed curiously at a piece of paper taped to another filing cabinet. It was a list written in Miss Gill's clear, firm script.

Refugee
Spanish
Comintern
Hoover, Edgar J.

"What's that?"

"Oh, some words I found in an old stenography notebook used by your predecessor. I thought they might be keywords to some files, but alas, no!" She crumpled the list and threw it in the trash. "Another false lead."

Miss Gill wasn't the only employee staying late. On her way to the corner office, Lois saw that Paula was still at her desk. Even more surprising was the presence of Paula's office mate. Herb was sorting through the messy piles of paper on his desk with an air of great purpose.

Lois completed the employee evaluations quickly but it wasn't until she was checking them for errors that she really read them. Paula's was practically a paean—at least coming from Mrs. Pierson. Lois devoured the words, as if they could bring her closer to their subject. "Creative, energetic, and ambitious," yes, that was her Paula! And then the caveat: "At times Miss Winstead can be a trifle arrogant, and emphasizes too frequently her international education." Oh how true, and yet that was one of the most attractive things about her!

Herb's was far less promising. Lois's eyes drifted from

one scathing remark to the next: "Perenially tardy with copy." "Loses sight of the big picture." "Does not adequately reflect Sather & Stirling image." Lois shook her head regretfully. Staying late wasn't going to do Herb much good! She felt sorry for the rumpled copywriter who always had a slightly lost look in his eyes, despite the snappy bow tie and man-about-town air he affected.

When she went to say good night to Miss Gill, Herb was standing in the file room doorway with a big stack of paper in his arms.

"But I don't want to put you to any trouble," he was saying. "I stayed late precisely so I could organize and file my campaigns myself."

"Filing is women's work," said Miss Gill, waving at Lois over his shoulder. "And as I've explained, the files are in some disorder. I'm revamping the system now."

"It would help me with the Smith's Sundries account, to learn a little about office supplies from the perspective of the women who use them," Herb said earnestly as Lois returned Miss Gill's wave and walked away. She looked back before she exited the office. There was something eerie about the scene, the darkened corridor, with the light from the file room throwing Herb's shadow, huge and menacing, on the wall as he stubbornly insisted that he file his campaign material. Is he going to stay there all night? Lois wondered.

She left the two of them still arguing.

Chapter Sixteen
Dictation with Paula

Lois selected a file cabinet at random and pulled opened the middle drawer. It slid out soundlessly, on metal wheels. She surveyed the drawer's contents before selecting a manilla folder labeled CAROLINA FILTERED-MARKETING ANALYSIS. Leafing through it, she came across a chart analyzing the appeal of filterless cigarettes versus filtered cigarettes. She took it out. That would work.

The file room was still and empty under the humming fluorescent bars. The air seemed cooler and drier here than it did in the rest of the office. The file cabinets concealed their secrets behind smooth, faceless, metal painted a pinky-tan. The drawers were labeled with enigmatic numbers.

Lois felt a powerful pull toward the wealth of information concealed in these gleaming cabinets. "I'll just look around a little more, while I'm here," she told herself, giving in to her pent-up desire.

The young secretary had found herself unexpectedly at loose ends that morning. When she walked in the door, she'd been met by the news that Mrs. Pierson wouldn't be in until ten o'clock. "She called and said she had a sick headache," Gretchen reported. "If you ask me, the name of the sick headache is Gloria."

Lois hardly thought that tough Mrs. Pierson would let another disagreement with a lowly model make her ill, but whatever the cause, she was left alone in the office, with nothing to do after she had completed her usual morning routine. Mrs. Pierson's mail (delivered, as always, by Miss Gill herself) was opened, date stamped, and arranged in order of importance on the upper-right-hand corner of Mrs. Pierson's desk, exactly two inches in from the top and side. Yesterday's letters were stacked in the signature box in the upper-left corner; the list of the day's appointments and the message list were side by side in the center.

After Lois had moistened her handkerchief and wiped the leaves of the rubber plant in the corner, she was at a loss until she recalled Miss Grimes's dictum, "There's no such thing as an idle hour." The brief moments of respite a secretary experienced should be spent taking inventory, tidying, or filing, her teacher had told the Business Methods class. "If nothing else is possible, make use of the time by practicing your typing or stenography, using whatever you can find."

So Lois had decided to find a chart to copy in order to practice her number technique, still the weak point of her typing. When she discovered that Miss Gill was closeted with the new paste-up artist, she reasoned that although Miss Gill had rejected her help in filing, there would be no harm in taking something *from* the files, so long as she made a note of where it went.

And she had to admit to herself, she wanted to satisfy her growing curiosity about the file room. When she thought about her predecessor's orderly desk and methods, she couldn't help wondering if Miss Gill was missing something. So often what people took for disorder was merely a system they didn't understand. If Lois could discover the guiding principle behind Miss Ravenal's reorganization, what a feather in her cap that would be!

Pulling drawers open at random and examining the contents, Lois's hunch grew stronger. The files were all neatly organized by product, and within each product the material was organized chronologically, back to front. Lois was delighted to find that her predecessor shared her preference for this method. If we're already thinking along the same lines, she reasoned, I should be able to figure out the rest.

The problem lay in how the products were ordered. Brochures for a beauty school followed personnel files for no reason Lois could discern; Norvell's "Fruits of Spring" lipstick campaign files were in one cabinet and its "doctor recommended" germ-killing mouthwash in another. In between Buskers Beer and Carolina Cigarettes was a file of Sather & Stirling organizational charts. Yet there was a method in the madness, Lois felt. All her instincts vibrated in recognition of an intelligence behind the apparent disorder.

"Miss Lenz! Stop what you're doing at once!" Miss Gill's furious voice made Lois drop the file she had pulled out to examine. She spun around guiltily, and there was Miss Gill glaring at her, arms akimbo. Lois had never seen the older woman so angry. Her dark eyes seemed to shoot sparks of fury, and her sallow cheeks were flushed red. Why, Miss Gill is still quite attractive, Lois noted, even as she stammered an explanation about filling idle hours.

This didn't appease the office manager at all. "I thought I made it clear that the file room was off-limits! Go back to your own work at once! If your free moments weigh on you so heavily that you must stick your nose into tasks that are none of your affair, I'll send you to the typing pool!"

Lois fled. It was only when she'd reached the door of Mrs. Pierson's office that she realized she was still clutching the cigarette chart. With a quaking heart, she returned to the file room. The volcanic rage of mild-mannered Miss Gill, triggered, it seemed, by anyone tampering with her files, frightened her more than Mrs. Pierson at her most furious.

But Miss Gill, busy replacing the file Lois had dropped, had reverted to her usual serene self. "I'm afraid I lost my temper," she said with a pleasant smile. "You see, I stayed rather late last night, and yet made so little progress—I'm a little tired today." She took out a small vial of pills and swallowed one. "This should pep me up!"

Lois ventured to explain her theory about the mixed-up files. "I have a hunch I could figure out Miss Ravenal's system," she continued, growing enthusiastic about her plan. "I'd work on it after hours. Perhaps it wouldn't take me very long at all!"

Miss Gill's eyes were wide with alarm. "No, no, no, no, no," she told Lois. "Master small tasks before large, remember. A secretary works under supervision, not independently. You must not seek to be a solo star. Resign yourself to being but a cog in the machinery that supports the work of others. Does the root of a plant try to produce a flower?"

Lois watched Miss Gill in amazement as she rattled off her secretarial creed at top speed. The office manager's behavior was distinctly off-kilter today.

"If you like, you may refile this chart," Miss Gill offered, as if granting a great favor. As Lois pulled open the drawer marked 630–660 and tucked the chart back into the proper folder, Miss Gill's eagle eyes never left her. "I believe in fresh approaches, Lois, but I must be certain the files are purged of all negative elements. Look at the unfortunate affair of Herb!"

The whole office had been in an uproar earlier that week. Miss Gill had discovered a misfiled letter in the file room. It was from a secretary in the typing pool at J. C. Birch, claiming that Herb Hathaway had stolen the "fits you, supports you, loves you" slogan from her. Herb had blustered that he wasn't going to stay "where people swallowed such arrant nonsense," and then quit, although it was an open secret that he was on the verge of being fired anyway. The secretary had been hired as a junior assistant copywriter in an effort to hush up the whole affair. But the real mystery was how the letter, which was dated April 4 and addressed to Mrs. Pierson, had ended up in the file room without anyone ever having seen it before.

Maybe I'd be upset, too, if someone was fiddling with my files, Lois thought, trying to excuse the office manager's behavior as she left the file room. But before she could ponder the nature of Miss Gill's possessiveness further, she found herself face to face with Paula Winstead.

The golden-haired girl was quietly elegant today, in a french blue pencil skirt and white blouse, a matching blue sweater draped over her shoulders.

"I see you've managed to escape from the hyena's lair, Lois," Paula greeted her gaily.

"Mrs. Pierson's in late today," Lois explained, breathing in Paula's enticing perfume with pleasure. "And I had to return something to the file room."

Paula's eyebrows lifted. "You add filing to your other accomplishments? I'm impressed—maybe because I'm so dumb about such things."

Paula's compliment was like balm to Lois's filing frustrations, and she puffed up with pride. "Filing is kind of my forte," she told Paula in a confidential tone. "In fact, I'm devising a new system I think will revolutionize the field of office systems!"

"You ought to apply your skills to our files. You know what a mess they're in."

"Yes, I've been thinking about them, and I do have a

few theories I'm testing," Lois boasted. She wasn't going to tell Paula how Miss Gill had just treated her like a child who barely knew A from Z.

"You know," Paula said as if struck by a sudden idea, "I've been wondering if you'd help me out someday by taking dictation from me. I found it so—well, so inspiring to dictate the Bongo Red copy to you."

"Why not today?" Lois practically tripped on her own eagerness. "Mrs. Pierson has a long lunch meeting with the Norvell people. We could do it then!"

"*Quel bonheur!*" said Paula, bestowing a smile on Lois so dazzling it made her shiver. "That would be a big help. And you can tell me more about your filing scheme."

Lois filled the rest of her idle time with another project. Even though Netta hadn't asked for any more help since their dinner, Lois had decided to try to re-create the missing half of the letter fragment Ramona had left behind. She'd had the idea of making a grid of boxes that represented the letters and spaces of the missing half, based on standard margins. Then she tried to fill them in, like a crossword puzzle. At first it was easy: "ition" became "ambition"; "idly" became "rapidly." After that it got harder. Lois wrote and scratched out, absorbed in her task. She set it aside when the phone buzzed.

"I thought you should know Mrs. Pierson's on her way," Gretchen said. "And listen, dear, today's not the day to cross her!"

Lois was glad Gretchen had warned her. Mrs. Pierson stormed in a moment later, her silver-blue hair electric with rage. She made a beeline for her desk and her eyes raked the tidy stacks and lists angrily. "There's no message from Miss Drake listed here," she said, shaking the message list at Lois. "Because she didn't call," Lois explained, only to have Mrs. Pierson crumple the list and throw it at her.

The next minute it was the snarl. "Who told you to open my confidential letters?" "Why, you did, Mrs. Pierson," said Lois in bewilderment. The confidential letters always went at the bottom of the stack; Mrs. Pierson had explained to Lois in a rare mellow mood that the majority of letters marked thusly were merely callow attempts by the hoi polloi to reach a busy executive. But now Mrs. Pierson tore the letter in question into fragments, barking, "If you can't distinguish between what's really confidential and what is not, you're of no use to me!" And so it went for the rest of the morning. Lois sagged in relief when the door clicked shut behind her boss as she departed for her lunch meeting.

"Thank heavens I have dictation with Paula to look forward to!" Lois said to herself as she straightened Mrs. Pierson's desk. She hoped this would be the beginning of a real friendship between herself and the cosmopolitan girl whose foreign flair made her irresistible to Lois.

Even in her eagerness for her dictation date, Lois conscientiously crawled under Mrs. Pierson's desk and carefully sorted through her boss's wastebasket looking for the letter Mrs. Pierson had torn up, so she'd have better judgment next time. Amid the lipstick-stained tissues and crumpled pieces of paper, she found three torn fragments of the letter that had been marked CONFIDENTIAL. Lois pieced them together on the peacock blue carpet.

```
YOU MUST DELIVER
BILLS TO P.O. BOX
CENTRAL POST OF
```

```
DO NOT DELEGATE        THIS TASK. TELL
NO ONE. YOU KNO        W THE CONSEQUENCES
OF YOUR FAILUR         URE TO COMPLY
```

Where was the missing piece? It must be that sodden bit that had been soaked by Mrs. Pierson's leftover coffee. But still—a strange and cryptic message, Lois thought. There was something disturbing, even threatening, about it. She crawled back out from under the desk, and put the torn pieces of paper in her purse. She'd study it later.

Today's secretary needs to be a bit of a cryptographer! she decided as she thought over her activities that morning. The thought amused her, and she was still smiling when she entered Paula's office, which the rising copywriter now had to herself.

"Lois," said Paula, looking up from the lacy brassiere she was contemplating. "You're an absolute darling to help me out."

Lois glowed as she seated herself. "I don't mind at all." She flipped open her notebook and, pencil poised, looked expectantly at Paula, waiting for her to work her verbal magic. A little prickle of excitement went through her when Paula stood up and closed the door.

Again Paula held up the pink froth of nylon, lace, and underwire. She peered at it so closely that her aquiline nose was only an inch away from the satin bow where the lacy cups met. She practically inhaled the brassiere, as if the scent of nylon had some secret to communicate to her. Lois watched her, spellbound.

"You deserve the best," Paula said dreamily. "That's why we use only the finest satin weave nylon in Helga's new 'Night and Day' brassiere. With double-stitched, double-waxed support, you'll feel both cared for and . . . caressed. Am I going too fast?"

"Oh no," Lois gulped. The small office seemed suddenly warm. Paula had seated herself just a few feet away from Lois and was absentmindedly running the brassiere through her fingers as she stared into space. Her perfume enveloped Lois like an elusive, spicy cloud.

"I need a better hook," muttered Paula. "Let me think. Let Helga hug you . . . Let the magic of Helga embrace you . . . with the finest satin weave nylon and three-way stretch lace panels, you'll have the comfort of knowing Helga will support you . . . whatever you do. But I have to mention the triple-waxed thread. The Helga people think it's a big selling point. With waxed thread and double stitching, a Helga brassiere . . . no, make that: Helga's Night and Day brassiere will follow you wherever you go. And like the best husband, this double-threat brassiere both forgives and forgets." Paula broke off and said in her normal voice, "No, no, no, scratch that. I can't end copy with the word 'forgets'—Mrs. Pierson would have my hide, and with good reason."

Lois felt a new awareness of her own undergarments, and she couldn't get her mind off Paula's distinctive scent, even as her pencil flew automatically across the page. "I liked the 'embrace you,' line" she said shyly. "Really?" Paula asked earnestly. She looked at Lois as if she'd forgotten all about the Helga brassiere, and Lois felt a strange, yet not unpleasant tension growing between the two of them. "What's that perfume you're wearing?" she asked.

"It's Norvell's *Inoubliable*," said Paula. "I'll never forget it. It was the first Norvell product I named. When I was a boarder at La Haute École, that was a nickname for someone you liked. You'd call them your '*inoubliable*.' "

"Does the agency require you to use the clients' products before writing about them?" Lois asked curiously.

"No, but *I* do." Paula leaned forward and unbuttoned the top two buttons of her crisp white blouse so that Lois could glimpse the lacy border of a cream-colored brassiere. "This is a Helga. You see, I'm very passionate about my work."

Lois fought to control a sudden wavelet of desire that splashed over her senses. Why, this was ridiculous! Faye was the only one she felt this way around, and that was only when they were practicing kissing, or practicing cheers, or when she got a glimpse of Faye's bare skin. She barely knew Paula.

"Lifts you, supports you, embraces you," Paula was saying as she leaned back. "That's still the theme, whoever came up with it, Herb or that secretary."

I've got to concentrate, Lois told herself in a panic. I mustn't allow my emotions to run away like this. But all she could think about was that Paula hadn't rebuttoned her blouse, and that when she crossed her legs, her narrow blue skirt rode up on her knees, giving a tantalizing glimpse of her inner thigh.

It's just that I haven't seen Faye in so long, Lois told herself. When she tried to picture Faye, she couldn't. All she could see was the girl in front of her, with the gilt-colored hair (Faye would say it's out of a bottle, Lois argued with her tempestuous desires), her chiseled cheekbones, her hooded green eyes, and her *Inoubliable* perfume.

"Goodness, we got right to work and I was going to order sandwiches," Paula recalled. "You must be simply ravenous!"

"Yes—that is, no," stammered Lois.

"You're dedicated to your job, aren't you? I think we have that in common."

"Not like you," Lois replied. "I'm not wearing a Helga brassiere. Mine is—"

Paula held up a hand. "Don't tell me, let me guess. May I?" Lois nodded jerkily, and Paula slowly unbuttoned the top two buttons of Lois's candy-striped shirtwaist dress, while a teasing light in her eyes seemed to dare Lois to pull away. But Lois leaned forward, mesmerized, as Paula slipped her hand inside Lois's dress. Her cool fingers brushed Lois's fevered flesh as she stroked the fabric of Lois's brassiere, felt the stitching, and slid up the elastic shoulder strap. "Wamarama!" she announced triumphantly. "One of our competitors."

Lois's heart was beating so hard she thought it would jerk out of her body. Her pencil fell to the floor from nerveless fingers.

"Why Lois!" Paula's green eyes widened. "You're all flushed!"

Paula didn't resemble Faye at all, but just then her eyes held the same look Lois had seen a hundred times before in Faye's eyes. A look that unleashed all the passion Lois had dammed up inside her young body.

They moved toward each other almost at the same time, and Lois crushed Paula's Bongo Red lips in a passionate kiss. Then Paula trailed a scarlet streak from the corner of Lois's mouth to a sensitive spot just below Lois's right ear.

Lois closed her eyes and caught her lower lip between her teeth as Paula slid her hand under the hem of Lois's full cotton skirt. This was a new experience—like nothing she and Faye had ever done! As Paula's hand climbed its way up Lois's nylon-clad thighs, it left a trail of gooseflesh behind. A stew of sensual excitement simmered somewhere deep in the center of Lois's being. Her muscles were like water and her breath came in little gasps, as if she were drowning.

"Tell me about your favorite filing system," Paula whispered in her ear before trailing her warm mouth along Lois's neck. Lois felt more buttons being unbuttoned, and then Paula's mouth was on her now bare shoulder. She clutched at Paula, bracing herself against the tremors that shook her.

"Well, I've been experimenting with a method that combines the ahhhhlphabetical with the chronological—ohhhh!"

Lois's legs fell open in response to Paula's questing hand. Paula's delicate touch, even through the layer of Wamarama underwear, sharpened Lois's desires in a way she'd never felt before. Was this what she'd been seeking with Faye? Was this what Miss Gilhooly, the hygiene teacher, had left out of their "mankind reproduces" unit junior year?

"Am I going too fast?" Paula murmured.

Lois wanted to answer, "Not fast enough," but all she could manage was a breathless "No!"

"It must be exciting to apply your ideas to Sather & Stirling's file room," Paula pursued.

"I haven't had a-a-ah chance," Lois confessed.

Abruptly the delicious stroking stopped. "You haven't? Why not?"

"Miss Gill won't let me," Lois explained. "She's kind of—touchy about the file room."

"But this morning you said you were filing," Paula said. She pushed back her chair and eyed Lois narrowly. "You weren't trying to mislead me, were you?"

"Oh no," Lois protested, not quite truthfully. "I was filing. But it was more an exception than the rule."

Suddenly the seductive ad girl was all business.

"Goodness, the time!" she exclaimed, glancing at her gold wristwatch. "This was fun, but you'd better scoot on back to Mrs. Pierson, before I get you in trouble."

Then Lois was out in the corridor, buttoning her dress, bewildered at her own behavior. What had she been thinking? How could she have forgotten Faye like that? And how like Faye Paula was, hustling Lois unceremoniously away when things began getting exciting!

Or could it be that Paula had lost interest in her because she wasn't as far along filing as she'd led the copywriter to believe?

Or was it both?

Lois sighed and mentally shook herself as she opened the door to Mrs. Pierson's office. But her sigh turned into a gasp when she saw Mrs. Pierson standing with her hands on her hips, glaring at Lois like a gorgon!

Chapter Seventeen
Mrs. Pierson Is Furious

Mrs. Pierson's eyes followed Lois as she inched nervously toward her desk. Then the whiplash voice froze her in midpath. "Miss Lenz," she said, swaying slightly like a cobra about to strike, "tell me what's on the wall behind my desk."

Lois looked obediently at the numberless clock. As always, it took her a few moments to puzzle out the time. Oh dear! It was one thirty-five—that dictation had taken much longer than she realized!

"There's a clock, Mrs. Pierson," Lois began contritely. "And I know I'm a little late. I'm—"

Mrs. Pierson let loose. "A *little* late? No, Miss Lenz, that's unforgiveably inaccurate. You are terminally late—as in terminated. You are suicidally late, because from now on, you are dead as a secretary in the advertising business, do you hear me? Moribund! Beyond rescusitation! Not even one of your Girl Scout friends could save you now!"

"Please, Mrs. Pierson, give me another chance," Lois said desperately. Tears started in her eyes. She couldn't believe this was happening to her, Lois Lenz, winner of the perfect attendance award three years in a row!

It's Paula's fault, she thought bitterly, blaming the gilt-haired girl. She wanted something from me and she didn't care if she got me in trouble getting it.

No, it's my fault, a small voice in her head said. It's those crazy impulses and strange cravings that ruin me!

And another voice was murmuring, Gosh, if I'm going to be fired, I wish we'd had a chance to—

"Another chance?" Mrs. Pierson was saying with a sneer of disbelief. "Can you give me back the thirty-five minutes I lost while you were shopping or gossiping or having your nails done?"

"But it wasn't any of those things," Lois pleaded. "I was taking lingerie dictation from Paula—Miss Winstead. And I didn't leave for lunch until twelve forty-five, so you see, I'm not as late as you think."

"Lingerie dictation?" Mrs. Pierson repeated. "With Paula? But we . . ." She narrowed her eyes, studying Lois. "You have lipstick on your collar," she remarked.

"Oh!" Lois turned bright red and scrubbed at the red streak with her handkerchief. "I'll do anything I can to make up for my tardiness, anything," she babbled as she rubbed the stain deeper into the candy stripes. Blot, don't scrub, said a cool, practical voice in her head.

Mrs. Pierson sat down at her desk as she contemplated her red-faced secretary, a small smile growing larger and larger. "Well, Miss Lenz," she said finally, "I must admit you surprise me!" To Lois's astonishment, she burst into her trademark hyena laugh. "Perhaps I should visit Elm Grove, or wherever it is you come from," she said, her eyes twinkling with malicious merriment.

"Walnut Grove," Lois corrected automatically.

"Same thing." Mrs. Pierson waved a hand as if swatting a fly. "Miss Lenz, I've decided to give you another chance, but only on one condition. I'm giving a small cocktail party tomorrow night, and my maid, Eunice, has chosen this week to have appendicitis. If you'll fill in, we'll forget about your tardiness. Do you know the difference between a Manhattan and a whiskey sour?"

"Certainly," said Lois, hoping Mrs. Pierson wouldn't call her bluff before she could look up "mixed drinks" in her *Secretary's Desk Reference*. Fortunately Mrs. Pierson didn't. "Yes, I think you're educable, Lois," she continued, contemplating the young girl as she swiveled back and forth in her chair. "I suppose I would have noticed your potential before if I hadn't been occupied elsewhere."

Lois felt a great wave of relief. Not only had she held on to her job, but Mrs. Pierson seemed to be taking a new interest in her progress. "I'll try not to disappoint you again," she promised.

"Good!" Mrs. Pierson smiled her wide smile that made her look a little wolfish. "Now fetch me some bicarb."

At the end of the day, Lois paused in Miss Gill's doorway a little more hesitantly than usual, but Miss Gill waved her in with a smile. "Any problems today, Lois? Any of Mrs. Pierson's quirks I can help you understand?" She poured Lois a cup of tea.

"No," Lois reported. "Mrs. Pierson was unusually pleasant today."

"Pleasant?" Miss Gill furrowed her forehead.

"There is one thing," Lois said. "I'm to help Mrs. Pierson at a cocktail party she's giving this Thursday, and since I've never been—"

"Mrs. Pierson invited you to her cocktail party!" Miss Gill exclaimed. Her furrow had turned into a frown line. "Why, everyone who's anyone in advertising will be there. How did this happen?"

"Mrs. Pierson said she thought I was educable, and—"

The word seemed to act on Miss Gill like a red flag on a bull. "Educable! I'm not sure this is a good idea, Lois.

It's too soon for a young girl like yourself to be thrown into such sophisticated surroundings. You'll be overwhelmed. You won't know how to behave."

Lois was dumbfounded. Miss Gill had done nothing but encourage her since she'd started at this job. Yet lately, she seemed to want to hold the young secretary back. Lois set down her teacup. "I think I know how to mind my manners!" she protested.

"When you started at Sather & Stirling, I was impressed by your humility, your willingness to take direction," Miss Gill said sadly. "You seemed to have a real understanding of the secretary's role. I'm sorry to see that being replaced by a certain recklessness and adventurism."

Lois could stomach no more of this discussion and excused herself as best she could, leaving Miss Gill still hoping she would achieve a "correct perspective on this matter before Thursday." She fumed all the way down in the elevator. Why on earth is Miss Gill so set against my attending this party? Does she think I'm some thug with no table manners? Lois's flats rat-a-tatted angrily across the marble lobby and she plunged briskly through the homeward-bound crowds, too full of irritated energy to take the bus.

And there won't even be any table manners or worrying about the correct fork! she thought scornfully. It's a cocktail party!

The warm admiration she'd once felt for Miss Gill had chilled considerably. It's true, a secretary's job is to serve, she argued mentally, but that doesn't mean there's no place for initiative or ambition!

What was that word Mrs. Pierson had used the other day when she was talking to Dr. Steinmetz? Sublimate. He'd said it wasn't healthy to sublimate one's desires, and Mrs. Pierson had said the advertising business was built on sublimated desires and they'd both laughed.

Well, Lois wasn't going to sublimate her ambition! Paula didn't!

At the thought of Paula, Lois froze in mid-stride, overwhelmed with a wave of want and need so strong it made her gasp. Whatever is the matter with me? she wondered. I must be sublimating my homesickness for Faye.

Would Paula be at the party? Lois resumed her walk. Miss Gill had said "everyone who's anyone." Surely Paula Winstead was someone!

Lois was passing Gruneman's Department Store now, each window a vignette from a life more glamorous than Lois could imagine. She looked enviously at a mannequin outfitted in a boat-necked cocktail gown of intricately draped gold lamé. "If I could just wear something like that to the cocktail party," she said aloud, "I'd dazzle Paula!"

But no—boatnecks made her look even shorter than she was. Something with a plunging neckline would be better, she decided. I'll ask Maxie as soon as I get home. She'll know what's appropriate. Maybe she'll even loan me one of her stylish ensembles!

Lois quickened her pace, eager to get home and eager to get out of the neighborhood surrounding the bus station, the seediest part of her walk home. This block was lined with disreputable businesses, everything from shabby bookstores that sold magazines wrapped in plain brown paper to bars, lurid with neon. Idle men stood outside them, playing dice and whistling at the girls who hurried by.

A man in a brown suit lurched out of the corner bar she was passing, holding the door open for a girl in a gaudy orange dress and too much makeup. Lois made a wide circle around them, looking at the pair with distaste. Then she stopped.

"Maxie?" she said.

Maxie looked swiftly up and down the street, and then told the man, "See you later, Bill, and thanks." She joined Lois, nonchalantly linking arms with her, and walking the dumbstruck girl away from the bar. "Hiya, Lois, how's tricks?"

Lois could smell beer on Maxie's breath, although the girl seemed fairly steady on her rhinestone-bedecked evening sandals. Suddenly, all that Netta had told her about Maxie's brush with the underworld came rushing back to her. Her heart sank. Had Maxie taken to the streets to support her habit? Was Bill her—her—Lois's mind refused to form the word.

"Who was that man?" Lois questioned the debutante anxiously. "What were you doing in that awful bar?"

Maxie made a face. "Relax, Mother," she said, taking out a handkerchief and carefully wiping off her orange lipstick. "Believe it or not, I'm working! I've finally found the career for me, just like the rest of you!"

Lois recoiled in horror. Could Maxie, indeed, have sunk so low? Yet looking at Maxie's pleased face under the garish makeup, Lois could hardly credit her own suspicions.

"But don't mention this to anyone," Maxie cautioned her. "It's a surprise."

"Surprise for who?"

"Pamela. And you know why, don't you? Surely you've figured it out by now that . . ."

But Lois was no longer listening. They were approaching Bay City's Central Post Office, and Lois had just spotted Mrs. Pierson, stepping briskly down the building's wide concrete steps. She didn't see Lois, and as the young secretary hesitated, wondering if she should call out to her boss, Mrs. Pierson got into a waiting cab and drove away.

Chapter Eighteen
The Party in Mrs. Pierson's Penthouse

The more Lois turned it over in her mind, the stranger it seemed. There was no earthly errand Lois could think of that would explain Mrs. Pierson's presence at the post office. A letter to send? Lois would mail it. A package to pick up? The office boy would be dispatched. Information she needed? Any one of a dozen people would be sent to find out what she wanted. Mrs. Pierson just didn't do errands herself, like ordinary people!

Lois eyed the executive covertly the next afternoon, as Mrs. Pierson sneered contemptuously over some copy and then ripped it decisively in half. Could Mrs. Pierson's strange visit to the post office have anything to do with the mysterious confidential letter that had upset her so the previous day?

"Good heavens, how did it get so late?" Mrs. Pierson turned to glare irritably at Lois as if the time were her fault. "Where's that memo, you fool? As soon as you've finished typing it, call the garage and tell them to send the car around." Lois pulled the memo on the Buskers Beer Slogan Contest from her typewriter and flew to do Mrs. Pierson's bidding, anticipation for the glamorous penthouse party driving all other thoughts out of her head.

Thank heavens Maxie, whatever her shadowy occupation, had come through with a dress. And what a dress! Lois thought with satisfaction of the cocoa-colored silk cocktail gown with a scoop-necked bodice and three-quarter-length sleeves. Embroidered gold vines and flowers climbed all around the harem skirt. Maxie had even loaned her gold slippers and a matching clutch. The whole ensemble was carefully tucked inside a dress bag, hanging in the office coat closet. Lois couldn't wait until Paula saw her in it.

The hard-driving executive began dictating orders to her at top speed as she led the way through the office. "Lois, the car is waiting!" barked Mrs. Pierson impatiently as Lois stopped to fetch her dress, then continued without pausing, "I want you to check the liquor supply as soon as we arrive at the apartment. Did you remember to call the caterer and my housekeeper to make sure they were on schedule?"

Lois was trying to take notes on her steno pad and carry her dress bag and purse at the same time. She finally managed by clenching the dress hanger in her teeth.

"'es 'issis 'ierson."

"We'll go over the guest list while I dress, and I'll tell you which cocktail each of the really important people prefers," Mrs. Pierson continued as they exited the building. Lois wrote busily as she followed her boss across the blistering yards of pavement to the car waiting at the curb. The heat wave hadn't broken, but when Lois got into the car, it was unexpectedly cool.

Air-conditioning! she thought, delighted. What luxury! Mrs. Pierson finished, "And don't forget to refill the cigarette boxes," and then opened up the evening newspaper. With one eye on *Confidentially* (FRIGID MOTHERS RESPONSIBLE FOR MOST AMERICAN COMMUNISTS), she fished out her cigarette case, extracted a Dunhill, and put it between her lips. Lois dove into her purse for the cigarette lighter she now kept to light Mrs. Pierson's cigarettes. Cigarette lit, Mrs. Pierson leaned back and sighed.

Maybe I should take up smoking, Lois thought. It seems to relax people. I could try those foreign-looking cigarettes Miss Ravenal left behind. As she tucked away the lighter, her fingers encountered the carbon fragment. She'd been working at odd moments on re-creating the missing half, and now she pulled it out and studied it for the hundredth time. The more she decoded, the stranger the letter seemed. Was she perhaps on the wrong track?

"Taking home carbons from the office, Lois?" said Mrs. Pierson, and Lois looked up, to find the executive's sharp eyes on her. She tucked the fragment back into her purse, and hastened to reassure her boss, who was a stickler for confidentiality.

"Oh no! It's something from my boardinghouse. A project for one of the other girls."

"Your boarding house?" asked Mrs. Pierson disinterestedly as she turned back to the paper. "Do girls still live in boarding houses?"

"The Magdalena Arms is one of the few left, I believe," Lois explained.

Mrs. Pierson looked at her suddenly, with an expression Lois couldn't interpret. But the car was sliding to a stop and Mrs. Pierson got out without pursuing Lois's living situation further. Lois followed her boss into an imposing limestone apartment building. With a nod to the man at the front desk, Mrs. Pierson sailed into the elevator, which seemed to have been waiting just for her. And knowing Mrs. Pierson, thought Lois, the elevator man had probably learned the hard way that he'd better have the elevator waiting for her—or else!

The elevator was as different from the elevator at the Magdalena Arms as day from night. Lois's feet sank into plush carpeting and the walls were paneled in dark wood, not covered in peeling paint. Lois felt excitement bubbling up inside her as she watched the floor indicator move from 1 to 20 before coming to a stop at PH.

Her mouth opened in a silent gasp when the elevator doors slid apart, revealing not an anonymous hallway but the gracious foyer of the penthouse apartment. Her eyes widened as they traveled over the vista of rooms opening out from each other and ending at a wall of windows that framed the lake. But she had no time to gawk. Mrs. Pierson had already disappeared from view around the corner.

Lois stepped tentatively into the cream-carpeted foyer, and the elevator doors closed with a soft whoosh behind her. The walls were lined with oyster gray silk, and the furniture was modern. "Mrs. Pierson?" Lois called as she stepped into the living room. She jumped when she saw someone looking at her, but it was just a painting of an empty-eyed woman with a long neck over the stark onyx mantelpiece.

"In here," came the familiar, impatient voice from a distance. Following the sound, Lois went down a short hallway, and opened a door on the right.

Mrs. Pierson's bedroom was as large as the Lenz living room in Walnut Grove. At the far end, in front of a triple-paned mirror, stood Mrs. Pierson, clad only in a black girdle and sheer stockings. Her cigarette hung from the corner of her mouth as she tweezed her eyebrows.

"Oh! I'm sorry," said Lois in confusion, backing out again.

But Mrs. Pierson said genially, "Sit down, Lois, and forget the girlish modesty. Do you have the guest list with you? Let's go over it now."

Lois crept back in the room and perched nervously on an ottoman at the foot of the bed. "Mr. and Mrs. Robert Norvell," she read.

"Manhattan and martini with a twist," said Mrs. Pierson. "She's allergic to strawberries. He likes stuffed olives. Keep Mamie McArdle away from him."

"Mamie McArdle?" asked Lois, taking notes. "She's going to be here?"

"Of course she is," said Mrs. Pierson haughtily. "Everyone who matters will be here. While we're on the subject, *she* likes her drinks strong and frequent."

Lois continued down the list, reading names and taking notes while Mrs. Pierson pulled a sleeveless cocktail dress of matte black satin from her closet and stepped into it. "Zip me up, Lois," Mrs. Pierson interrupted.

As Lois obeyed her, a strange sense of déjà vu came over her. Maybe it was Mrs. Pierson's surprisingly shapely figure, but she was suddenly transported back to that day in the locker room, when Faye had asked Lois to zip *her* up. The day her life began to change.

And look at me now, Lois thought in sudden delight. In a penthouse apartment, zipping up the most powerful woman in advertising! Mrs. Pierson had the same athletic physique as Faye did, Lois noted. Did she play badminton, too? She had to stop herself from smoothing the dress over Mrs. Pierson's hips and kissing the nape of her neck, as she used to do with Faye. I mustn't let my excitement make me giddy, she told herself sternly.

"You look stunning," she complimented the older woman as Mrs. Pierson sat down at her dressing table and wielded a dark red lipstick.

"Thank you, Lois. You'd better change, too. The maid's uniform is in the closet in the maid's room."

"Maid's uniform!" Lois was aghast. "But I brought a party dress! I can serve just as well in that, can't I?"

Mrs. Pierson looked in the mirror at the reflection of Lois behind her. "I thought we had an agreement, Lois. I thought you were aware that I was doing you a great favor."

Lois knew she was defeated. She wanted to keep her job, more than anything! But I'll never let myself get in such a—a humiliating situation again, she vowed privately, as she slunk down the hall. And someday I hope Mrs. Pierson learns how such humiliation feels!

Mrs. Pierson tapped on the maid's room door a few minutes later. "Need any help?" she asked, entering without waiting for a response. "Let me zip you up. There! You look very nice!" She tugged familiarly at the skirt and adjusted the shoulders. "I put out some shoes for you," she said as she exited. "Those red flats won't do at all."

The maid's uniform was actually quite attractive, a company-occasion dress of black taffeta with a dainty white voile apron and a little flirtation of a lace ruffle at the low round neck. It even fit well, although the bodice was a little snugger and the skirt a little shorter than Lois liked. But still, it was a maid's uniform. She was a servant. Lois's spirits plummeted lower than the basement. How Miss Gill would delight in her situation!

And she'd dreamed of making gay small talk with Paula! Now she'd only be serving her canapés!

Oh well, Lois reminded herself. It's only this evening.

She put on the shoes Mrs. Pierson had left out, black patent leather pumps with four-inch heels. "They're not very practical," she said dubiously, but Mrs. Pierson declared them perfect. The more downcast Lois became, the more encouraging and friendly was Mrs. Pierson. "You'll be an ornament to the party!" she said gaily. "I'm quite pleased Eunice had to have her appendix out!"

A buzzer sounded and Mrs. Pierson picked up the phone and listened for a moment. "Thank you, Eddy, send them up," she said, and hung up. "The caterers are in the kitchen; they'll explain the service to you. I think, Lois," she lectured, "that this evening will be quite educational. I hope you approach it in that spirit." The elevator dinged softly, and Mrs. Pierson squared her shoulders. "Here we go!" Lois made a dash for the kitchen.

Half an hour later she had her hands full with the thirsty hordes, circulating through the apartment with her tray of highballs and rushing back to the kitchen, where the barman from the catering company was mixing as fast as he could. Lois thanked heaven more than once for her photographic memory, as she made sure that Gwen Mac-Gowan, the hatchet-faced marketing director at Helga got her martini with a pickled onion, or that Roger Forsythe from the J. C. Birch Agency got an extra dash of bitters in his Manhattan.

And few guests seemed to notice Lois as she squeezed through the increasingly crowded rooms, although one plump woman in a gray moire satin suit and a hat with an ostrich feather did grab her arm, burbling, "You must be Martha's new cupcake! Let's go somewhere and have a talk, just the two of us." Politely Lois refused, wondering how strong the barman was mixing his drinks. "Cupcake"?

But for the most part, Lois was as much a part of the background as the furniture. And as the rooms grew more crowded, and the guests more flushed, the cigarette smoke thicker and the din of chatter louder, Lois began to find advantages in her anonymity, eavesdropping on the conversations of the powerful and well-to-do, picking up snippets of advertising gossip. "I hear Birch is pitching Buskers," Gwen MacGowan murmured to Mrs. Pierson as they stood by the grand piano, while "Lemon ice will be *the* color this fall," one man advised another in the hallway.

Then Lois spotted Paula.

She was on the terrace, chatting with several other girls cut from the same cloth: attractive, assured, and probably ambitious.

To Lois's eyes, Paula stood out. She was wearing a

stunning bell-skirted gown of chartreuse printed chiffon, and as Lois watched, she laughed at something one of the other girls was saying, a silvery sound that floated over the din of the party.

Lois gripped her tray firmly and headed toward the group as if magnetized. They were talking about their fiancés when Lois approached.

"Where's yours?" a brunette in glasses asked Paula, taking a highball from Lois's tray. Lois waited for the answer with the rest of them.

"In Ankara, with the Foreign Service," Paula replied. With a queer smile she added, "I expect it will be years before he gets a better posting."

"Ankara, that's good," said the brunette appreciatively. "Mine's just in the Army, stationed at Fort Dix." She gave a theatrical sigh. "I don't know *when* I'll be able to see him again!"

"Mine's in the Foreign Legion," broke in a sporty-looking girl with a flushed face. "Maybe he'll die." She popped a canapé into her mouth, seeming quite nonchalant about the tragic prospect.

"I suppose you read *Beau Geste* as a child," Paula said, and the group burst into knowing laughter. Then Paula noticed Lois and dropped the stuffed olive she was about to take a bite of. "Lois! What's the idea sneaking up on us pretending to be a maid?" she snapped.

"I'm helping out Mrs. Pierson just for the evening," replied Lois, taken aback at the sudden accusation. "Her maid has appendicitis."

"Helping out, is that what they call it now?" murmured the brunette, looking Lois up and down over the top of her glasses. The other girl laughed.

"This is Lois Letz, girls, Mrs. Pierson's new secretary and apparently maid for the evening," Paula introduced her, a trifle flustered.

"Lois *Lenz*," corrected Lois.

"Freudian slip," whispered the flushed girl, and she and the brunette laughed even harder.

"Lois, this is Pat Moutarde"—Paula indicated the sporty one—"and Gay Tallent."

Conversation languished after Paula had made the introductions. The girls eyed Lois speculatively.

"You know, I think we may have a friend in common," Lois said to Paula, to fill the silence.

"Oh?" Paula raised one eyebrow. "Who?"

"Netta Bean, one of the girls at the Magdalena Arms. She stopped by the office the other day—"

"I don't know a Netta Bean," said Paula decisively. She turned to her friends. "Time to mingle?" and the trio of sophisticates sailed off. Lois heard Pat ask, "Isn't the Magdalena Arms that disreputable boardinghouse on the west side?"

Lois took her highball tray, her aching feet, and her bruised spirits to the far corner of the terrace. Setting down the tray, she leaned on the limestone parapet, still warm from the day's heat. There was only the faintest pink glow on the horizon from the vanished sun, and lights from the windows around were beginning to dot the deepening blue dusk. A hint of a breeze lifted the dark curls from Lois's heated cheeks. Finally, a break in the weather, one part of her noted, but her thoughts were on Paula.

What did she want from Paula? Did she merely admire the older girl and want to emulate her? Or was there more to it than that? Do I want to be her? Lois asked herself, Or do I want to have her? As my new best friend, that is.

She was a little disturbed by her own fickleness in forgetting Faye. Lois closed her eyes tightly and conjured up a picture of Faye, lolling on her canopied bed doing algebra problems. The way she caught her full lower lip in her upper teeth as she studied, the languorous way she waved one crooked leg in the air as she lay on her stomach with the math book spread open in front of her. Lois could almost see her, looking up from her books, pushing up her gold-framed sunglasses as she slowly licked her lips with a pointed pink tongue—

But wait a minute, thought Lois in confusion. Faye never wore sunglasses while studying algebra!

She put the picture out of her mind. She had no business mooning over memories of home anyway. Collecting empties and orders as she went, she shouldered her way back through the crowd to the kitchen. "Two Manhattans, a Scotch and soda, and another martini with an onion," she told the barman.

"We're low on whiskey," said the barman as he poured.

Lois stood frozen. Clear as a bell, she heard Mrs. Pierson's voice as they left the office: "As soon as we get to the apartment, check the liquor supply." This was far, far worse than being late for lunch!

"Take over, will you?" She thrust her tray at the barman and then pushed her way desperately through the dining room, her head in a whirl. Should she make a quick trip to the nearest liquor store? Where would that be? A phone directory, she thought frantically. Where would Mrs. Pierson keep her phone directory? She darted into Mrs. Pierson's bedroom, and began pulling open drawers and riffling through the dressing table. Nothing! She'd have to find Mrs. Pierson and confess her mistake. She opened the door to the hall, feeling as if she were walking the plank.

The next minute she'd collided with a woman in a green dress and was stumbling backward.

"Sorry, I was looking for the powder room," said the woman.

"Pamela!" cried Lois thankfully.

"Lois?" Pamela peered at her in puzzlement. "I keep meeting you when I least expect it! Why on earth are you dressed up as a maid?" Pamela looked stunning, her creamy skin and auburn hair accentuated by the jade-green shantung silk sheath she wore.

Lois clutched at her former pep squad captain's arm. "Oh, Pamela! I'm in terrible trouble! The barman's running out of whiskey and I can't find a liquor store! I was supposed to order more before the party started and Mrs. Pierson will fire me if she finds out!" Tears started in Lois's eyes as she recounted her dire situation.

Pamela took charge immediately. "Where's the phone?"

"There's one in here," said Lois breathlessly. The two girls reentered Mrs. Pierson's bedroom, and Pamela picked up the phone by the bed and dialed 0. "Desk? I'm calling from the penthouse. Where does Mrs. Pierson get her liquor?" She listened a moment, as Lois stood by on tenterhooks. "Oh? You could? Yes, whiskey. You know her brand? By the case? Wonderful." She turned to Lois. "Are you low on anything else?" Lois shook her head and Pamela said into the phone, "No, that'll do it. Thanks!" and hung up. "The deskman will phone in the order. Your whiskey's as good as on its way," she reported.

Weak with relief, Lois sank down on the bed. "Pamela,

you've positively saved my life!" she said, her voice trembling with emotion.

Pamela brushed aside her gratitude. "It was nothing. What are friends for?" She sat down next to Lois. "But honestly, Lois, what's with the maid outfit? It's not exactly what the up-and-coming career girl wears to cocktail parties in Bay City."

Lois blushed miserably. "I *am* the maid—for tonight, anyway." She explained Mrs. Pierson's wrath and her threat to fire Lois. "And I want to keep my job!" she ended. "I know it's humiliating, but what else could I do?"

"Yes, I think humiliation was Mrs. Pierson's intention." Pamela clenched her fists. "That hyena! I've a good mind to tell her what I think of her!"

"No, don't! It would only cause more trouble."

"You bring out my protective side," Pamela told her seriously. "The big city is a jungle, and sweet-natured girls like you are just so much raw meat for the lions."

"Oh, I'm not so dumb and helpless as I look." Lois's breath quickened. Pamela had put her hand on Lois's knee and the ex-cheerleader felt again the powerful magic of her old crush.

Pamela looked deep into her eyes. "Oh, I've never doubted your intelligence," she said, her voice low and husky. "You know how much I admire your ambition and dedication. It's just, you're so naive . . ."

Pamela's face was close to Lois's, and Lois felt as if there were a magnet drawing them together. "Maybe I'm not as naive as you think," whispered the younger girl. She could see herself reflected in Pamela's eyes. She thought of Faye and the nights she'd lain awake in her bed in room 504, wishing her best friend would suddenly appear for some practice kissing; or those other nights she relived the way she'd felt when Paula gave her dictation. Suddenly it occurred to her that she could practice kissing Pamela to keep in practice for practice kissing Faye! What was the ultimate purpose of all this practice? Lois couldn't think, with Pamela so close.

Lois never knew what might have happened next, because the door opened, and a lilting voice said, "Oh dear, *this* isn't the powder room!" It was the woman in the ostrich feather hat, and instead of backing out the door, she came in, beaming at them and peering curiously around the room. "This must be the queen bee's nest itself!" she cried with pleasure, pulling out a small notebook and a gold pencil.

Pamela jumped up. "The powder room is down the hall, Miss McArdle!"

Lois looked at the newcomer with interest. So this was the influential *Confidentially* columnist! Why, she looked like a garden club lady back in Walnut Grove! Yet Pamela was glaring at her, as if the plump woman were one of the predatory jungle animals she'd just been telling Lois about. Of course, remembered Lois, she blames Mamie McArdle for the break-in at the Magdalena Arms.

"Pamela!" gurgled Mamie McArdle. "What a pleasure to see you again!" Her glance took in Lois. "Is this *your* cupcake? Poor Maxie!" She shook her pencil at Pamela. "I don't think you value Miss Mainwaring as much as you should; really, I don't!" she scolded.

The odd remark affected Pamela strangely. Her face turned a splotchy red as she fought to control her emotions. "I have to get back to the party," she choked, and shot out the door.

Mamie sat down in the place Pamela had vacated. "Touchy girl, isn't she? But tell me all about *you*. I love a new face!"

"I'm Lois Lenz and I come from Walnut Grove," Lois

explained. "I work as Mrs. Pierson's secretary at Sather & Stirling."

"Oh, you must tell me *everything* about Walnut Grove!" Mamie exclaimed enthusiastically. "I'm gathering material for a series of articles about small-town girls who sink to degradation in the big city, and I need a few really good tidbits about small-town life for contrast."

Happy to be helpful, Lois told her about the summer picnics on the bluff, the garden club's annual luncheon benefiting the home for unwed mothers, and other sundry details.

"Oh, this is wonderful, great stuff," Miss McArdle kept exclaiming, writing busily in her notebook. "You're much more helpful than that copywriter, what's her name, Miss Woosted?"

"Do you mean Paula Winstead?" Lois queried. "But she's never lived in a small town!"

"Oh no, I was trying to get some background material for a book I'm writing under a *nom de plume*—it's to be called *Boarding School Girls*. But she was terribly tight-lipped."

Mamie closed her notebook and put away her pencil. She leaned toward Lois so that her strong scent practically slapped the young girl in the face. "Now tell me. Confidentially and off the record. Are Martha Pierson and Gloria Drake an item, or is it true that Gloria threw her over for a hairdresser?"

"Why, Mrs. Pierson and Miss Drake just know each other in a business way!" said Lois, astonished by Mamie McArdle's suggestion.

"Aren't you the cutest little country cousin!" laughed Mamie. "In spite of the French maid outfit."

"I believe they had a professional disagreement about Miss Drake's stylist, not her hairdresser," Lois added as an afterthought.

"That's better," approved Mamie. "You're wise to the bit, aren't you?"

"The bit?"

"You're just a little new to the twilight world, am I right?"

"Twilight world?" Mamie McArdle was talking gibberish. Then Lois understood the implication, and was offended. "I have no need of the twilight world, thank you very much! I'm not even married, much less pregnant!"

"Pregnant?" Now it was Mamie's turn to be confused. Then she began to laugh until tears squeezed out of her merry brown eyes. "Oh my dear, I said twilight world, not twilight sleep! Oh, this is too good to keep to myself. Good night, Miss Lenz, and I look forward to seeing you again!"

Lois wondered if she'd been mistaken about Miss McArdle's meaning. But she remembered clearly her classmate Vera, who had to get married their junior year. Lois had visited her right before her twins were due, and Vera had told her about the "twilight world," where you gave birth without experiencing pain. Could she have meant "twilight sleep"?

Lois tidied up the room before she left, thinking of Mamie's question about Mrs. Pierson and Gloria Drake. Why she'd talked about them almost as if—as if—

She was straightening the contents of the nightstand drawer, when something caught her eye. Underneath the eyedrop bottles and reading glasses, there was a photograph—what Lois had learned to call an eight-by-ten glossy. She pulled it out curiously.

The girl in the photograph was Dolly Dingle—Dolly wearing a dark wig, and a strange sort of black leather girdle with lots of straps. She was holding a riding crop, raised as if to strike a young blond girl, clad only in brassiere and panties, who was kneeling at Dolly's feet. The blonde was looking up at Dolly with a mixture of terror and delight on her face. But the most surprising thing about the photo was that the shoes Dolly wore were identical to the ones Lois had on her feet that minute!

Chapter Twenty

Some Advice from Mrs. Pierson

Lois made a last circuit through the apartment, empty-ing overflowing ashtrays and collecting abandoned glasses. In the kitchen, the caterer's men were packing up. The housekeeper had gone home hours ago. Lois con-templated the full dishrack and the overflow of dirty glasses in the sink and wondered if she should wash them or leave them for the real maid.

"Well, that's everything," said the caterer, rolling his cart into the service elevator. "Good night, miss."

"Good night, thank you," replied Lois wearily as she dumped the glasses in the sink. I'm not going to worry about the dishes, she decided defiantly. I'm going to tell Mrs. Pierson good night and I'm going home!

She knocked on Mrs. Pierson's bedroom door, and then entered. "Mrs. Pierson, I'm all done so . . ."

Her words trailed off. Mrs. Pierson hadn't even looked up. She was sitting on the edge of her bed smoking and making notes on the guest list. Lois's heart sank. She wouldn't put it past Mrs. Pierson to give her those notes and demand imperiously that they be typed up and on her desk by 9 A.M.!

As she watched, Mrs. Pierson took her cigarette and

put it on the edge of the nightstand, where its smoldering ash burned dangerously close to the finish. Lois ground her teeth. Of all the—suddenly, her patience snapped.

"For heaven's sake, Mrs. Pierson, use an ashtray!" Lois stalked over to the bedside table. "Leaving your cigarettes on top of furniture is the surest way to scar the finish—it's a nasty, filthy habit!"

Mrs. Pierson looked up with astonishment as Lois stood over her in the too-snug maid's uniform and four-inch patent leather heels brandishing the cigarette threateningly.

"Would you like to have a hole burned in you? Well, your nightstand doesn't like it either!"

"I'm sorry, I—I never thought of it that way," faltered Mrs. Pierson. Her eyes followed Lois as the young girl ground the offending cigarette out in a ceramic ashtray.

"There!" said Lois. "Now if you don't need me any further, I'm tired, and I'm going home."

Mrs. Pierson grabbed her arm. "No, don't go!" she said, looking at Lois with a mixture of fear and delight that was strangely familiar. "I'll be good!"

Lois hesitated and Mrs. Pierson asked, "We've never really talked about your ambitions, have we?"

"I didn't think you were interested in them," said Lois, surprised by the sudden turn the conversation was taking.

"That's because I thought you were just a dumb little high school girl," said Mrs. Pierson. "But tonight, I suddenly see you for what you really are—a kind of jungle cat, beautiful—and cruel!"

How differently people perceived her, Lois thought. First, Pamela wanted to protect her from jungle animals, and then, Mrs. Pierson was acting as if *she* needed protection from Lois. She must have had too much to drink. "I'm just a girl from Walnut Grove," Lois replied soothingly, but Mrs. Pierson overrode her. "Every day you come to the office and pretend you're merely my minion, but all the while you're secretly gloating because you know that *you* hold the upper hand!"

By now Lois was truly confused. "But I *am* merely your minion," she protested.

Mrs. Pierson held up a hand. Her eyes were glowing like two gray coals. "I'll tell you a secret"—she lowered her voice—"I don't mind. You remind me a little of myself when I was your age. Understanding power—that's made me a successful saleswoman. I create the fantasies—but in order to create them, we must also live them, mustn't we?"

Lois was torn between flattery and concern. Concern won as Mrs. Pierson continued breathlessly, "Let's play a little game. You'll be the Roman empress, and I'll be the Greek slave."

"I don't know anything about the Roman Empire," Lois tried to excuse herself. "I took French."

"All right, then you'll be the Nazi commandante, and I'll be the captured resistance leader," continued Mrs. Pierson determinedly.

"I don't want to be a Nazi!" protested Lois. "Let's play we go to the kitchen and I force-feed you some coffee." Lois stepped forward, prepared to pull Mrs. Pierson to the kitchen by force if necessary, but Mrs. Pierson was obediently rising and Lois ended up gouging the executive's stockinged foot with the heel of her patent leather pump.

"Ohhhhh!" cried Mrs. Pierson, her face a mask of pain and pleasure.

"Oh, Mrs. Pierson, I'm so sorry," Lois gasped, even as she felt a shameful delight in bruising Mrs. Pierson's foot. It was small enough revenge for having to wear the maid's uniform all night long.

"You're punishing me, aren't you, you cruel minx?" said Mrs. Pierson. And before Lois could answer, the older woman added, "I deserve it. I've been a bad girl."

Even in the midst of her worry, Lois was glad Mrs. Pierson realized she'd gone too far.

"You just went a little overboard," she told her boss judiciously.

"But sometimes, isn't it good to be bad?" Mrs. Pierson was following her own train of thought. She gripped Lois tightly. "Lois, let's be bad together!"

Mrs. Pierson's burning lips were on her neck, and Mrs. Pierson's hand was wound in Lois's hair. There was an instant of total shock, when Lois stood rigid in the executive's arms. Then the siren call of Mrs. Pierson's lips, hands, the soft curves of her breasts pressed up against Lois's (in heels, Lois was the same height as her superior), awakened the desire the secretary had kept caged for so long (more than two months not counting the interlude with Paula), and that desire leapt up and rattled the bars of its prison.

Lois captured Mrs. Pierson's mouth with her own and felt the dizzying sensation of her own power as the icy Mrs. Pierson melted beneath her onslaught. She was only vaguely aware that her short taffeta skirt had gotten hiked up around her waist so that Mrs. Pierson's hands were caressing the bare flesh above her stockings. She knew only one thing for sure: Mrs. Pierson had had much more practice kissing than either Faye or Paula.

"Don't stop," Lois gasped when she came up for air.

"I should," whispered Mrs. Pierson hoarsely, "but I can't. You little vixen!"

What would a vixen do in a situation like this? Lois wondered, newly eager to please her boss. Experimentally, she pinched Mrs. Pierson's bottom through the black satin. Mrs. Pierson moaned, inflaming Lois still further.

The older woman tugged urgently at the new Helga underwear Lois had bought only the other day.

"Pretend I'm your new secretary," she panted. "Tell me to type!"

"Type!" Lois gasped. "Type an urgent memo as fast as you can!"

The next moment Lois's head fell back and she quivered uncontrollably. Would this "memo" unveil the secret that had so far eluded her?

As if from far away, she heard the click of a door opening. A voice was saying something. The fog of pleasure cleared abruptly, and Lois clutched Mrs. Pierson in confusion, and then simultaneously they disentangled, Lois, scarlet, pulling down her skirt, and Mrs. Pierson blinking her eyes like a diver coming up for air.

Miss Gill was standing in the doorway, her lips compressed, holding a portfolio in one hand and some suits in their cleaner bags in the other.

"I stopped by to give you the West Coast sales figures, and I thought I'd drop off your cleaning as well," she said, efficiently hanging the suits in Mrs. Pierson's closet and taking a folder from her satchel.

"Thank you, Ivy." Mrs. Pierson nervously lit a cigarette, and then with a glance at Lois, stubbed it out in the ashtray.

Miss Gill looked at her wristwatch. "Party's over already? I hope you made some useful contacts." The sharp eyes which saw everything fell on the guest list with Mrs. Pierson's notations. "Shall I take this to type up?" Her eyes flicked to Lois. "We can share a cab if you're ready to go." Then to Mrs. Pierson: "You don't need Miss Lenz any further, do you?"

"No, that will be all, Miss Lenz," said Mrs. Pierson with a pitiful attempt at her old peremptory manner.

"I'll just change my clothes," said Lois and fled.

In the maid's room, where she'd hung her day dress and the unworn brown silk, Lois unzipped the uniform with trembling hands. Her whole body still quivered with unsatisfied desires, and her mind was churning with a mixture of frustration, relief, and injured pride. If only Miss Gill had come a moment later! And then again, thank goodness she'd come when she had. But if only it had been anyone but Miss Gill! And then, the nerve of her, taking Mrs. Pierson's notes to type—that was Lois's job!

She dressed hastily, gathered her belongings, and returned to Mrs. Pierson's room.

"I'll just say good night to Mrs. Pierson," she told Miss Gill, who was coming out of the bedroom.

"Mrs. Pierson is on the phone with her analyst," said Miss Gill cheerfully, closing the bedroom door behind her. "I'm sure it will be fine if you just slip out. The cab is waiting."

As soon as the cab was on its way, Miss Gill began. "I think you see now that you had a more difficult time at this party than you expected. It might be hard to admit that you lack the level of understanding of a mature secretary—"

"I think I showed great adaptability," Lois defended herself, "which the *Secretary's Desk Reference* lists as one of the four most important characteristics for a secretary."

"Doesn't the *Secretary's Desk Reference* also advise against following instructions without thinking?" Miss Gill asked gently.

"You've always said, 'Be tractable with your supervisor.'"

"I've also advised you to limit your tasks to those which fall within your purview. I've seen in you a tendency to involve yourself in the affairs of all sorts of departments—copywriting, reception, filing, and now, er, entertaining. I'm afraid you're spreading yourself too thin, Lois, when you should be digging deeper into the fertile fields basic secretarial tasks offer to the discerning eye."

Lois remained stubbornly silent and Miss Gill changed tactics.

"It's out of a real regard for you that I say these things." Her soothing voice spread like syrup over the cab. "When you started at Sather & Stirling, you were such a simple young girl. Is this the adjustment you make to city life? Twisting your normal impulses into those of a man-hating neurotic?"

"Why, some of my good friends are men!" said Lois in astonishment.

Miss Gill ignored her. "The path of such women is a torturous and difficult one, Lois; it takes intelligence and character to walk it. I'm not sure you have either." The cab was pulling up to a nondescript apartment building in a middle-class neighborhood midway between Mrs. Pierson's penthouse and the Magdalena Arms. Miss Gill gave the cabdriver several bills and the address of Lois's residence.

"Just promise me you'll think about what I've said, and start limiting yourself to the real duties of a secretary," Miss Gill advised as she got out of the cab.

Chapter Twenty-One
In the File Room

"Real duties of a secretary! Real duties of a secretary!" Lois fumed to herself as the cab turned toward the Magdalena Arms. Her emotions were churning in a volatile stew, like the night air that came through the open cab window in hot oppressive waves, laced with undercurrents of electricity. This evening had brought so many new experiences to sort out that her brain wouldn't work properly, but kept running around in circles, chasing the same questions.

Why had Mrs. Pierson suddenly switched from calling her "country clod" and "Miss Frumpsville" to "minx" and "vixen"? What did Miss Gill mean when she warned Lois about turning into a "man-hating neurotic"?

Why did Paula blow hot and cold for no apparent reason?

What had Mamie McArdle been talking about?

What was Dolly Dingle's photo doing in Mrs. Pierson's desk drawer?

Lois opened her purse and pulled out her handkerchief to blot her heated brow with a little lemon-verbena-scented toilet water. A folded piece of paper fell into her lap. Lois unfolded it and read:

YOU DON'T KNOW A FROM Z.

GO BACK HOME BEFORE IT'S TOO LATE.

The threatening message was scrawled in big block letters with a blunt pencil.

Lois had reorganized her purse only that afternoon. Someone at the party must have written this!

But who? Enigmatic Paula? Mysterious Pamela? Gossipy Mamie McArdle? Mrs. Pierson, who had revealed a new side of herself tonight?

Suddenly Lois was tired of the mystifying conversation and behavior of her city friends. Figuring them out was like trying to file a document she didn't fully understand. She longed for the clarity and order of Miss Grimes's Business Methods class, the simple satisfaction of filing correspondence in date order.

Filing! If only she could file, she'd feel better!

"Driver," she said suddenly, "take me to 333 Lake!"

The driver spun the wheel to the left and Lois was thrown against the door of the cab as it made an abrupt U-turn. Lois smiled as she resettled herself. Despite the dirt, heat, and the strange behavior of many of its inhabitants, there were lots of things about city life she liked, and prompt service was one of them.

Minutes later, she was climbing out of the cab in front of the deserted plaza at 333 Lake. The night guard was a lone figure in a pool of light at the front desk, and he seemed to take forever, unlocking the door and pulling out the log for her to sign in. It was so late he had to turn on the elevator for her.

In spite of her sense of purpose, Lois felt uneasy. She had to remind herself that she'd seen Miss Gill enter her apartment just moments ago. There was no chance of the file-fixated office manager surprising her!

And she'd been frustrated so many times in the last few days, she felt she had a right to some sort of fulfillment, even if it was only putting files in order.

She pushed to the back of her mind the other factors in her sudden desire to file: Paula's snub, and Miss Gill's evident urge to take her down a notch.

It was strange being in the office this late. When she got off the elevator, the reception room was dark, the receptionist's desk barely discernible in the faint glow from the city lights.

She switched on the receptionist's desk lamp and went through the door to the corridor. Where was the light switch? She inched forward feeling along the wall, then stopped. Was that a flicker of light ahead, where the corridor turned? She squinted into the dark. Had she imagined it? But no—there it was again, a splash of light on the wall.

It's the flickering of a flashlight, Lois realized, recalling her days at Girl Scout camp. Someone else is in the office!

She crept forward, and peered carefully around the corner.

It was as she thought. The wavering light was coming from the file room!

The back of Lois's neck prickled with fear. She knew she ought to report this to the guard right away, but she just *had* to see who the intruder was, and what he was doing.

She inched forward until she could put her eye to the crack of the file room door, which the intruder had left slightly ajar.

A dark figure was hunched over an open file drawer, flipping through its contents. The flashlight illuminated the manila folders and white papers, but left the intruder shrouded in shadow.

Now the intruder pulled out a file, opened it, and after

studying it briefly, shoved it impatiently back into the drawer, crumpling a corner.

Inadvertently Lois leaned forward, and to her horror, the door swung open with a loud creak!

Instantly the intruder swung around and shone the flashlight full in Lois's face. Blinded, she reacted instinctively, swinging her foot up and at the hand that held the flashlight with a high kick that would have done the Nutshells proud. There was a muffled gasp of pain, and the flashlight fell to the floor, uselessly illuminating a swath of metal filing cabinet. Lois kicked again, this time aiming at the intruder's legs. Another gasp and a hoarse curse. Before she could gather herself for a third kick, the figure rushed at her. They grappled briefly, before Lois's assailant thrust her to one side. Lois was left with a vague impression of desperate strength, and the rough fabric of a trenchcoat before the miscreant fled down the corridor. As soon as she recovered her balance, Lois raced in pursuit, following the sound of the receding footsteps. The intruder had blundered, retreating into the office, away from the elevator.

He'll be trapped, thought Lois exultantly. Now I'll get the guard.

The footsteps stopped and there was a distant bang. Oh no! Lois hurried past the art room and the art supply closet, as a mechanical whirring noise began. But she was too late. He'd taken the freight elevator!

Lois bit her lip in vexation. If only she'd called the night guard as soon as she saw the flashlight, the whole mystery might have been cleared up by now! But it was too late.

Slowly she retraced her steps. Wouldn't it be better to say nothing? She could only imagine what Miss Gill would say if she knew Lois had been visiting the file room after hours! Besides, Lois suspected the intruder might be a Sather & Stirling employee; for the intruder knew the office layout better than she did. A scandal was the last thing Messrs. Sather & Stirling would want!

There'd been something else, too—an impression of familiarity in their brief moment of contact. What was it? Lois shook her head. The fleeting impression was gone.

Back in the file room she switched on the lights and picked up the flashlight, turning it off. It was an Acme brand, she noted, an agency client. She looked at the file folders that had spilled on to the floor. There was nothing of interest that she could see—they were client files from a campaign for Regal Margarine. The open drawer was labeled 630–660.

These numbers. They were the clue. Examining the file she'd picked up more closely, Lois saw there was an incompletely erased number penciled on the tab. These numbers must be part of the organizing scheme!

A noise made her jump. It was just the flashlight, which she'd set atop the cabinet, falling over. But Lois's heart was pounding and she went out to the corridor and looked nervously up and down.

This was no good, she decided. She was as jumpy as a jonesing dope fiend. I'll come back, she promised herself, replacing the files in the drawer. I won't give up until I figure this out!

At the night guard's desk she examined the sign-in sheet as she wrote "10:21" next to her name. All the names had sign-out times next to them from earlier in the evening. The intruder had covered his tracks well.

There were distant rumblings and flashes of light in the west as Lois hurried through the oppressive heat, breaking into a run when she saw an empty bus lumbering to the stop at the corner. She sat in a seat by the window. It felt odd, not having to fight her way aboard.

Her visit to the file room had only added to the mound

of mysteries. As she watched the familiar buildings slip by, the skyscrapers turning to haughty town houses and then crumbling tenements, she decided that it was time to start finding answers to the questions she'd been asking! Deep in thought, unconsciously fingering her silver whistle, Lois's mind leapt about in queer tangents, from Mamie McArdle and her proposed series about degraded small-town girls to Miss Gill and her insulting implication that Lois was too simple-minded to travel "torturous and difficult" paths. As the bus rolled past the corner bar where she'd seen Maxie the other day, Lois worried again about the troubled debutante and the unsavory activities she was pursuing. From Maxie, her thoughts jumped to the other girls on the fifth floor. Dolly with her wig and whip; Janet with those glasses she didn't need; Netta and her mysterious missing friend. The whole fifth floor was bubbling over with secrets. What were they all concealing?

Chapter Twenty-Two
Advice from Pamela

A strange wind was spinning the refuse on the street in frenzied whirlpools as Lois hurried along the dimly lit block. It was just a few minutes before curfew, and Kay was bolting the front door as Lois ran up the steps.

"Just made it," said Kay with a big yawn, letting Lois in. "And I don't mean curfew. It's going to start coming down any minute."

With hurried thanks, Lois left Kay to lock up and headed to the stairs. She couldn't bear being cooped up in the tiny elevator tonight. She needed room to think!

"You forgot your mail, Lois," Kay called after her, holding out a handful of correspondence.

Lois took it, glancing over it as she climbed the stairs. A postcard from Faye; Rod had taken her dancing, Daddy and Mummy had redone the rumpus room, she was planning her fall shopping—goodness, was it August already? A letter from Mom. There was a note from Billy, too. Probably another request for a hard-to-find jazz recording.

The fifth-floor corridor was dark and quiet when Lois reached the top, except for a gleam of light under Maxie's door. Lois hesitated, then put her ear to the wooden panel. She recognized Pamela's voice in the low murmur. The two friends must be having a late-night bull session.

Maybe Pamela could help unravel the mysteries that were puzzling her, Lois thought. Maybe she'd insist Maxie tell her just what she was doing in that seedy bar.

Suddenly she was tired of living in this twilight of uncertainty and doubt. She wanted to know what was going on!

She tapped lightly on the door. "Girls, it's Lois, mind if I join you?" she called softly. "I have your dress, Maxie, I didn't even wear it." There was no reply. Had they heard her? Lois tapped again and, opening the door, stepped boldly into the room. "Sorry to burst in on you like this," she began, then stopped.

Maxie and Pamela were kissing passionately, entwined in a tight embrace!

Her eyes took in the whole scene in a split second—Maxie in her silk kimono, half lying on the bed, Pamela still in her green sheath, her shoes kicked carelessly to the floor, bent over the supine girl, the pink comforter twisted and crumpled underneath them.

Why, this must be what Mrs. Pierson and I looked like to Miss Gill, Lois realized.

And then, just like Lois and Mrs. Pierson earlier, Pamela and Maxie became aware of her and pulled apart. Maxie tugged her kimono closed, and Pamela sat up and smoothed her hair.

"Why, Lois!" she faltered. "We were just—I was just showing Maxie—That is, Maxie had a muscle cramp . . ."

Then she threw up her hands. "Oh, I give up! Maxie and I are lovers, Lois!"

"Lovers!" Lois gasped.

"Sort of like steadies," Maxie put in helpfully. "Like you and your boyfriend Bobby."

"Billy, and we broke up before prom," Lois corrected.

"Whoops, sorry!" murmured Maxie sympathetically.

"It's all right," Lois reassured her. "We're still good friends."

"We're Lesbians!" Pamela broke in desperately. "You know, deviants! I know even Walnut Grove has heard of deviants!"

"Deviants . . ." Miss Gill's phrase, "man-hating neurotic," echoed in Lois's head. "Girls, do you know something?" she said in an awed voice. "I think I'm a deviant, too!"

Pamela and Maxie stared at Lois, mouths agape.

"Good Lord," said Pamela at last. "How could we have been so blind?"

"Suddenly it seems obvious," agreed Maxie. She gave Lois a wide smile. "Welcome to the secret world of Lesbian career girls, Lois!"

Lois sank down on the pink satin pouf feeling dazed. It was as if the past few months had suddenly come into sharp focus.

"So that's what Dolly meant when she asked if I liked girls?" she asked eagerly.

"Exactly!" chorused Pamela and Maxie.

"And I bet Netta's in a twist about Ramona because they were lovers, too?"

"Precisely!" cried Pamela and Maxie.

"And Janet and Phyllis are also—"

"More Lesbian career girls!" the two said triumphantly. Maxie added, "The fifth floor has always had a reputation to keep up."

Why, it was like joining a sorority! Lois felt aglow with satisfaction at her new membership. Then her brow puckered.

"But is it right?" she wondered. "Is it normal? Miss Gill told me tonight that I was on a tortured path to becoming a neurotic! And Mom saved a magazine article

on the use of electroshock therapy in treating neuroses—
I'm sure it must be good for the sick people, but it didn't
sound very pleasant!"

Both Pamela and Maxie tried to reassure her at once.
"It's perfectly normal," declared Pamela forcefully, while
Maxie put in gaily, "And even if it's not, who cares?
You're not hurting anyone."

"As for electroshock therapy," Pamela continued, "are
you neurotic?"

"No," admitted Lois. "I don't think so."

"There!" said Pamela triumphantly.

"You just have to be careful who you talk to about
your special predilections," Maxie advised. "Don't con-
fide in anyone unless you know they're wise. And stay
away from psychiatrists!" She gave a mock shudder. "My
family had me see one after an incident with Mingy Patter-
son at Miss Gratton's, and he was loonier than I was!"

Paula was rummaging in her purse. "A homophile group
I belong to put out a pamphlet you should read . . ."

But Lois wasn't paying attention. She heard again Mamie
McArdle asking her, "You're wise to the bit, aren't you?"

"Why, is Mamie McArdle . . ." she began.

"Yes!" said Maxie gleefully. "Doesn't that just flip you?"

"But she was going to do that 'exposé' on women-only
boardinghouses!" Lois protested. "That doesn't seem
right!"

"Just because she's a Lesbian career woman doesn't
mean she has scruples," remarked Pamela. "But tell us,
why would Miss Gill call *you* neurotic?"

"Actually, she said I was becoming a 'neurotic man-
hater,'" Lois corrected. "And I think it was because she
saw me kissing Mrs. Pierson after the party tonight."

"Good heavens!" cried Pamela. "You were kissing the
hyena?"

"Well, she started it," Lois defended herself. "And she sort of reminded me of Faye for a minute or two."

"Faye?" Pamela's eyes widened. "Why, that little hussy! Do you mean to tell me that the whole time she was accusing me of favoritism and hinting to Miss Kreplach that I had unnatural desires for you, she was . . . you two were . . ." Pamela sputtered to a stop.

"I'm sure she didn't mean any harm," Lois defended her best friend feebly.

"And did you?" Maxie demanded suddenly.

"Did I what?" said Pamela in confusion.

"Did you have 'unnatural desires' for little Lois here?"

"Why . . . why no, of course not," said Pamela. "You know I was with Carol then."

Pamela's response seemed unsatisfactory to Maxie. Goodness! Maxie is jealous of Pamela and me! Lois realized all at once.

But that was silly. Lois pushed away the memory of Pamela's hand on her knee earlier that evening. Anyway, I'd never steal a friend's girlfriend, she decided. Certainly not after Maxie loaned me the Balenciaga off her back!

"And you're still faithful to Faye?" Maxie interrogated Lois now.

"Well, sure," said Lois, even as her thoughts sped guiltily to Paula Winstead.

"Stay away from Mrs. Pierson," Pamela advised. "That woman goes through girls like I go through handkerchiefs in pollen season! I hope this Miss Gill who caught you doesn't make a stink about it."

"I don't think she will," said Lois thoughtfully. "She was much more upset the time she caught me in the file room without permission."

"She sounds like she's a little neurotic herself," interjected Maxie. "Is she one of the repressed kind?"

"Repressed?" asked Lois.

"You know—the gay boys and girls who hide their deviancy so well from the world they forget it themselves," Maxie explained.

Lois was thoughtful. "That sounds like some balancing act, hiding from the world and being honest with yourself."

"The balance is a bit different for every girl," Pamela put in. "I think Maxie judges some of the kids pretty harshly, considering she was once engaged as a blind!"

"Well, I didn't go through with it, did I?" Maxie threw an embroidered velvet pillow at Pam. "Besides, Lois, it makes things kind of exciting. 'Kissing in a shadow' can be a lot more stimulating than kissing in a spotlight!" She winked at Lois, who sat up alertly, ready to hear more. But Pamela frowned.

"You thrill-a-minute rich girls," she scoffed. "Is it all just a 'kick' to you?"

"And you career girls with your groups and your pamphlets," retorted Maxie, "do you have to take everything so seriously?"

Pamela got off the bed and stretched. "Speaking of careers, I have an early-morning department meeting I should be fresh for. I ought to be heading home." She donned her evening wrap and hat slowly.

"All right then!" said Maxie a little too brightly. "See you later, alligator!" But almost as soon as the door closed behind Pamela, she burst into tears.

"Oh Maxie," said Lois in distress, "why didn't you ask her to stay? Anyone could see she was just waiting for you to ask her!"

"She's tired of me," sobbed Maxie. "She thinks I'm useless and frivolous and she wants to get rid of me for someone like you!"

"No, no, that's not true!" Lois protested, even as she wondered if Maxie had hit the nail on the head.

"That's all right," said Maxie, wiping her eyes and blowing her nose. "I'm going to show her—I'm going to show everybody!"

"Show them what?" asked Lois anxiously.

"That I'm not as frivolous as you all think!" said Maxie fiercely.

"Do these plans have anything to do with that awful place you were in the other night?" Lois demanded.

"You heard what Pamela said—I was looking for kicks," said Maxie defiantly.

Lois had read in one of her mother's mystery magazines that you could tell if a person was lying by watching the pupils of their eyes, which would expand and then contract. Maxie's pupils had done just that!

Suddenly Maxie threw her arms around Lois and gave her a tight hug. "You're awfully sweet, Lois," she whispered. "I'm glad you're one of us."

And then Lois was back out in the corridor. The fifth floor looked the same as always, but Lois felt as if the whole building, the whole world even, had shifted on its axis while she'd been in Maxie's room. A flash of lightning suddenly illuminated the dingy carpeting and stained walls of the corridor, and a few seconds later there was a distant rumble of thunder.

Chapter Twenty-Three
Netta's Confession

A cool breeze was flapping the ruffled organdy curtains Mom had made as Lois closed the door of room 504 behind her. At last, the storm. She'd leave the window open as long as possible, she decided, drinking in the fresh air. She switched on her desk lamp and gave a sudden shriek when she saw a figure lying on the bed.

The figure sat up, blinking its big gold-green eyes, and groping for its spectacles. "I'm sorry, I didn't mean to startle you, I must have dozed off," it apologized.

"Netta! You cut your hair!" gasped Lois.

There was another flash of lightning, and the rumble of thunder following sounded louder.

"Why yes." Netta raised one hand self-consciously to the gamine cut, which framed her face in feathery wisps of pale chestnut. "I'm still not used to it. It feels strange—so light."

"It's very becoming," Lois said in admiration. "You must give me the name of your hairdresser. But Netta, what are you doing here?"

"I got a card from Ramona today! It was postmarked New York." She pulled a picture of the Statue of Liberty from the pocket of her dressing gown and gave it to Lois.

Lois turned it over. Written in bold, black handwriting was a brief message: "Forget about the key. It's not safe. And forget about me. R."

Netta was sitting up now, looking a little more like herself with her spectacles firmly on her nose. She was wearing a threadbare cotton robe over her thin night-gown, and was slipping her feet into equally worn scuffs.

"I wanted to take another look at that carbon scrap you found, and I guess I fell asleep, waiting for you," she said. "Goodness, it's late! Have you been at Mrs. Pierson's cocktail party all this time?"

Lois sat down on the bed next to Netta. "No, I—well, lots of things happened tonight, and then I was talking to Maxie and Pamela. Netta, they told me—I mean, I kind of guessed anyway, but—"

"They told you I've been using the passkey to let myself into your room and search it for clues to Ramona's whereabouts?" Netta finished her sentence. "I'm to blame, and no one else! The rest of the gang disapproved, but Lois, I was desperate!" Netta's voice trembled with emotion. With her new knowledge, Lois realized that the young school teacher concealed a furnace of passion beneath her staid exterior.

"So turn me in—tell Mrs. DeWitt! If I lose my job and get evicted, I don't care! Ramona may be in trouble—even in real danger!"

"But I do understand!" cried Lois. "What I'm trying to tell you is, I know now that you and Ramona were lovers and Lesbian career girls! I'm a Lesbian career girl, too!"

A flash of lightning and a loud crack of thunder punctuated Lois's declaration, followed by a sudden shower of rain. Simultaneously the two girls leapt up to close the window.

"Oh!" said Netta. "So Dolly was right!"

"And anyway, even if I wasn't, I would have been

happy to help you search for clues," said Lois. To her chagrin, she was blushing again. For some reason, she felt much more embarrassed discussing her new discovery with Netta than she had with Maxie and Pamela. Trying to be businesslike, she tapped the postcard. "Is this the first clue you've had Ramona might be in danger?"

Netta shivered and drew her robe around her more tightly. "There's something I haven't told anybody," she said. "Ramona wrote me a letter the day she left. She put it under my pillow. She said that she had to get out of town because things were getting too hot—"

"That would have been early June, it was awfully warm then," Lois concurred.

Netta rolled her eyes. "She was referring to the break-in, Lois. I don't think Ramona thought for one minute it was someone from the *Confidentially* column. I think she knew who it was and what they were looking for!"

"But who? And what?"

"I don't know! But in her letter she wrote that I should 'Look in the closet for the key' if I wanted to cash in on her 'project.' She said that I'd probably be too much of a straight arrow to use it, but it would be good insurance." Netta took off her glasses and wiped her eyes. "That's why I've been so worried! And that's why I need to find this key. If Ramona's in danger, I have to help her!"

Lois's heart twisted in pity for Netta's predicament. This Ramona sounded like she'd been a headstrong handful! It was on the tip of her tongue to tell Netta she was better off without such a wild girlfriend, but she realized that wouldn't be tactful. And who am I to be giving advice? she asked herself with an inward sigh.

"I've searched the closet over and over and haven't found any key," Netta concluded. "That carbon is the only clue left."

"I've been working on re-creating the missing part!" Lois told her excitedly. "I've filled in quite a bit—maybe it will help."

She snatched up her purse and began to dig through its contents. "I know I put it in here, I looked at it earlier," she murmured. As Netta watched, she upended her purse over the desk and sorted through the contents. "Why, it's gone!" she cried finally, in distress. "And so is the confidential letter Mrs. Pierson tore up!"

"What's this?" Netta's capable fingers plucked out a crumpled piece of paper. But it was only the threatening note Lois had received earlier. "Goodness, Lois, what on *earth*?" Netta asked after reading it.

Quickly Lois recounted the events of the evening, the penthouse party and its aftermath, Miss Gill's unexpected interruption, the discovery of the note, her decision to visit the file room, the intruder and his escape. Netta was a good listener; she did not interrupt once but sat attentively on Lois's bed.

"Don't you see what this means, Lois? Somebody at that party must be connected with Ramona! If only we still had the carbon!"

Lois jumped up. "But it isn't really gone, Netta," she exclaimed. "With my photographic memory, it will be simple for me to re-create it." She pulled her steno pad from the jumble of possessions on her desk, and flipped it open. A gust of wind hurled rain against the window as the lightning tore a jagged line in the sky and the thunder roared. Netta leaned forward breathlessly.

Lois paused a moment, mentally flipping back through her mind's orderly files to the moment in Mrs. Pierson's car when she'd last scanned the fragment. Then she put pencil to paper and wrote swiftly, without pausing. "There!" she said. "I'm pretty sure that's it. I tried to re-create the missing portion, based on the spacing and the most likely words," Lois explained. "Here's what I came up with."

The two girls bent their heads over the steno pad.

---

we have an acquaintance in common, someone *from your early days as* a publicity girl, when your politics *were* pinker than the current color scheme permits. *She's shared with me* so many mementos from that period; membership cards that others would be sure to ?

    I wonder if you might find a place in your organization *for someone like myself* who has such a knack for finding out others.

    I can assure you?
    ~~Please be assured~~ that I am a competent typist and filer, *and I have been taking a night* course in stenography, in which *my expertise has grown rapidly.*

    I have a burning ambition to get ahead, something you *should have some sympathy* for. I feel sure you and I can *come to terms in a way that* will be beneficial to both of us.

    the phone numbers to the Federal *Bureau of Investigation* at hand.

The two girls stood shoulder to shoulder studying Lois's re-creation. "Putting in *Bureau of Investigation* was a stretch," admitted Lois. "But I counted out the spaces and it was the only thing that fit and made sense. Except it doesn't, really."

"Oh, Lois!" Netta burst into tears. "It makes only too much sense! Don't you see that Ramona must have blackmailed her way into a job by threatening to report someone's early political affiliations to the FBI?" The distraught teacher collapsed back on Lois's bed, trying to suppress her sobs.

Lois looked at the letter again, and had to admit that Netta's theory fit with her re-creation. "Maybe I made a mistake," she tried to comfort the weeping girl. "Perhaps there's a more innocent explanation." She put an arm around Netta's shaking shoulders. "Don't take on so," she begged the usually self-contained student teacher.

Netta wiped her eyes, and heaved a sigh. She managed a watery smile. "Sorry to go all to pieces on you like this, Lois."

Lois told Netta she understood. In truth, she felt closer to Netta after seeing the other girl's soft, romantic center under her hard, practical shell! To distract Netta, she said cheerfully, "It's too easy to jump to conclusions from little things. Why, I've been imagining all summer that you girls were up to something dreadful, and all the time you were just a bunch of Lesbian career girls!"

Netta grinned weakly. Lois continued, "And then there were moments today when I imagined someone was blackmailing Mrs. Pierson! Just because of that confidential letter she tore up and threw away and then seeing her coming out of the post office last night."

But now Netta was sitting bolt upright. "Someone's blackmailing your boss! Then there *must* be some connection between Sather & Stirling and Ramona! It's too much of a coincidence, your purse searched, a blackmail letter, and a blackmail victim all the same day!"

Lois objected. "But what connection could there be?"

"Maybe Ramona got a job at Sather & Stirling," suggested Netta. "Tomorrow ask everyone at the office if they've heard of Ramona Rukeyser. Maybe she worked in the typing pool!"

"All right," Lois agreed dubiously.

Netta continued, "And I'm going to break open Ramona's trunk tomorrow. Tomorrow evening I'll tell you what I find out and you tell me what you find out. Promise?" She put out her hand solemnly.

"Promise." Lois gripped her hand.

The thunder and lightning had receded but the rain still beat against the window. Despite the late hour, Lois felt alert and energetic. There was something magical about staying up through the storm, the two of them awake while the city slept. The wall between Netta and herself had disappeared, and Lois liked their new intimacy.

And she was suddenly physically aware of Netta's soft warmth and the way the contours of her body were revealed by the thin cotton nightgown. Lois had never noticed how—how *shapely* Netta was. The young girl's breath quickened as something stirred inside her. The unsatisfied desires from earlier in the evening awoke again, aroused by the touch of Netta's hand, which still lay clasped in her own.

Stop it, Lois told herself sternly. Am I turning into some sort of Lesbian fast girl?

With an immense effort she sublimated her arousal into research.

"Netta, do you know a book called *Something Whirlpool*, or *Whirlpool Something*? It's about a girl who's been attacked by a vagrant, so she doesn't like to date, and then she goes to college and there's her roommate—"

Netta interrupted. "*Winter Whirlpool*, that's a good one! Except for the last chapter. I tore that out."

"Well, there's the part where the two girls are chatting late at night, and then the author writes, 'And she fell into a whirlpool that spun around until she floated away on a sea of rapturous release.'" Lois paused, and then demanded urgently, "Can you tell me what on earth that means?"

"Yes, I could tell you," said Netta thoughtfully. She took off her spectacles and wiped them on her robe. "Or," she said after a moment, "I could just show you." Putting her spectacles on the desk, she leaned toward Lois.

Netta's kiss was like a long sip of fresh water, and Lois's lips clung to hers, with the unquenched thirst from earlier that evening. Netta lay back on the pillow and pulled Lois down on top of her, wrapping the petite girl in her strong arms. How lovely it felt to lie down with someone! I've been doing all my kissing standing up, Lois realized. This is so much more comfortable! She said as much to Netta, who replied, "Lois, you're the limit," as she unzipped Lois's dress. Eagerly, Lois helped tug the dress over her head, and then unable to restrain herself, pushed Netta's robe down to reveal the curve of her freckled shoulders. "Mmmmm," she sighed appreciatively. She was seized by an impulse to bite Netta, she wanted to possess her so thoroughly. She ran her hands down the other girl's strong arms. "Do you play tennis?" she asked her. "No," said Netta nibbling on Lois's ear, "just jujitsu."

Lois felt her brassiere slide away, and Netta's cool hands cupped her breasts briefly then slid tantalizingly over Lois's torso. "You look as cute undressed as you do dressed," whispered Netta. "You mean, you've thought about me before?" Lois asked as Netta shed her robe and nightgown. "More than once," admitted Netta. "The way you combine common sense with such . . . such . . ." She licked her lips as she looked at Lois, and Lois felt as if she were drowning in desire—her own at the sight of naked Netta, and what she saw mirrored in Netta's eyes. With an urgency that matched Lois's own, Netta straddled the other girl so that her bare breasts brushed Lois's stomach, as Netta began tantalizing and teasing Lois's nipples with lips and tongue.

Lois arched her back in pleasure. "Such what?" she gasped, clinging with one hand to the headboard of the bed, while the other hand convulsively grabbed a handful of her blue-and-white-striped bed linen.

"Such . . . naiveté." Netta's hand slid between Lois's legs. "It's an irresistible provocation to a dedicated teacher like myself."

The pounding of the rain on the window and the pounding of Lois's heart blended together in a rising tide of passion. "Oh, Netta," gasped Lois. "It's too much!"

"Too much?" replied Netta, "Or not enough?" She slid up the length of Lois and kissed her mouth lightly, teasingly; then harder, as if she, too, had a thirst that must be slaked.

Lois's passion peaked, like floodwaters overflowing the dam walls, crumbling them and bursting their imprisonment, roaring through valleys, tearing up trees by their roots, and leaving whole towns destroyed and submerged in their wake. Then she floated away on a sea of rapturous release.

And the rapture went on and on.

Later, much later, when the rain had subsided to a gentle patter, Lois turned and snuggled into the crook of Netta's arm. She opened her mouth to ask if Netta was still awake, but the older girl forestalled her. "Go to sleep," she murmured. "Go to sleep, Ramona."

Chapter Twenty-Four
An Unpleasant Surprise

Lois stood, clinging to a strap, swaying with the crowd as the bus lumbered toward the business district. The city's dirt had been washed away and the whole metropolis gleamed like a new penny.

Lois felt brand new, too. Her whole body was alive and alert in a way it had never been before. Even the morning routine of rushed breakfast and crowded bus couldn't dim her glow.

She lurched into a man reading a newspaper as the bus ground to a stop. He looked up and leered at her, "Feeling lonesome, sister?"

Why, he doesn't know I'm a Lesbian career girl! Lois thought. He doesn't have the faintest idea!

She had an impulse to tell him, but remembering Maxie's advice, she restrained herself and merely gave him a cold glare.

Then she lost herself again in pleasurable recollections of the previous night. Netta's sweat-slick thighs wrapped around her waist. The flutter of Netta's eyelids as Lois put into practice what the school teacher had taught her. What a walking textbook of knowledge Netta had turned out to be!

Then, all too swiftly, pictures from their night of passion were replaced by more painful memories. Lois's instinctive recoil when Netta had called her "Ramona"; Netta's intense embarrassment and abrupt departure.

That had been bad enough, but then this morning at breakfast Netta had been clipped and businesslike, reminding Lois to ask at the office if anyone knew a Ramona Rukeyser. Lois had begun to wonder if Netta was one of the "repressed" girls Maxie had warned her about, when Netta had added brusquely, "About last night—let's just consider it a question answered. Put it in the file-and-forget basket, all right?"

Lois wanted to say that wasn't where *she* would file last night's experience, but Netta had hurried away.

Should I have stopped her? Lois wondered now as the driver called out "Lake Street!" Should I have told her that forgetting anything goes against all my secretarial training?

But it wouldn't have done any good, Lois told herself miserably. In her heart, she knew there was only one explanation for Netta's remoteness. She was still in love with Ramona. It was only the sudden storm and her teacherly instincts that had sparked their night of pleasure.

And what do I have to offer? Lois thought unhappily as she hurried across the marble lobby. She'd heard plenty of stories that summer about the ravishing Ramona with her daring and dash. I'm so green and dumb, Lois thought bitterly. I can't seem to hold anyone's interest for longer than an hour or two!

Yet her spirits rose with the elevator. After all, Ramona's in New York and I'm here, she reasoned. And if Ramona *is* involved in a criminal enterprise, surely Netta will begin to feel differently about her special friend?

Why—is this love? Lois wondered. This up-and-down

feeling? This breathless, fizzy sensation? For the first time since the party, she thought about Faye. I was never in love with Faye, she decided with the wisdom of experience. It was never more than simple lust!

Getting off the elevator, she hurried directly to the receptionist. "Gretchen, do you remember a girl by the name of Ramona Ruk—"

But Gretchen was saying at the same time, "*There* you are, Lois! Miss Gill wants to see you at once—she's awfully steamed about something."

She'd barely finished speaking when Miss Gill loomed up in the doorway behind her. There was a stern, forbidding look on her face, and she snapped at Lois, "Come with me at once, Miss Lenz!"

Bewildered, Lois followed as Miss Gill whirled through the corridor to the file room. The office manager threw open the file room door, saying, "Can you explain this Miss Lenz?"

Lois gasped. The file room was a mess. Drawers were pulled out, files were piled haphazardly on top of the cabinets, and some had slid onto the floor, spilling their contents over the speckled linoleum. One stapled sheaf of papers had caught on an open file drawer, and hung defenselessly in midair. It was a sight to make any secretary worth her salt weep.

"But I didn't do this," Lois cried in distress.

"Then who did?" countered Miss Gill. "You were the only person to visit the office after I left last night. I examined the night guard's logs."

"Miss Gill, I swear to you on my *Secretary's Desk Reference*, I'm not responsible for this mess," Lois began. But then she faltered—was she responsible? How to explain her failure to alert the guard to the intruder? "I *was* in the file room, but—"

Miss Gill's voice dropped several degrees below freezing. "Can you explain *what* you were doing in the file room last night, after I'd made it quite clear the files were none of your concern? Can you tell me *why* you chose to come here last night, not half an hour after I saw you under quite different circumstances, with filing apparently far from the forefront of your mind?"

"I—I had some folders to file," said Lois feebly.

Miss Gill slammed a file drawer shut with a violence that made the young secretary jump. "I'm sending you to the typing pool today," she announced grimly. "Judy Hartnell will take your place with Mrs. Pierson. We'll discuss your future at Sather & Stirling at the end of office hours, but right now I don't have any more time to spend on this disruptive dilemma. I have an office to manage!"

Lois felt she was living in a nightmare. Numbly she made her way to the noisy typing pool room and sat dispiritedly at Judy Hartnell's desk. All around her, heads were bent over typewriters and the constant clatter filled her ears. Her fingers automatically picked up a sheaf of corrected catalog copy from the in basket and set it on her typing stand. She pulled out the right-hand drawer, looking for typing paper and carbons.

The intruder *must* have returned after Lois's departure. It was the only explanation. But would Miss Gill believe Lois? The story sounded far-fetched, even to Lois herself.

She's just got to believe me, Lois told herself desperately. She's got to!

The carbons were in the left-hand drawer. How Lois missed her own little desk of blond wood, with everything in its proper place! How she missed Mrs. Pierson's morning growl, the routine disparagement of the coffee Lois fetched, the relish with which she browbeat her unlucky underlings!

"Good morning, Lois," said a low voice at her elbow, and Lois smelled Paula's perfume before she turned and saw the gilt-haired copywriter standing by her desk, a quizzical smile on her lips. "What are *you* doing here?"

"I've been demoted," said Lois shortly. The sight of Paula reminded her of last night's slight, and she still smarted from the snub.

"Oh!" Paula looked concerned. "I'm sorry to hear that."

"I've got a lot of typing, Paula," Lois said stiffly. "Was there something you needed?"

"Look, Lois, I know I was a boor last night. But—well, you were in that faux French maid outfit, and when influential people like Mamie McArdle and the Norvells are present, it doesn't do a girl like me any good, being *intime* with the hired help!"

Lois couldn't hold a grudge against such nakedly matter-of-fact ambition. "I really *am* busy," she said less coldly. "What is it you need?" For if Paula was being friendly, it must mean she wanted something!

"I want to take you out for a drink after work." The copywriter laughed her silvery laugh. "I want to pick your brains again—about filing."

Filing! "I wish I knew just what it was you wanted from me," Lois said bluntly. "Maybe then I'd be able to help you."

Paula pretended indignation. "Why must you suspect me of some dark motive?" she protested. "Maybe I just like you." Then she smiled disarmingly. "And if I do have a problem you could help me with, what's the harm in that? The lobby at five, *d'accord?*"

"All right." Lois shrugged. It would distract her from her own problems, at any rate. She looked after Paula as she exited the typing pool room. Her jaw dropped.

Paula was walking with a limp!

Lois heard again the gasp of the mysterious intruder as she'd kicked out and her foot connected with flesh and bone. And that flashlight. What had Paula said? She made a point of using agency-represented products. Had Paula written the slogan "Look for an Acme—it lets you see more clearly"?

Why, it was her perfume I smelled last night! Lois realized. That was the strange feeling of familiarity!

She rose from her desk, intending to go after the duplicitous blonde and confront her then and there, but Miss Klopcek, the harried head of the typing pool, intercepted her. "Have you finished the catalog copy?" she asked breathlessly. "I need you to start on the board meeting notes as soon as you're done. We're absolutely swamped today."

Thwarted, Lois returned to her desk and pounded away at her typewriter the rest of the morning. To think she'd almost ended up here, doing nothing but typing all day long! How deadly dull it was!

I've gotten attached to my job, Lois realized, feeling more homesick than ever for Mrs. Pierson's office. The thought that she might lose it filled her with a sickening feeling of panic. And what if I don't even keep my position in the pool? she thought. What if I'm fired without a recommendation? Would she be reduced to answering those "Earn money at home sewing aprons" ads she used to read in the back of *Teenaged* magazine?

I can't go home to Walnut Grove, she thought desperately. I can't leave all my friends on the fifth floor, not now when I'm just beginning to figure out city life! I can't leave Netta!

She fed a fresh sandwich of typing paper and carbon into her machine. I'll show Paula what ambition looks like! she thought grimly. I'll make her admit to Miss Gill that she was in the file room last night, if it's the last thing I do!

At noon Lois sprang to her feet and was half out the

door when Miss Klopcek put a restraining hand on her arm. "Half an hour, Miss Lenz, and not a second more," she warned. "I need every minute from each of my girls today."

Lois nodded impatiently and hurried off in search of Paula. Her office was empty. Lois tracked her down at last, in the art supply closet. Paula was sorting through tubes of paint.

"What are you doing in the art department?" Lois asked accusingly.

Paula looked up in surprise. "I'm looking for tubes of Delavalle brand paints. Mr. Saloman is planning to pitch them. What are *you* doing here?"

Lois switched tactics. "Do you own an Acme Super-Seeing Flashlight?"

"Of course I do," said Paula, more bewildered than ever. "They're durable, long-lasting, and their beam is twelve percent brighter than the competitors'!"

"Where is it now?" pursued Lois.

"At home in my kitchen drawer," replied Paula. "Why are you asking me these questions? If you want a flashlight, there are at least a dozen samples in the storeroom."

So that was the tack Paula would take! Lois was stymied, but only briefly.

"I don't need a flashlight," Lois bluffed, "because it's clear as day to me that you're hiding something!"

Paula paled in sudden alarm. But just as quickly, the copywriter recovered her savoir faire. "You're not making sense today, Lois," she said smoothly, easing past the glaring secretary. "And all this double-talk is giving me a headache. Which reminds me, I have some aspirin copy due." And she limped swiftly away.

Lois was gnashing her teeth in frustration when a sound caught her attention—the creak of the freight elevator. Of course—if that was how Paula left, that must be how she'd arrived as well. And that would explain why the night guard's log pointed to Lois as the culprit.

At least I can tell Miss Gill *that*, thought Lois, hurrying back toward the office manager's sterile little cave.

The door was closed with the IN CONFERENCE sign hanging on the knob.

"Hurry, hurry," Lois muttered in frustration. She had only ten minutes of her lunch break left. The voices inside Miss Gill's office rose in argument.

"But her replacement doesn't know where anything is! She's on the phone half the time to her boyfriend, and I caught her actually filing her nails, while her in basket was piled sky-high! And she had the nerve to tell me she was on a coffee break! Please, Ivy!"

"Lois stays in the typing pool." Miss Gill's voice was firm. "It's for your own good, Martha."

"You're making a mountain out of a molehill!" Mrs. Pierson's voice had an unfamiliar pleading quality. "You know the strain I'm under—those anonymous demands—I'm at my breaking point!"

"Another reason to keep Lois in the typing pool. Oh, Martha! Models and illustrators are one thing, but your own secretary . . ." Miss Gill's voice grew harsh. "Do you think I've forgotten what happened the last time you were—attached—to a secretary? Do you think I want to stand by and watch it all over again?"

Just at this interesting juncture, a hand fell on Lois's shoulder. "There you are!" It was Miss Klopcek. "Back early! Miss Gill told me you were a dedicated girl." She hustled the unwilling secretary along the corridor to the typing pool. "But Miss Klopcek," Lois protested, "I must speak to Miss Gill—"

Miss Klopcek chuckled. "She'll still be here at five. You know our Miss Gill! Sometimes I wonder if she has a home to go to!" and shaking with merriment, Miss Klopcek handed Lois a stack of paper filled with close handwriting and bristling with columns of numbers and statistical charts. "The latest report on beer drinkers from the research department," she said. "I hope you can get it done by five. Miss Gill said you were adept at numbers."

In spite of her frustration, Lois couldn't help feeling pleased to hear that all her practice in number technique had paid off. But wait—Miss Gill seemed to be giving everyone different accounts of her presence in the typing pool! She'd foisted the young girl off on Miss Klopcek as a typing whiz, apparently explained her demotion to Mrs. Pierson by the post-party incident last night, and only told Lois about the file room fiasco!

But why? Lois wondered. Why tell everyone a different story? Was it simply her pride in running a tight ship that made her conceal the file room's true state?

And what to make of the references to Mrs. Pierson and an earlier secretary? Could it be that Mrs. Pierson had once been "educating" Miss Ravenal? Gretchen had said she was always taking her to places like Le Cheval Blanc, and the theater, Lois remembered, mechanically typing the average quantities of beer drunk at different ages.

None of it added up. Lois's thoughts chased fruitlessly around all afternoon, her speculations getting mixed up with statistics on how important foam was to the average beer drinker. Or the mental image of Netta's face, her red lips slightly swollen with kisses, would make the names of the most popular ballpark beers go all blurry.

Something jostled her shoulder and made her type "palette" instead of "palate." It was one of the other typists.

"It's five o'clock," the typist told her. "The typing will still be here tomorrow. Gretchen said to tell you your friend's here."

"Oh!" Lois looked around. The typing pool was rapidly emptying. Hastily she covered her typewriter, picked up her purse, and smoothed her skirt. My friend, she thought with growing excitement. Did Gretchen mean . . . ?

Netta stood up from a lounge chair as Lois entered the reception area, and Lois's heart leapt up. How was it she had once thought Netta homely? Her pixie haircut was as attractive in the daylight as it had been last night, and she was wearing a crisp white blouse and a pair of pedal pushers in a madras plaid of gold and orange, which accentuated the gold flecks in her eyes. Even Netta's freckles seemed newly scrubbed. The sight of Netta in pants made Lois's stomach do a funny flip, and despite her many woes, she couldn't prevent a smile of gladness from spreading over her face.

"Lois, there was nothing in the trunk. Perhaps you're right and I am jumping to conclusions," Netta began, rather subdued.

"I wasn't able to ask about Ramona, because of something else, unrelated." Lois suddenly remembered her unfulfilled inquiry.

Paula entered the lobby, putting on her sunglasses. Seeing Lois, she instinctively took a step back, then said coolly, "I'll have to cancel that drink, Lois. A previous engagement."

"But—" said Lois helplessly. Nothing was going right. The clues she and Netta had come up with were dead ends, and now Paula, the real file room culprit, was slipping away.

But Netta was staring at Paula narrowly. "Paulette?" she asked her. "Paulette Wolgstadt?"

Paula turned as white as snow. Without another word, she leapt into an elevator just before it closed.

"Quick, Lois, after her!" said Netta.

Chapter Twenty-Five

Paulette?

"The freight elevator," said Lois instantly. "Maybe we can get downstairs before she does." She and Netta dashed through the office, Lois in the lead, nearly knocking over a shocked Miss Gill in their headlong flight.

"That's neither safe nor becoming to a secretary!" sputtered the office manager, flattening herself against the wall.

"I hope this doesn't cook my goose with Miss Gill," Lois panted as the elevator began its creaking descent.

"I hope this isn't a wild-goose chase," said Netta, watching the floors glide by impatiently. "But I have a feeling that Paulette might hold a clue to this puzzle. It's just too much of a coincidence." She turned to Lois. "That copywriter you're so fond of is Paulette Wolgstadt, who was elected Corn Queen of the senior class at the Minnesota State Teacher's College when Ramona and I were just frosh!"

"That's impossible," protested Lois indignantly. "Paula attended a finishing school in the Swiss Alps! She's told me loads of stories about the hijinks she and her international chums got into!"

"She's told you a lot of hogwash," Netta retorted as the elevator ground to a halt. "And if we catch up to her, you'll hear her eat her words." She pulled open the freight elevator's wooden gate and leapt off the loading dock in one fluid motion. Lois followed her, glad she'd worn a full skirt and flats to work that day.

Together they raced up the alley and paused on Lake, anxiously searching the crowded street for a blond girl clad in a dark pink blouse and gray-and-white-striped skirt. Lois grabbed Netta's arm. "There!" She pointed. Paula was walking briskly along Lake straight toward the two girls. But at the very moment Lois spotted her, as if alerted by some sixth sense, Paula saw them. She immediately turned around and began running in the opposite direction, toward Broadway. Instantly Netta and Lois were after her.

It was a strange chase, the two young girls pushing their way desperately through the afternoon rush hour crowd, with Paula's blond head bobbing always beyond reach. They almost caught up with the fleeing copywriter at Broadway and Second when the light changed, but at the last second, Paula hurled herself into the traffic and crossed the street to the angry blare of horns.

"Where is she? Can you see her?" Netta squinted helplessly through her thick glasses across the stream of traffic. "She's turning," said Lois, "down that side street." The signal turned green and they raced across the street and down the block to the corner where Paula had turned. The two girls were just in time to see her duck into a bar at the end of the block, her limp more pronounced than ever.

It was a small establishment, with only a tiny smudged window in its brick exterior. Netta pushed open the padded swinging door, and Lois followed her into the cool dimness. They immediately spotted Paula at a booth in the back, as she swallowed in one gulp the contents of a shotglass the waiter set before her. When she saw the two girls approach, she made a convulsive move to get up, but Netta forestalled her escape by sliding into the seat next to her. "Enough running," she said. "We've got to talk, Paulette."

Lois sat down across from Paula. The golden-haired girl was a shadow of her usual collected self. Sweat had matted her hair, and formed dark stains on her pink blouse. She'd lost an earring and her mascara had started to run. She looked at Lois bitterly.

"I suspected you were in cahoots with Ramona!" she lashed out at the younger girl. "Pretending to be so naive when all the time you were part of her filthy blackmail scheme!" She turned on Netta. "And you want a share, too, I suppose? Well, forget it. Tell the whole world I was Corn Queen—I don't care anymore!"

"Ramona was blackmailing *you?*" gasped Netta, turning pale. "I don't believe it!"

Lois sympathized with Netta's feelings. Even after hearing it from Paula's own lips, she was having a hard time believing that the cosmopolitan career girl she idolized was nothing more than a manufactured fantasy, a dream as false as any advertising promise.

"Believe it," said Paula—or Paulette—grimly. "Since the day she started work at Sather & Stirling, I haven't had—"

"So Ramona *did* work at Sather & Stirling!" Netta said. Paulette looked from one girl to the other. "You two didn't know that Ramona Ravenal, as she calls herself now, was Mrs. Pierson's previous secretary?"

A waiter stopped by their table. "What'll it be, folks?"

"A martini," Lois heard herself say.

"Same," echoed Netta.

"A beer, and a chaser, a double," said Paulette, pointing at her shotglass.

So it was *Mrs. Pierson* that Ramona had blackmailed into giving her a job, Lois realized. From the look Netta gave her, she guessed that the school teacher, too, had come to the same conclusion. I seem to be following in Ramona's footsteps, Lois thought to herself, in bed and in the office!

"Begin at the beginning," ordered Netta when the waiter had departed. "Ramona left town suddenly at the end of May, after someone broke into her room searching for something." She peered at Paulette closely. "It wasn't you, was it?"

"No," said Paula, sitting up indignantly. "I may be a former Corn Queen, but I'm no thief." Then she slumped back down. "Who am I kidding? Another few weeks of her demands and I'd have been driven to anything.

"It started the first day she spotted me at the office, oh, back in March. She laughed and laughed at the idea of me in the Swiss Alps. I begged her not to say a word—my reputation for the cosmopolitan touch was my bread and butter. She promised she wouldn't, and then asked me to loan her $20.

"I knew which way the wind blew after that. Oh, it was never anything as direct as 'give me $50 every Monday.' She'd just ask for a 'loan' every week or so, or she'd admire an outfit I wore, and say she wished she had my finishing school taste. I'd take the hint and give her the clothes she wanted.

"It was like living in a nightmare. It wasn't the material demands so much as the constant torment—the jibes, the hints, the way she'd look at me with a little smile when anyone referred to my boarding school days."

Paula put her head in her hands and shuddered. The waiter set down their drinks and Paula took a long draught of the foaming beer, then tossed back the whiskey. She shuddered again.

"When she didn't show up for work and Gretchen said rumor was she was gone for good, I was ecstatic, but still, I kept waiting for the other shoe to drop. And the next day it did. She sent me a letter at the office, thanking me for all my 'assistance' and saying since she wouldn't be needing it anymore, she'd filed the picture of me being crowned Corn Queen where it belonged, like a good secretary should. In the file room. I could practically hear her heartless laughter! The file room, where anyone might come upon it! Thank heavens Miss Gill took it into her head to reorganize the files. But that was a problem, too—she wouldn't allow anyone into the file room, on any excuse, until she was done."

"So that's why you played up to me—you thought *I'd* get you into the file room!" exclaimed Lois.

"It wasn't all business," murmured Paulette low.

"And it was you who attacked me the other night, wasn't it?"

"I attacked you? Who's the one limping today from a bruised ankle?"

Netta asked, "And you didn't find the picture?"

Paulette put her head in her hands again. "I may as well go back to Minnesota and take a job teaching little brats their ABCs!" she moaned. "There are too many files and I haven't a clue where Ramona would have put mine!"

"Teaching is not something you fall back on when you fail at your first choice," Netta lectured. "It takes talent, intelligence, and aptitude."

"The key!" Lois sat bolt upright. "I've got the key!"

Netta and Paulette stared at her.

"Don't you see? Both times I looked at the files, I sensed a pattern, an organizing method that eluded me. But now that I know it was Ramona who reorganized the files, it's clear as day! With her library training, it's a cinch she used the Dewey Decimal System!"

Lois saw again in her mind's eye the incompletely erased number on the file folder. What a fool she'd been, not to figure it out sooner.

"The key she wrote Netta about will undoubtedly list the Dewey Decimal number to the folder where she's filed the photo," Lois explained.

"So all this time I was searching your closet for a key to a door or a trunk, I should have been looking for a piece of paper with numbers," said Netta thoughtfully.

Even in the midst of these revelations, Lois noticed that for the first time Netta had automatically referred to room 504 as Lois's room, instead of Ramona's. Could Netta finally be forgetting the amoral charmer who'd broken her heart?

They sat for a moment, each busy with her own thoughts. Paulette was the first to break the silence. "Then there's hope of finding this picture and destroying it forever?" she asked eagerly. "And I can continue on my path to becoming the most-sought-after copywriter in the business?"

"Possibly," said Lois cautiously. She didn't want to raise Paulette's hopes only to dash them again. "We still need to find that key. Even though we know the files are in Dewey Decimal order, still, classifying files is a highly personal process. Ramona might have filed the picture under 'corn' or 'queen' or even 'teaching college'!"

Netta roused herself from her abstraction. "I've searched that closet pretty thoroughly," she said pessimistically. "But it's true, I wasn't looking for a piece of paper. I guess we should try one more time."

Paulette rose with new determination. "I'll pay the tab and get us a taxi," she said.

Chapter Twenty-Six
An Unexpected Visitor

The cab inched at a snail's pace through the down-town traffic as Paulette nibbled on her nails and Lois glanced at her wristwatch and then past Netta, out the window. Forty minutes and several astounding revela-tions after they'd raced out of the office, they were back outside 333 Lake. Looking up at the familiar building, Lois could practically see the invisible thread connecting the elite advertising agency on the twenty-seventh floor to the down-at-heel women's residence across town. The struggles of a group of girls trying to make it in the big city had sent a vibration through that invisible thread that tangled into a knot in the Sather & Stirling file room. I'm going to untie it today! vowed Lois silently.

Was one of the Magdalena girls secretly Ramona's confederate? For *someone* was still blackmailing Mrs. Pierson, even while Ramona was sending postcards from New York saying she was through drawing the wages of fear. Lois hated to think that any of her new friends were capable of such behavior. If only we knew *what* Ramona had on Mrs. Pierson, and where she got it, she fretted to herself.

The driver cursed, and leaned on his horn, then swung

around a delivery truck, missing a black Cadillac by an inch. "Paulette, you went back to the file room after our, er, encounter last night, didn't you?"

"No, I went home and put some liniment on my ankle," said Paulette. "Why?"

"But someone was in the file room after I left!" exclaimed Lois. "It was a mess this morning! That's why Miss Gill demoted me to the typing pool—I was the only one signed in last night."

"Maybe it was whoever's blackmailing your Mrs. Pierson," Netta spoke up.

Lois glanced at her sharply. So she'd been thinking along the same lines as Lois.

"Blackmailing Mrs. Pierson?" Paulette was puzzled. Lois told her about the confidential letter, Mrs. Pierson's presence at the post office, and the conversation she'd overheard that afternoon.

"Could it be Ramona has returned?" Paulette shuddered at the thought. "She might have run low on money."

"No!" said Netta. "I'm sure she's through with this—this prank."

"Prank!" Paulette was incensed. "Is that what you call her infamous demands, which cost me several hundred dollars, my favorite suit, and quite a few sleepless nights?"

Netta flinched. "I'm not saying what she did wasn't wrong, terribly wrong, but—but—"

"But—but—what?" jeered Paulette.

"Netta! Paulette!" Lois interrupted before the two were at each other's throats. "We don't have time for spats! We've got to work together if we're going to solve this puzzle!"

The driver left downtown and picked up speed as the three girls fell silent again.

"I've been thinking about the problem of Mrs. Pierson,"

Lois said after a few minutes. "We know Ramona blackmailed her way into her job, and Gretchen said Mrs. Pierson was glad to see her go. But when I overheard Mrs.
Pierson this afternoon, she talked about 'anonymous demands,' and that's not the way Ramona operated." She
turned to Paulette. "The only thing that makes sense is
that whatever Ramona had on Mrs. Pierson fell into the
wrong hands before she could file it. I think Netta's right,
Paulette—Ramona's not behind this."

Paulette shrugged. "I hope you're right. And Lois . . ."
She leaned toward Lois and her perfume enveloped the
young secretary. "I wish you'd call me Paula. You know
I'm awfully fond of you, don't you?"

Lois gazed at the attractive girl—it *was* easier to think
of her as "Paula"—and was surprised to feel not even a
flicker of her old desire. She still admired Paula's beauty
and ambition. She could even understand the older girl's
drive to reinvent herself as the person she felt she should
have been born. But the magic spell of attraction was
broken.

"I'm fond of you, too, Paula," Lois said. Netta was
looking out the window at the tenements flashing by, pretending she wasn't listening to the two girls. Lois hastened to turn the conversation from the personal to the
practical. "Who knew about the freight elevator, as a way
to slip in and out of the building without signing in?"

Paula shrugged. "Probably anyone who'd worked at
Sather & Stirling long enough."

The cab pulled up to the Magdalena Arms, and the
three girls slid out. While Paula was paying the driver,
another cab pulled up behind them. Out jumped a girl
wearing jeans, tennis shoes with no socks, and a sleeveless red turtleneck. Her black hair was tousled and she
was breathing hard as she ran up to the trio.

"Netta! Lois! I've been looking all over for you!"

"Maxie?" Netta raised her eyebrows at the disheveled debutante. "What is it?"

"I need to talk to you about Ramona! There's something I haven't told you—I thought it would be better if you didn't know, but after Dolly told me what Janet told her you told Phyllis—"

"Hush, Maxie, not now!" Netta tried to stop the flow of words.

"—I couldn't let you go on carrying a torch for that girl!"

"None of you understand—" Netta tried to interrupt again.

"Oh sure, she's fun and sharp-looking and the life of the party, but she's not the girl for you!"

Lois was wondering what on earth madcap Maxie was up to now. She was dressed like a beatnik poet.

"If you're trying to tell us Ramona's a vicious blackmailer, we already know that," Paula broke in impatiently.

"Blackmailer?" Maxie looked startled. "Ramona's been selling reefer! That's how she financed her move to New York!"

Netta reeled back a step. "That's not possible!" she gasped. "Between her job at the ad agency and her blackmail scheme, how on earth did she find the time?"

"How do you know this?" Lois demanded.

"I was just at the Buzz Bixby Quintet rehearsal, and everyone was complaining that their supplier had split for New York. They were moaning because this girl had some nice stuff from Vera Cruz, no lemonade or sassafras. Well, my ears perked up at that, because Dolly told me Phyllis told Janet that Ramona had sent you a postcard from New York, and Ramona had often said . . ." Maxie bit her lip, then plunged on, "Well, she'd often said when she wanted to blow town, she had a pile of weed sticks she could unload for some quick cash.

"She got into the business through a fellow she met at that after-hours jazz club we went to, the time you and Pamela both blew your stacks. You know how Ramona was—always looking for a way to make an extra dollar, and she never minded if it wasn't quite on the up and up! This cat used to pay her to roll the cigarettes. I'd help her sometimes, the nights you were at your jujitsu class. She must have—"

"She must have found her own supplier among the Mexican dock workers," broke in Lois. "That's why she was studying Spanish!" And I'll bet those are marijuana cigarettes in my office drawer, she thought to herself, half horrified, half intrigued.

"I asked Buzz, what did his supplier look like? And he described Ramona to a T!" Maxie was continuing. She wound up: "So you see, Netta, Ramona just isn't worth breaking your heart over. You and she were all wrong for each other and she won't thank you for making a stink about her departure. She's like a cat—she'll always land on her feet."

The front door to the Magdalena Arms opened and Pamela poked her head out. "What are you kids doing out here?" she demanded. "Maxie, I've been waiting for you for half an hour, and I was just about to give up and go home. What's the big news you had to tell me? What's the cause for celebration?"

Maxie turned toward Pamela, her face radiant, and practically waltzed into the front hallway. "I have a job!" she caroled.

Good heavens, thought Lois, as she and Paula and Netta followed Maxie inside, I hope she's not going to tell Pamela that she's taking over Ramona's cigarette-rolling job!

But Maxie's next words took all of them aback. "I've been working for Mamie McArdle as a research assistant on a trial basis, and today she made it permanent!"

Pamela said weakly, "Why that's—that's fine, Maxie!"

Paula murmured to Netta, "The Magdalena Arms is certainly living up to its reputation."

Netta said to Lois, "I think Kay's trying to get your attention."

And Kay at the desk called to Lois over the hubbub, "You have a guest in the visitor's parlor—a Faye Collins."

Chapter Twenty-Seven
The Secret in the Closet

Faye stood up when Lois entered the dusty little visitor's parlor. "Surprise!" she cried gaily. She was wearing a powder blue dress with a matching bolero jacket. Lois was struck by a provincial quality about Faye she'd never noticed before. Was it the little veil on her powder blue hat? Or her conservative heels? Or that she was still wearing Strawberry Ice on her lips while Lois had moved on to Bongo Red?

"What are you doing here?" was all Lois could muster.

Faye pouted. "Aren't you glad to see me? I came up to do some shopping. Classes start in a few weeks, you know, and rush week begins even sooner."

Am I glad to see her? Lois wondered. She'd thought, when she looked at Paula in the cab and felt nothing, that her raging desires were finally under control. But one glance at Faye and that old prickling, tickling sensation crept over her like a drug. She experienced again that familiar impulse to rip Faye's clothes off and feed on her succulent young flesh.

"I can't believe you've been living in this grubby little boardinghouse all summer," Faye continued, looking around the parlor with a wrinkled nose. "Did I write you that Daddy and Mum are redoing our house from top to bottom in Tudor?"

Desire faded as quickly as it had flared up. Was that its last flicker? Probably not, Lois admitted to herself. She'd begun to realize she was an awfully susceptible sort of girl, and Faye was her first love after all. But she was done letting her physical reactions overwhelm her better judgment. And meanwhile—

"That's nice." Lois sat down on the stiff horsehair sofa and Faye sat down, too, looking expectantly at Lois. "I *am* glad to see you, Faye, I'm just surprised. You see, I'm in the middle of something right now—"

"I thought we'd get a bite to eat, and I could show you the marvelous outfits I bought today," Faye said as if she hadn't heard a word Lois had said. "I'm staying at the Abigail Adams with my cousin Denise. Then tomorrow we can go shopping."

"My budget won't stretch for new clothes right now," said Lois. "And anyway, I'm trying to figure out—"

"But you'll need some new fall fashions for Rush!" Faye was aghast. "First impressions are very important at Epsilon Epsilon Chi."

"But I'm not going through Rush," Lois tried to explain as gently as possible. "I'm not going to Northridge Junior College this fall. I'm going to keep working at Sather & Stirling, and take some night courses at the City College here."

For a moment there was a look in Faye's eyes that was so nakedly lost, Lois forgot about the girls in the hallway, and the many mysteries that swirled around her. "Faye," she began softly.

But Faye switched gears as rapidly as ever, and in the space of a moment her mood changed. "Well, fine!" she

snapped, getting to her feet and gathering up her hand-
bag and shopping bags. "Stay here in this nasty city, if
that's what you want! I thought there was some hope for
you, or I wouldn't have come! But now I see the city's
corrupted you beyond rescue!" She seemed to get angrier
as she spoke. "After I told everyone this was just a phase
and you were coming back in the fall! After I sent an
anonymous note to Mr. Phillips so he'd break up Billy
and Jane's clandestine romance!"

"You didn't!" gasped Lois in dismay as the door to
the visitor's lounge opened and Lois's friends piled into
the room. "Lois, we need you," began Netta urgently,
but Faye was continuing, louder and shriller than before:

"I should have known from all those boring letters you
wrote about filing and stenography that you weren't even
worth trying to save! The way you acted like living in this
run-down, ramshackle slum was heaven!"

"Hey!" said Maxie indignantly.

"I only wish I hadn't wasted even a second of my
shopping trip on you—you career girl!" And with that
final slur, Faye turned on her powder blue heel and
roughly elbowed her way through the silent gaggle of
girls. She slammed the door behind her. Almost instantly it reopened and Dolly poked her head into the
room.

"So that was the high school sweetheart?" she asked
curiously. "Phyllis told me Kay told her she'd come for a
visit. Good looker, but what a temper!"

"Dolly!" Lois's mind left the past behind and fast as a
freight train raced back into the present. That photo in
Mrs. Pierson's drawer—that was another link between
the Magdalena Arms and her boss! "Do *you* know who's
blackmailing Mrs. Pierson?" Lois demanded.

Dolly was all wide-eyed innocence. "Blackmailing Mrs. Pierson! But how would I know such a thing? I don't even know the woman!"

"Well, your picture is in her nightstand drawer!"

The other girls were turning their heads from Lois to Dolly as if watching a tennis match.

"Oh, all right! I do know Mrs. Pierson—rather well, in fact. But it's not something I talk about. Gosh, she's more of a sentimentalist than I thought, keeping that picture by her bed! Which one was it? The one with me and Amy, or the one with me in the feather boa?"

"That doesn't matter right now," said Lois impatiently. "Ramona blackmailed Mrs. Pierson into a job, and now someone else is blackmailing her. Do you know who? Or why?"

"Ramona didn't know anything about us, if that's what you're getting at," Dolly said defensively. "I can be discreet when I need to be! Martha *did* say recently that an old mistake had come back to haunt her, but I didn't pay much attention. When we get together, she's always talking about what a bad girl she's been, so . . ." Dolly shrugged expressively.

Lois was stumped. Something from her past? A thought tickled at the edges of her mind.

"We're wasting time," said Paula impatiently. "Maxie has an idea about where Ramona hid the key . . ."

Out in the hall, Mrs. DeWitt was reciting her favorite poem.

> "A whisper, and then a silence:
> Yet I know by their merry eyes
> They are plotting and planning together
> To take me by surprise."

"Mrs. DeWitt!" Lois raced back across the entrance hall to catch Magdalena Arms's House Mother, who was just unlocking the door to her apartment.

"Mrs. DeWitt, who was it who wanted to see the picture from the benefit for the Spanish refugees?" Lois demanded. The other girls looked at each other blankly, except for Netta, whose eyes gleamed with sudden comprehension.

As always, it took Mrs. DeWitt some time to emerge from her fog. "The Spanish refugees? Are they still having difficulties?"

"You remember," begged Lois. "The benefit with Edgar Villiers, the famous Iago! And one of your girls here was so interested?" Once again she thanked heaven for her photographic memory as understanding dawned in Mrs. DeWitt's eyes.

"Ah yes! What a night that was! And young Miss Rooker—"

"She means Ramona," whispered Netta.

"—was *most* interested in my account! Do you know, I think she borrowed that picture and forgot to return it!"

"Thank you, Mrs. DeWitt." Lois motioned the other girls to follow her. They gathered in a group at the bottom of the stairs. "So now we have a fair idea *what* Ramona was using to blackmail Mrs. Pierson. How could this picture Ramona took from Mrs. DeWitt have fallen into someone else's hands?"

"Maybe it hasn't. Maybe it's in the file room. Don't you think that we should go look?" Paula said hopefully.

"And at least get *your* photo," muttered Netta.

"We still need to find the key," said Lois doubtfully. A babble of talk broke out. "That's what we were trying to tell you!" "Maxie says she can show us where Ramona—" "Evidently, Maxie has some inside knowledge—"

"I can show you where the key is!" Maxie said cheerfully. "Follow me!"

As the troop of girls headed up the stairs, Lois told Netta, "I hope the blackmailer doesn't turn out to be someone else at the Magdalena Arms."

"The only possibility I can think of is Mrs. DeWitt herself, which I doubt. Most likely the person who broke into Ramona's room took it, although Ramona claimed nothing was missing," said Netta. Unexpectedly she smiled. "How you've changed, Lois. At the beginning of the summer you would have been reporting Mrs. Pierson yourself, not trying to protect her!"

Lois was startled. She *had* changed, in so many ways, without even realizing it. And she wasn't the only one. There was Netta's new haircut, and ahead of her Maxie was telling Pamela about gathering background color for "Bus Ride to Hell," the first in the series of articles about small-town girls and their demoralization in the big city.

"I've been having the most fun, going to dance halls, and strange little bars like that place Lois saw me in the other day," Maxie burbled. "It's the perfect job for me! I make my own hours, I'm not shut up in an office, I get to dress up in different outfits, and best of all"—she paused a little shyly—"I'm good at it! Mamie says I have a real knack for getting the juicy stuff!"

"How long has this been going on?" asked Pamela.

"Almost all summer." Maxie threw a sly smile over her shoulder at Netta. "That *Confidentially* card we found on the stairs the night of the burglary attempt? That was mine! Mamie gave it to me that day."

"I'm proud of you, honey," said Pamela hesitantly, "really I am, but—"

"And my whole new career is all due to Lois," Maxie was earnest now.

"Me!" said Lois in amazement.

"I'd just been letting myself drift, and then when you came along and Pamela was always talking about how organized and ambitious and bright you were—it really woke me up! I wanted to prove—but here we are."

The girls crowded around as Lois unlocked the door to 504, and followed her inside. Maxie went directly to the closet and pulled out Lois's shoes, a hatbox, and two suitcases, handing the items to the waiting girls as she cleared a patch of floor in the back right corner. "Anybody have a nail file?" she asked. Immediately a selection of nail files was offered. Netta reached for Lois's hand as Maxie delicately pried up a section of floorboard, revealing a small tin box, nestled next to a joist. Lois gripped Netta's hand tightly.

"This is where she kept her marijuana cigarettes," Maxie said. "Many dope fiends use this kind of hidey-hole to 'stash' their 'fix.' Mamie's going to put that in Part 3, 'Reefer: The Road That Ends in Despair.'"

"I can't believe it," said Netta, a little miffed. "I've been over this closet dozens of times!"

"I'm afraid, Netta, you're too nearsighted to pursue a career as a detective!" Maxie laughed. But Maxie's light-hearted humor was wasted on the anxious girls. "Open it," urged Paula. Lois picked up the box and unhooked the simple metal clasp. Inside was a gold ring and a single slip of paper folded in two.

Netta drew a breath. "That's Ramona's class ring from Minnesota State Teacher's College," she said. "Or mine, actually. I gave her mine, and she gave me hers."

"Now you have two," Dolly consoled her. "Sometimes two rings and no girl is better than one ring and a girl like Ramona!"

Lois unfolded the paper. There were two columns— one of words, one of numbers.

SCW	946.08
Corn	633.15
Plagiarism	808
Lingerie	658.11

"That's it!" said Paula, who was looking over Lois's shoulder. "Let's go!"

Chapter Twenty-Eight
The Other Two?

Once again, the three girls were in the back of a speed-ing cab, Lois in the middle.

Paula had tidied herself up in the Magdalena Arms bathroom, and looked a little like her old self, except for the tense, determined expression she wore.

Netta's face was unreadable, her eyes opaque behind her thick-lensed spectacles. Lois couldn't help wondering why she'd insisted on coming along. Was she still worry-ing about Ramona? Was Lois a fool to hope that one day Netta would forget that hoodlum heartbreaker and real-ize there was someone right next door, someone who val-ued the young teacher's high standards, common sense, and dependability?

Why, Netta's been helping me since the first afternoon in Bay City, when she carried in my luggage! Lois re-minded herself. Of course she knew now that Netta had been looking for another opportunity to search 504's closet, but still. It was her I leaned on when I had too many martinis, Lois's mind continued tabulating; she piqued my pride and made me poke into the files that first time. Why, we wouldn't be here if it wasn't for Netta!

Netta! It had always been Netta, Lois thought, heart-sick. Even while I was distracted by Paula, Pamela, and Mrs. Pierson.

"Who could the other two be?" asked Paula for the twentieth time, interrupting Lois's train of thought.

That had been the main topic of speculation since reading Ramona's key. Four numbers—four blackmail victims. Lois was sure SCW stood for Spanish Civil War and referred to some political indiscretion Mrs. Pierson had committed; Corn meant the past Paula was trying to hide; but what of the other two?

"I think I know what plagiarism means," said Lois thoughtfully. "Herb Hathaway."

"Of course!" exclaimed Paula. "That night we both stayed late—he was trying to outwait me, and I was trying to outwait him! And of course, neither of us could outwait Miss Gill."

"As for Lingerie . . ." Lois tapped the paper she held. "I don't know. But Ramona seems to have listed these numbers in the same order in which she found her victims—first Mrs. Pierson, then Paula, then Herb. Probably she started blackmailing Herb after she opened that letter the J. C. Birch secretary sent to Mrs. Pierson in April.

"So this last number is the last person she black-mailed—maybe the person who broke into her room, and frightened her enough to make her leave town."

"In other words, someone dangerous." Netta's face was worried.

"Are you girls prepared?" Lois looked at the other two seriously.

"I am," said Paula, her face set. "We were trained to fence at La Haute École—"

"Paulette, you didn't *go* to La Haute École de whatever," Netta interrupted impatiently. "And anyway you haven't got a foil."

Paula responded stubbornly, "Well, then I'll hit anyone who tries anything with my purse."

Lois had a nagging feeling in her head, like an idea was trying to rise to the surface of her consciousness, but couldn't. It was as if she were collating presentation copies and had gotten the sections in the wrong order. Something should be adding up, but what was it?

The cab pulled up to 333 Lake Street, and the girls piled out, Paula paying the cab. Lois was grateful to the older girl for funding the transportation portion of their investigation. She really did act like the affluent graduate of a Swiss finishing school.

If you act like it, do you become it? Lois wondered.

The patches of sky visible between the tall skyscrapers were streaked with red from an unseen setting sun as the trio hurried into the deserted glass and steel tower.

"Aren't you working awfully hard these days?" said the night guard as Lois signed in. "Ought to take a night off. Specially Friday night!"

The tightlipped girls ignored him and got on the elevator. Lois thought of Dolly, Pamela, and Maxie, who were waiting for them back at Francine's. "You kids get this file stuff straightened out, and we'll round up Janet and Phyllis, and have a big celebration when you get back," Dolly had proposed. I hope we have something to celebrate, Lois thought grimly. Aloud, she said, "Let me handle Miss Gill." Netta and Paula nodded.

They got out of the elevator and strode across the empty reception room like the three Fates. Paula jerked open the door behind the reception desk, and they turned toward the file room.

Chapter Twenty-Nine
The File Room Again

Grim, determined, and a little excited, the trio burst in on Miss Gill. She was, as usual, bent over a drawer, thumbing through the files.

"What's this?" she demanded. "Lois, I took your abrupt departure as your resignation. Paula, if you've work to do, it's not in the file room. And you—who are you?" She peered at Netta suspiciously.

"Miss Gill, I have *not* resigned," Lois began boldly. "In fact, I've returned because these very files you've been guarding so carefully are being used in an evil blackmailing scheme! Devised," Lois continued as Miss Gill recoiled in horror, "by my predecessor Ramona Ravenal, aka Ramona Rukeyser." She indicated Netta. "This is Miss Bean, who has helped uncover this pernicious plot. Why, just tonight we located the key which will allow us to find Ramona's blackmailing files and destroy them."

Miss Gill was trembling with shock. "Blackmail! In the file room! I can't believe it! How could this be happening right under my nose?" She turned to Lois. "I underestimated you, Lois. I'm sorry. Please—consider the file room your own." Her sweeping gesture encompassed the roomful of gleaming cabinets as she stepped aside.

Lois stepped forward, the key in her hand, while Paula, Netta, and Miss Gill formed a little semicircle behind her. "Ramona reorganized the files according to the Dewey Decimal System," she explained to Miss Gill. "Which means, incidentally, that after we've gotten rid of the files Ramona hid, it shouldn't be too difficult to put the real files back in their previous order. Although . . ." She turned to the office manager thoughtfully. "I'm wondering if the Library of Congress system mightn't be a better fit."

"Lois, get on with it," Paula begged.

Lois located the drawer labeled 630 and pulled it open. There was file 633.15, the numbers ever so faintly penciled on the edge. She took a quick peek inside it, just to make sure. Yes, that was Paula—Paulette rather—bending her head to receive an enormous bristling crown constructed of ears of corn. She was holding a scepter made from corn, too. Paulette Wolgstadt looked . . . wholesome was the only word for it. Lois could see why Paula Winstead would want that picture suppressed. She handed the file to Paula, who glanced inside and then closed the file tightly, a look of relief spreading across her patrician features.

"Next the mysterious lingerie file." Lois quickly located 658.11 and opened it up. Inside was a photostat of an ad for Helga's new Simplex Girdle. Lois frowned, puzzled. "I don't understand," she said. "There's nothing incriminating about a girdle ad!"

"Let me see." Netta took the folder from her.

Lois slid the third file from its place in drawer 940. Inside were two items. One was a card identifying Martha Pierson as a member of the Communist Party, and the other was a photograph, yellowed, that had been clipped from a newspaper. It showed a group of people sitting in a large semicircular booth in a restaurant. The caption read: "Fundraisers relax after the benefit performance of *Ah, How Gay*, which raised money for refugees from the current crisis in Spain."

"Why, that's Mrs. Pierson!" Paula was peering over Lois's shoulder with undisguised curiosity.

"That looks like Mrs. DeWitt," added Netta, glancing over Lois's other shoulder. Then she looked back at the Helga girdle ad. "You know, there's something funny here . . ."

But Lois was looking at the woman between the young, smiling Mrs. Pierson and Mrs. DeWitt (who was wearing a hat Lois had seen her in just a few days ago). The woman was a strikingly beautiful brunette, captured in profile, as she looked adoringly at Mrs. Pierson. And a whole series of clues began to click together like so many pieces of a puzzle. The list of words Miss Gill had taped to the file cabinet one night. Miss Gill's bitter voice earlier that day, saying, "Do you think I've forgotten what happened the last time you were—attached—to a secretary?" The way Miss Gill had looked when she'd gotten angry at Lois over the files, almost as vibrant and beautiful as the girl looking at Mrs. Pierson in this yellowing photo.

There was another click, this one audible to everyone in the room, and they all looked up. Miss Gill had released the safety on a snub-nosed revolver she was pointing at Lois.

"It was you!" burst out Lois. "You all along!"

"Give me that file, you meddling typist!" snarled Miss Gill.

Gingerly, Lois held out the file to the office manager. Miss Gill's usually calm demeanor was contorted with fury, spite, malicious glee—a whole panoply of emotions which played over her features like a deranged orchestra. She snatched the file from Lois.

"Up against the files!" Miss Gill waved her gun menacingly at the little group, who hastened to comply.

"It was you who broke into Ramona's room," Lois couldn't help saying, "because she was blackmailing you about your Communist past!"

"I'll take that," the double-faced office manager said to Netta, snatching the girdle file, and then she took Paula's Corn Queen photo, adding, "This may come in handy, too!"

"I think you mean Communist present. The double stitching on the girdle said, 'Women of the world unite,' if you looked closely," murmured Netta.

"Quiet, you! The Bay City branch subcommittee on the Woman Question is not going to fail now!"

"And it was you who made the file room such a mess!" continued Lois indignantly. "You probably did it this morning, before anyone else was here!"

"I needed to get rid of you—it was bad enough that you lived in Miss Ravenal's old room, then you stumbled across the blackmail letter I sent Mrs. Pierson!"

"Mrs. Pierson was once in your cell," said Lois, trying to piece it all together, "and after you frightened Ramona away, you started bleeding poor Mrs. Pierson yourself with those anonymous letters!"

"It wasn't my cell," the older woman corrected her with some asperity. "It was the cell of all the comrades who belonged to it. It was a communally owned cell, if you will. I was the secretary. 'Poor Mrs. Pierson'—that's rich! After she abandoned the party in 1939, just because of that unfortunate Molotov-Ribbentrop Pact. The same time she abandoned me for that little blond chippy who was in the chorus of *Ah, How Gay*."

"But how did you know—" Paula had scarcely begun before another clue fell into place in Lois's head.

"You've been steaming open Mrs. Pierson's letters!" The words popped out almost involuntarily. "That kettle always bubbling on the hotplate—the way her letters would be a little damp lots of times when you brought them—"

"A steam iron would have worked better," admitted Miss Gill. "But how to explain its presence?"

They were lined up against the first row of file cabinets, and Miss Gill stood just inside the door, facing them. Netta was nearest the wall; if Lois could just catch Netta's eye, and if she could inch over to the light switch—

"And you really blackmailed your former comrade?" demanded Paula. Thank heavens the astute copywriter knew enough to keep the conversational ball rolling! Leaning forward infinitesimally, Lois succeeded in catching Netta's eye. She looked at Netta, then at the lightswitch, then at Netta. Netta looked at the lightswitch and then at Lois. She gave an imperceptible nod.

"—more for the fun of watching her squirm than anything," Miss Gill was saying with relish. "She actually confided in me—asked me for my help! After all those years of treating me like her lackey, while she paraded her latest conquest through the office! How little she knows about any kind of loyalty, much less party loyalty!"

Lois could almost pity the tormented woman, who had let one bad girlfriend drive her to a political zealotry that had spun out of control!

"And now you're planning to use Sather & Stirling's new Helga Simplex Girdle campaign to send secret Communist messages throughout the world, is that it?" asked Netta. She stepped forward, and when Miss Gill waved the gun at her, she stepped back to the left.

"Ingenious, isn't it?" Miss Gill looked delighted. "I was able to hire a clever paste-up artist who's also a party member, and she altered the mechanicals. If you look closely you'll find all sorts of slogans in the stitching—'In the Communist family, the father does the dishes,' for example, and 'Communism means higher wages for women.' It's a new technique called 'Subliminal Suggestion.'"

"But—not the Helga Simplex Girdle campaign." Paula was appalled. "I wrote most of the copy! If this ever comes out, my career is over!"

Miss Gill ignored her. She addressed Lois: "I was sincere earlier, Lois. I *am* sorry I underestimated you. I told Martha she should get someone young and dumb for her secretary, someone too thick to catch on to anything. It was bad enough you were living in Ramona Ravenal's old room, but you weren't quite as dumb as I hoped either."

Lois kept her eyes fixed on Miss Gill, sensing without

seeing Netta's slow progress toward the light switch. "So you've decided I know A from Z?" she asked.

Miss Gill laughed, in a way that made chills run up and down Lois's spine. "I'll throw in most of the alphabet, but it's not going to help you—I'm keeping the G, U, and N."

"But what do you intend to do?" demanded Paula boldly. "You can't kill us all and hide the bodies in the filing room!"

"There's a lot of room in these file cabinets," said Miss Gill, and the three girls froze with fear. "But I'm not a murderer. You'll be kept under wraps, until the Helga Campaign is launched. But first . . ." She held the newspaper photo out toward Netta. "You, come here. Hold this. And no funny business. Paula, light me a match."

Lois could have wept. Netta had been close, she knew it. Now the schoolteacher stepped hesitantly forward and took the photo from Miss Gill. Miss Gill took the lit match from Paula and put it under the yellowed paper. The edges of the clipping turned black and curled under, and the flame licked the brittle paper. The smell of smoke filled the file room.

Lois coughed and coughed again. She brought up her hands to cover her mouth, and covering her face with one hand, coughing all the while, she fumbled her silver whistle into her mouth. Miss Gill's eyes were intent on the burning piece of paper. Lois blew.

Netta dropped the newspaper photo and deftly chopped at Miss Gill's gun hand, just as Miss Gill pulled the trigger. The explosion was deafening in the metal-lined room. Netta chopped again, and Miss Gill dropped the gun, grabbing her wrist in pain. Netta kicked the gun neatly across the floor to Lois, who was already bending to pick it up.

"Is everyone all right?" asked Lois anxiously.

Paula nodded. "I think the bullet went there." Paula pointed to a hole in the drawer just left of Lois's knee.

Netta was restraining Miss Gill, who had lunged after the gun. The office manager was panting, her eyes glittering feverishly.

"What on earth is all this hullaballoo?" Mrs. Pierson stood in the doorway, hands on her hips, frowning at them all. "Whistles, bangs." She sniffed the air. "Smoke! Is it the Fourth of July?"

Then she saw the half-burned clipping on the floor and her face paled. "Ivy—" She looked in dismay at the deranged office manager.

"Miss Gill has been blackmailing you since Ramona left town in June," Lois told her. "In fact, she's planning to use the Helga Simplex Girdle campaign to spread subversive Communist messages!" Mrs. Pierson looked at Lois in utter disbelief. But at Lois's words, Miss Gill collapsed completely, sinking to the floor as she dissolved in tears. "No!" she wailed. "It can't end like this! This was supposed to be my triumph! This was supposed to be my—revenge." Her head drooped. "I lost you long ago and now I've lost my cause. I have nothing left."

"Ivy, Ivy." Mrs. Pierson knelt by the office manager's side. "You still have the office!"

"The office!" Miss Gill's head snapped up. "Did you really think that these petty bourgeois crumbs could satisfy me after I had tasted the heady wine of the proletariat?"

"I thought you had left the party with me when the nonaggression pact was signed," protested Mrs. Pierson. "I thought we were both disillusioned!"

"You didn't care what I did!" snapped Miss Gill. "You'd left on a holiday to Florida with that peroxided chorus girl!"

Mrs. Pierson looked around helplessly. "Sometimes, when idealism dies, love dies, too," she defended herself.

"Mine didn't," sobbed Miss Gill. "Neither one!"

"Come to my office, dear," said Mrs. Pierson. "I'm going to call Dr. Steinmetz for you." She helped Miss Gill to her feet. "He's very good with this kind of repressed hostility and sublimation." The two women staggered out of the file room, Miss Gill sagging against Mrs. Pierson, who supported her former comrade.

Chapter Thirty-One
Permanent Secretary

By the time Dr. Steinmetz had arrived, with an ambulance and some orderlies, the three girls had joined Mrs. Pierson in her office and told her everything she needed to know.

"We'll have to hush the whole thing up," she said immediately. "This is the kind of thing that could send clients flocking to other agencies." She looked speculatively at Miss Gill, who moaned as Dr. Steinmetz injected a sedative. "Of course, Miss Gill will get the best of care. She's been a loyal employee, and was a good friend before this, er, incident. And I'd like to hear more about this 'subliminal suggestion' technique she's devised."

Mrs. Pierson heaved a sigh, and turned back to the three girls. "But it does leave us shorthanded. I'm already worried about who's going to write the Busker Beer copy, now that Herb's gone. They're preparing to launch a new lager!"

Paula perked up. "I don't believe I've told you, Mrs. Pierson, that I spent part of my youth in a small town in Minnesota. There's nothing about beer I don't know!"

"Really?" Mrs. Pierson looked at the elegant girl doubtfully.

"I love lager!" said Paula with an intensity no one could doubt.

"Well, we'll discuss it tomorrow. Or better yet, you can ride in the ambulance to the rest home with me and give me your ideas." She looked at Miss Gill, whose eyes were closing. "I don't think Miss Gill will be much for conversation tonight. Careful, you! She's very fragile!" This to the ambulance man as he strapped Miss Gill on to the stretcher.

As the men rolled Miss Gill out of Mrs. Pierson's office, the busy executive turned to Lois. "Lois, I want to tell you I think you've behaved splendidly through all of this. I commend and applaud you and I hope you'll stay on as my permanent secretary."

"Really?" Lois's eyes were shining. "You're not just asking me so I won't reveal your Communist past?"

"Well, of course that's a factor," said Mrs. Pierson somewhat testily. "As is the fact that I spent several frustrating hours looking for an ad-buy report, before that gun went off. Make up your mind, Lois, do you want the job or not?"

"I want it," said Lois with all her heart.

"Good! Have that ad-buy report on my desk in the morning." Mrs. Pierson and Paula hurried after Dr. Steinmetz and the departing stretcher.

For the first time since the previous night, Lois was alone with Netta. She felt awkward and shy. "I'm surprised Mrs. Pierson didn't offer *you* a job," said Lois, just to be saying something. "After all, it was your adeptness at jujitsu that saved us! And you know as much about Mrs. Pierson's Communist past as I do," she added as an afterthought.

"While you and Paula were talking to Dr. Steinmetz, Mrs. Pierson told me she was going to endow a housing scholarship at the Magdalena Arms and she was sure I'd be a wonderful candidate," Netta replied as she gazed out the window at the city skyline. "It's funny." She played with a wisp of hair. "Ramona thought I could benefit from her blackmail scheme, and I guess I have. Fate plays odd tricks, doesn't it?"

Lois straightened the contents of Mrs. Pierson's in basket. "Maybe you want to write her a thank-you letter," she said, resentment creeping into her voice in spite of her effort to be fair-minded. "Maybe you want to join her in New York."

"Don't be silly, Lois," said Netta impatiently. "I could never care for someone who made money from other people's misery! The rest of the gang may have thought I was carrying a torch, but I guess part of me has known for some time that it was over between Ramona and me."

"Over?" Lois couldn't believe what Netta was saying. "But you've been so upset all summer—"

"Old habits die hard, I guess. When we exchanged rings back at Teacher's College, we promised we'd always help each other, through thick and thin. I had to hold up my end of the pact. But that's all done, now that she's returned my ring."

"You mean . . ." began Lois, scarcely daring to hope.

"Oh, Lois," cried Netta passionately. "When I saw that pistol pointed at your head by that crazed office manager . . ." In an instant she was at Lois's side and had taken the young girl in her arms.

"But why were you so distant this morning at breakfast?" Lois murmured against Netta's soap-scented neck. She drew back. "Why did you tell me to file and forget last night? That was a terrible thing to say!"

"How could I be sure you felt the way I did? You're so young, and from what I've heard, you've been running around all summer like a puppy, picking up a new scent every two seconds."

Lois would have felt offended at the comparison if Netta hadn't kissed her at the end of it.

"I'm hardly a puppy—I'm a permanent private secretary!" Lois said, kissing Netta back. She surveyed her domain. "Netta, I know that the rest of the gang is waiting for us at Francine's, but do you suppose . . ."

"You want to do some filing, don't you?" Netta's eyes twinkled in understanding. "I could help. I still know my alphabet. Besides . . ." She gently pushed Lois into Mrs. Pierson's chair, and then straddled the sitting girl. Lois caught her breath. "It's Friday night. Francine's will be open for hours." She unbuttoned Lois's blouse. "We've got all the time in the world."

And as Netta bent her head, Lois lifted hers to meet Netta's kiss.